THE
INN
ON
Amelia Island

SEVEN SISTERS
BOOK SEVEN

HOPE HOLLOWAY

Hope Holloway

Seven Sisters Book 7

The Inn on Amelia Island

Copyright © 2024 Hope Holloway

This novel is a work of fiction. Any references to historical events, real people, or real locales are used fictitiously. Other names, characters, places, and incidents are the product of the author's imagination, and any resemblance to actual events or locales or persons, living or dead, is coincidental. All rights to reproduction of this work are reserved. No part of this publication may be reproduced, stored in or introduced into a retrieval system, or transmitted, in any form, or by any means (electronic, mechanical, photocopying, recording, or otherwise) without prior written permission from the copyright owner. Thank you for respecting the copyright. For permission or information on foreign, audio, or other rights, contact the author, hopehollowayauthor@gmail.com.

The Seven Daughters Of Rex Wingate

Born to Charlotte Wingate

Madeline Wingate, age 50
Victoria "Tori" Wingate, age 46
Rose Wingate D'Angelo, age 44
Raina Wingate, age 44

Born to Susannah Wingate

Sadie Wingate, age 36
Grace Wingate Jenkins, age 34
Chloe Wingate, age 30

Chapter One

Susannah

Susannah angled her phone in the sunlight, slowing her step to read a text that had come in just as she reached the end of Wingate Way. Then she let out a soft groan.

Chloe was canceling to go to Jacksonville with her boyfriend? Oh, that was a disappointment.

Susannah had set aside this entire morning to spend with Chloe and two of her other daughters to discuss the wedding that would be taking place right here at their family-owned inn on…on…she sighed because they hadn't yet set a date. It would be sometime this summer. And that was daunting, because they were well into May.

If they didn't start planning the details now, they'd never pull off Raina and Tori's "double-ring ceremony"—which sounded to Susannah's ears like something they'd played as little girls.

Okay. This would still work today without Chloe, even though she'd volunteered to help with the logistics. Susannah would spend the time with the brides, and they'd bring Chloe up to speed later. They had to, at the very least, pick a date.

And they'd do that today. Nothing could stop them.

Tucking her phone back in her bag, she stood with one hand on the wrought-iron gate outside of Wingate House, taking a moment to gaze at the three-story Victorian mansion with the swelling heart of a mother. No surprise, since Susannah sometimes thought of this glorious place as her eighth daughter.

Like those seven wonderful women, this Wingate was a great lady—classically beautiful, deeply appealing, always charming, occasionally quirky, and forever a tremendous source of pride to the family.

Silly, she knew, to ascribe human characteristics to a building, especially one tucked into a tree-lined neighborhood that boasted many century-old houses. Every corner in this historic section of Amelia Island featured a sprawling home painted in pastels, topped with turrets, and wrapped in precious porches built to comfort and impress.

But not every house had *this* family's history, reputation, and legacy, nor did any share the name of the street it was on, the riverfront avenue known as Wingate Way.

Wingate House had been built as the stately home of the first Reginald Wingate, her husband's grandfather, who'd arrived on this island at the turn of the twentieth century. Mid-century, it had been redesigned as a venerable inn, one of the finest on Amelia Island. But this past year, Susannah had reimagined the sprawling property into a glorious backdrop exclusively for picture-perfect weddings.

Since transforming the aging B&B into a weddings-only venue, Susannah had been pleasantly surprised by the success of her venture.

But why should she be? With wide white beaches along the eastern coast and the deep blue waters of the Intracoastal Waterway on the west, Amelia Island had long been a highly in-demand destination for weddings. Brides had plenty of options for larger events, but few for what the trade called "micro weddings."

Like her marketing materials said, Wingate House offered "a small wedding option with an elegant Victorian atmosphere and Instagram-worthy manicured grounds on the banks of the Amelia River."

Over the past few months, several top bridal websites had run feature stories on the inn, pronouncing Wingate House ideal for intimate weddings. Those nuptials were frequently older couples getting married for the second time—like two of her daughters would do right here... *soon*.

There always seemed to be a delay in their planning sessions, usually because the venue was booked. But that, Susannah reminded herself, was a high-quality problem to have.

One more time, pride in her work, the outcome, and the inn's exciting future zipped through her, enough that she pushed the gate wide open and chastised herself as she entered.

Hadn't she listened to the pastor on Sunday when

he'd talked about the sin of pride? It went before the fall, after all.

Following the stone walkway to climb the steps of the wraparound porch, she forced herself to think about the day's work, not bask in her resounding success. After Tori and Raina left today, she would—

"You must be Susannah."

Startled by the voice, she whipped around to see a woman lounging on one of the porch sofas. She held a cardboard cup in one hand while she casually twirled sunglasses with the other.

"Hello." Susannah stepped out of the morning sunshine into the shadow of the overhang, flipping through a mental snapshot of today's appointments. Only her daughters were on the schedule, she was certain.

But all that success she'd just been thinking about frequently made some brides pushy when they wanted a date that wasn't available.

"Can I help you?" Susannah asked when the visitor stayed silent.

For a long moment, the woman stared back at her, a direct dark gaze that could be described as beady, however uncharitable that might sound. She had shoulder-length black hair and a fringe of bangs, and looked to be in her forties.

Thin to the point of scrawny, she wore a yellow tank top, white shorts, and filthy sneakers...currently resting on Susannah's coffee table.

"I don't even know where to begin," the stranger finally said, slowly pushing up to no more than five-foot-three. "But I'm right? You're the great and glorious Susannah Wingate?"

The bitter sarcasm wasn't lost on Susannah, who winced, briefly wondering if her overdose of pride had brought on that insult.

"I doubt anyone would call me great or glorious," she said with a smile that felt necessary if not natural.

"Surely Rex would."

Susannah drew back, more from the ice in the tone than the fact that this stranger knew her husband's name. Many people did, that was for sure. Few spat it out like that.

"Do I know you?"

"Not yet, but you will." She tipped her head toward the double leaded-glass doors that led to the inn's entry hall. "I'd like to see it."

"I'll be happy to make an appointment, Miss..." She lifted her brows, waiting for the name.

"Button. Ivy Button."

The name was so precious and unexpected she almost smiled. But nothing about this woman made her relax. She had a razor's edge and Susannah didn't want to get cut.

"Hello, Ms. Button. I am Susannah Wingate, as you've guessed."

"The one they call Suze," the other woman said.

Had her nickname been in one of the articles written about Wingate House? Possibly. She didn't remember, but how else would this stranger know?

"Yes, that's what they call me. When is your wedding?"

She gave a derisive snort. "Never again, thank you very much. Once was enough for me, along with the cliché ugly divorce. That's not why I'm here."

"Oh?" And then it made sense. "Ah, Ms. Button. I realize Wingate House is still listed in many directories as an inn, which we were for decades, but now we're exclusively used as a wedding venue," Susannah told her, relieved that this was likely a mistake. "Perhaps I can refer you to another of the many fantastic B&Bs on Amelia—"

"I'd like to see it." She ground out the words and pointed to the doors. "Now."

Despite the early summer heat, chills blossomed on Susannah's arms. "I can't show it to you now." Not true, but she didn't want to be alone in the house with this off-putting woman. "Why don't you give me your number—"

"My name is *Ivy Button*," she repeated, slathering the name with significance, as if Susannah had to recognize it.

"I'm sorry, I don't..."

The other woman muttered a curse under her breath. "Of course she never mentioned me. Or her sister, did she?"

"She..." Now Susannah was completely confused. "Who are you talking about?"

"Doreen Parrish. Please tell me you haven't forgotten her."

"Doreen?" Okay, *maybe* this was starting to make

sense. "Of course I haven't forgotten her. Doreen's only been gone a year but gave us a lifetime of service at this inn before a heart attack took her last year. You knew her?"

"She was my aunt."

"Oh...oh." Susannah pressed a hand to her chest, suddenly ashamed for any unkind thoughts she'd had about this person. "I didn't know she had a niece."

The other woman rolled her eyes. "Please. You didn't know a *lot* about her, it seems."

Finally, the puzzle pieces began to fall into place.

This was about...the *baby*. Well, the man was now fifty-five years old, so no baby. But this woman had no doubt discovered that Doreen Parrish had an illegitimate son that she'd given up for adoption many decades earlier.

Did she know that baby was the result of an ill-advised liaison with Rex Wingate when he and Doreen were not even twenty years old? Or that the adopted child now had a son of his own who currently lived on Amelia Island?

With all the DNA tracing available these days? Probably.

"You must want to meet Blake," Susannah said, certain this was what had brought on the unorthodox meeting.

The other woman scowled. "I have no idea who that is."

"Blake Youngblood. Well, he was raised Blake Young,

but he changed his name," she said. "He's Bradley Young's son."

"Who is Bradley Young?"

Dear heavens, maybe she *didn't* know. She searched the other woman's face, trying to see past the expression of distaste, knowing that the history and secrets could get very complicated. But Doreen's niece had a right to know everything.

Susannah gestured toward the sofa. "Why don't we sit down and—"

"Who is Bradley Young?" she demanded.

Susannah sighed, so not having expected this today. "Doreen had a child in 1968 and gave him up for adoption. His name is Bradley Young. His son is—"

"There was a *baby*?" Her voice rose in disbelief. "From...Rex?"

"It took us all by surprise." Now there was an understatement.

"Rex is the...the father?" she sputtered the last two words.

"He is, but we're used to—"

"That son of a..." The woman clenched her teeth and fumed, her nostrils flaring. "Well, there you go. It wasn't enough to rape a poor lovestruck woman who had the IQ of a dust mop—Rex got her pregnant, too!"

Susannah swayed at the word...*rape*. Was she talking about...*Rex*? Her Rex? A man so kind, loving, and caring that he couldn't think about something like that, let alone do it?

"He didn't...take advantage of her," she said, her voice strained and breathless.

"Oh, really. Were you there?" she fired back.

"No, I...I...hadn't met Rex yet, but he told me—"

She snorted. "I'm sure he has a story, but I have the truth. *In writing.*"

Susannah stared at her, all the blood in her head pooling into a hot pit in her stomach.

"You're mistaken," she managed. "They did have a brief...alliance. They were quite young, teenagers, really, and she left without telling him she was pregnant. After she gave the baby up for adoption, she came back to Amelia Island but never told anyone about the baby. There were no hard feelings, and no...no. Nothing like...*that*. How could there be? She worked here, as the inn manager, for fifty years, and was practically a member of our family."

"Family?" She arched a brow, seemingly amused by Susannah's panicked verbal spew. "The family that called her 'Dor-mean' and barely spoke to her? That family?"

Susannah couldn't stand for another second, her knees were so weak. She felt them buckle as she dropped into the closest chair, staring up at the woman.

Yes, the girls had called her Dor-mean—not to her face—because she *was* mean. The woman had been nasty, hateful, and rude. She was also possibly on the spectrum, but none of them realized it or even discovered her secret baby until after she'd died and they'd cleaned out her apartment on the third floor of the inn.

But they'd taken care of her for fifty years! They'd given her a place to live, let her manage the inn with a lot of help from Susannah, and never once did Doreen say anything about Rex or that one night in the past.

In fact, she and Rex barely spoke... They hardly looked at each other...

More blood drained. No. *It wasn't true.* Rex would never hurt anyone.

"I'm so sorry you're here for a sad errand," Susannah said, digging for composure and a way to get rid of this stranger. "I'm also sorry we don't have any of Doreen's belongings anymore. We didn't know she had family."

"Yes, you have her belongings," Ivy said, pointing to the house. "I'm looking at it."

Susannah glanced over her shoulder, not sure what she meant. "I'm sorry, but after Doreen passed, we went through her apartment. We gave everything to charity or...or..."

The woman wasn't listening. She was looking past Susannah, at Wingate House, at the arched windows and mahogany doors, at the corbels and balustrades, all the way up to the freshly painted wood overhang.

She looked at it with greed and hunger and...purpose.

"What exactly do you want?" Susannah croaked the question.

"The house," she said as if it were obvious. "The one your dead father-in-law gave to my aunt. My mother is Aunt Doreen's heir, and she's sent me here to let you know it's been more than a year. Time for you and all Wingates to get out of this place. We're taking over."

Susannah choked softly. Her dead—did she mean Rex's *father*? He'd been gone for more than two decades.

"No one gave Wingate House to anyone," she ground out the words, ire rising. "It's been in our family for more than a hundred years and it will stay that way for a hundred more."

"I have the contract and her letters," the woman said. "And a good lawyer. I'm happy to use all that to get you out of here, if I have to."

"We're not going anywhere," Susannah said.

"Then I will tell every person on Amelia Island and beyond that your husband is a rapist who took advantage of a mentally disabled woman." She gave a soft snort of satisfaction. "And now, thank you very much, I can add the colorful fact that his assault resulted in a child he wouldn't even acknowledge. Oh, the press will eat that up, don't you think? Might not be good for business...this one, or all of the shops your daughters run on *Wingate Way*."

She dragged out the last two words, covering them in revulsion.

"No, no." Susannah tried to stand, but her legs wouldn't support her. "You can't do that. It's not true. You can't slander a man like that. He's done nothing to you."

"He ruined my aunt's life and she never got to collect her hush money. But I'll be happy to. This place has to be worth a few million, right? Don't worry. If me and my mom don't like living here, we'll sell it back to you. For a nice high price."

She couldn't do that. It was blackmail! And not true, not one word of it. Rex didn't have an aggressive bone in his body.

With a smug smile, Ivy tossed back the rest of her coffee and slammed the empty cup on the table.

"Obviously, you're not letting me in. Fine. I will be back. Oh, and by the way, the contract says we get it furnished, so don't try to take anything out of this place or we'll sue you until you can't see straight. By the time we're done, Rex Wingate won't be able to walk down the street that's named after him and look a single person in the eye. So, uh, see ya around...*Suze*."

With that, she pivoted, jogged down the steps, and sauntered along the walkway like she...well, like she owned the place. She opened the gate and walked out, leaving it gaping wide open, exactly like Susannah's mouth.

What just happened?

The fall, she thought. The one that took a person down right after committing the sin of pride.

On a soft moan, she walked over to the cup, gingerly picked it up, and walked around to the side of the house to deposit it in the trash. Which was exactly where it, and Ivy Button, belonged.

Only then did the tears spill, because Susannah had absolutely no idea what to do next.

Chapter Two

Raina

"You can't cater your own wedding, Tori Wingate!" Raina reached over and jabbed her sister playfully. "You can manage another caterer, and Suze has a ton we can pick from."

Tori rose from her comfy position on the floor, kneeling next to Charlie's tiny body, getting a gooey smile from the four-month-old baby lying on a bunny blanket.

"Uh, Charlotte Wingate, will you please tell your mother it's not just *my* wedding." She bopped her button nose. "It's both of *our* weddings. Not to each other, dear niece of mine, but to our dream men. And you better not cry during the ceremony." She shifted to the right and gave little Charlie's twin sister the same face. "Or you, lovely Lily."

A foot away and also on the floor, Raina dropped back against the sofa. "They'll be perfectly well-behaved," she promised her sister. "And if not, who cares? That's why we're having two weddings on one day. It's an excuse for a Wingate party."

Tori tore her attention from the babies, leveling her

gaze on Raina. "It's more than that, Rain. Didn't you hear me? We're marrying our dream men."

"That we are," Raina agreed. "And if you'd have suggested that to me when these two were but mere seedlings and you forced me to take a pregnancy test, I'd have never believed you."

"Remember? You found out you were pregnant and discovered the baby's father was a snake all in the same five minutes." Tori brushed back a long lock of strawberry-blond hair with a chuckle. "It does seem like I'm always there for the pivotal moments in your life, doesn't it?"

"Yep." Raina smiled and stood. "My butt's asleep. And we'd better get going to Wingate House. Suze is chomping at the bit to get this double wedding on the schedule and start ordering whatever we need. Although we've got dresses, flowers, and dessert covered by our sisters."

"And catering."

Raina rolled her eyes. "And we're back to square one. You are not catering your own wedding and that's final."

"Okay, okay." Tori leaned back on her hands, glowing as she had been since the day Dr. Justin Verona proposed to her. "I guess we'll have more fun that way, although I hate to give up the control."

"Please. If I can give up control of Wingate Properties to my fiancé, anyone can give up control of anything."

"It's going well with Chase at the company, though, isn't it?" Tori asked.

"Dad's happy," Raina said, thinking of her last

conversation with the man whose name was on the door, the street, and seven birth certificates.

Rex Wingate had been the one to put Chase Madison in charge when he recognized what Raina already knew—motherhood trumped her career, at least at this tender time in her life. "Chase may not be a Wingate—"

"Not yet, but he can change his name when you marry him," Tori joked.

Raina laughed, then grew serious. "I'm not sure about my name. What about you?"

"Of course I'm changing it. Tori Hottypants. Has a ring to it, don't you think?"

"Definitely, but I've never been anything but Raina Wingate, and, if I'm being honest, I'm worried Dad might be disappointed."

"Why?"

"I don't know. No sons to carry on the Wingate name."

Tori lifted a shoulder. "Do what feels right to you."

"I will. I'm giving it some thought. Whatever my last name, I know I'll be happy with Chase. He's so amazing," she added, not caring that her voice cracked with emotion that she didn't try to hide. "Did I tell you he's already started the adoption process to become the girls' father? We have our first consultation with the lawyer tomorrow."

"Oh, I love that," Tori gushed. "Let me know how it goes every step of the way."

Raina eyed her. "You're not thinking about having Justin adopt Kenzie and Finn, are you?"

"As if my ex would ever allow that. No. It's perfect for you, though, since Jack backed out of their lives completely." Tori pushed up from the floor. "All right, let's get moving before we're late. I'm glad I came early to get some time alone with you and help you pack up the babies. Where do you hide the diaper bags?"

"Hang on." Raina lifted her phone. "Text from Suze." She read it and frowned. "Oh, dang. Chloe canceled."

"Really? When are we going to plan this thing?"

Raina skimmed the text, definitely confused. "Suze is on her way over here—"

"All right, we'll do it without Chloe. But Suze doesn't even know I came here to pick you up, does she?" Tori pulled out her phone. "I didn't get a text from her."

Raina shook her head, holding up her hand. "She says she wants to talk to me. Privately. In fact, she wanted to be sure Chase wasn't home."

Tori drew back and made a face. "Well, then, I guess I'm officially chopped liver. Why wouldn't she want me here? It's both of our weddings."

"I don't know, ask her when— Oh, look!" She squealed and pointed. "Charlie's pushing her arm. She's gonna turn over!"

But Raina's raised voice startled the baby, and she stopped mid-roll to look at her mother and let out a little cry of distress.

"Oh, darling, I didn't mean to scare you." Raina was

next to her in a flash, folding next to the bunny blanket to love on her sweet pea.

Charlie thought about it for a second, stared at Raina, and opened her mouth to wail.

"You'll get it, little one."

"So am I just squeezed out of my own wedding?" Tori asked, sounding more concerned about that than a baby rolling for the first time.

"Don't be ridiculous," Raina said. "It's probably about something completely different." But she had to acknowledge that the text was kind of odd, and not at all like their mother.

"You think it's about Chloe canceling? Is something wrong? Or something with Dad? What—"

Raina lifted the crying baby and tipped her head toward the front door at the sound of a car pulling into the driveway. "That's probably her. Feel free to ask."

Lily started crying, too, so Tori picked her up.

They were both holding babies and trying to calm them down when Susannah tapped lightly on the front door and called Raina's name.

"Come on in," Raina said. "Brace for crying babies."

She pushed the door open and stepped inside, looking surprised when she saw Tori.

"Oh, I didn't realize you were here," she said.

Tori lifted a brow. "I thought I'd come here first to help Raina get the babies over to Wingate House," she said.

Susannah stared at them, a blank look on her face.

"For our meeting," Tori reminded her. "You know, the one we scheduled before Chloe bailed?"

Holding Charlie, Raina took a few steps closer. "You okay, Suze?"

The fact was, her mother looked pale and troubled, and not at all like her usually joyous self.

"Yes, yes...I'm...fine." She closed her eyes as she placed her bag on the entry table.

She didn't seem fine. "Look, Grannie Suze is here," Raina whispered to the baby, searching her mother's face for a clue.

"What's going on with you?" Tori asked, coming closer with Lily in her arms.

"Oh, nothing, I just...wanted to check on my grandbabies," she said with what sounded a little like false brightness. "I'll take Lily, since you're leaving, Tori."

Tori handed over the baby. "And the wedding meeting?"

"Oh, well, we'll have to reschedule. I wanted to talk to Raina."

Tori's gaze flickered. "All righty, then. Now that I have an open window in my schedule, I'll swing by the café and see how it's going after the breakfast rush."

"Okay," Susannah said absently, glancing at the baby in her arms, but not giving her usual expression of delight. "What were you two talking about?" she asked, still sounding way too fake and, frankly, weird.

"We were talking about Chase adopting the babies," Tori said. "Raina was going to tell me the process."

"Oh? You've started?" Susannah asked, suddenly

very interested—or just jumping on the change of subject.

"Chase set up the first appointment," Raina told her. "He thinks we can do it fast. Like, if we're lucky, right after the wedding...or maybe before, if we can't nail down a summer date. How long did it take you, Suze?"

Her mother looked up from her intense study of Lily, who was attempting to get her tiny thumb in her mouth. "Take me...to do what?"

"To adopt us," Raina said, frustration growing.

Susannah stared at her, then at Tori, then down at the baby.

"Suze?" Tori pressed.

"I, um, never did adopt you four girls."

For a moment, Raina's world tipped. How could she have not known that?

"Excuse me?" Was that why she'd let them call her Suze all these years, and never insisted on being "Mom" like she was to the three youngest?

"I didn't get around to it," she confessed. "And I know it sounds ridiculous, but I had my hands full. Four new daughters and a new husband."

Raina could have sworn her voice cracked on the last word. "It's fine, Suze."

"Is it?" she asked, sounding like she was on the edge of a breakdown. "I...I...I should have..."

"Susannah Wingate," Tori said, swooping in to put an arm around her. "It's a little late to worry about technicalities."

Susannah looked up, her eyes filled with unshed tears.

"Suze!" Raina and Tori exclaimed at the same time.

"Here. Take Lily." She held the baby out to Tori and backed away. "Excuse me for a minute."

Before either of them could react, she rushed out of the room, disappearing into the hall and, presumably, the powder room.

Tori and Raina just stared at each other, gobsmacked.

"What the heck is going on?" Tori asked on a whisper. "And also, she never adopted us? Did you know that? Do Rose or Madeline?"

Raina shook her head. "I never really thought about it, you know? I just assumed we were as much hers as we were Dad's."

"I know." Tori carefully placed Lily on the bunny blanket. "She clearly wants to confide in you, so I'm going to skedaddle."

"I don't know why you can't stay."

Tori shrugged. "Neither do I, but I can't."

"Girls," Susannah called as she came down the hall. "I think I'm going to take off."

Raina did a double-take. What the heck? "You just got here."

"I know, but I...I have to...do something." She looked like she'd dried her eyes and dabbed at any mascara that might have smeared, and smoothed her chin-length blond bob. But even with all that, her complexion looked pale and her lips drawn to a tight, unnatural smile. "So let's reschedule when Chloe's available."

"I thought you had something you wanted to talk to me about," Raina said, truly baffled by this change of heart.

"Oh, it can wait." She waved off any more questions and hustled over to the entryway to get her bag. "I'll call you. Bye!"

She was out the door before they could breathe—and without saying goodbye to the babies.

"Something is really wrong with her," Raina muttered as Charlie fussed in her arms, squiggling like she didn't want to be held anymore. Or maybe she was put out by Grannie Suze's unusual departure.

"Do you think she just remembered she forgot to legally adopt her four oldest daughters and is headed off to the courthouse?" Tori asked.

"She was upset before we brought that up. But, honestly, that is so wrong." Raina walked to the blankets and carefully laid Charlie next to Lily. "I thought she'd adopted us, I really did."

"But imagine what those days were like," Tori said. "She was a brand-new wife. You and Rose were not a whole lot older than these twins, and she had two more daughters looking at her to be their replacement mom. Madeline was an angel, but I'm sure I was a holy terror."

Raina felt a smile pull, but her heart dropped. "I wonder if that's weighed on her all these years."

"She could still do it, you know," Tori said. "People adopt adult children all...the...Raina? Oh, Raina. I know that face. That's your Fix-It Face. What are you cooking up in that problem-solving brain of yours?"

"Well, I can't fix whatever is bothering Suze today, but the adoption thing? I'm about to go through the whole process of adopting stepchildren. What if I nudged whatever powers that be so Susannah could legally be our mother? Would that be crazy?"

"You could ask her."

"Or..." Raina lifted both brows. "We could surprise her."

"Oh!" Tori shuddered and rubbed her arms. "That just gave me chills."

"Right? Can you imagine how happy that would make her?"

"That would be the best gift ever," Tori agreed. "But it doesn't address what's eating at her now."

"My guess is Chloe told her something that upset her," Raina said. "She was all ready to meet with us and plan, then she suddenly got a text from Chloe and the wedding was forgotten. So probably— Oh!" She covered her mouth to keep the exclamation quiet, pointing at Lily with one hand. "Look, Aunt Tori. Lily just turned herself over."

Now on her stomach, Lily lifted her fuzzy head, bracing herself with her tiny hands, her face about an inch from the blanket. Her big eyes looked surprised at first, but then she looked right at Raina and grinned.

"Lily!" Raina snagged her phone and stabbed at the camera button. "You did it!"

"I'll leave you to your inevitable photo shoot," Tori said as she slipped her purse on her arm and walked toward the door, pausing as she opened it. "Let me know if you hear from Suze. Also if you do *something* to finally get us a legal mother."

Raina chuckled. "I'll do my best."

"Good, because if anyone can pull off the surprise adoption of four adult women, it's you, Raina Wingate." She crinkled her nose. "Or soon-to-be Raina Madison."

Raina held up her hand. "Not sure yet."

"Hyphenate?"

"Ugh. No, thanks."

"We can't all be Mrs. Hottypants," Tori quipped. "If you figure out what's bothering Suze, call me."

"I will," Raina promised, and meant it. Something was wrong with Susannah, and she intended to find out exactly what it was.

Chapter Three

Chloe

Chloe canceled her long-overdue wedding planning session that morning for one simple reason: Travis had asked her to ride with him to Jacksonville, told her it was important, and announced he needed her with him.

She didn't require more than that from this man she had fallen head over heels in love with. But when she got in his truck and didn't see his quick smile or that warm light in his eyes, she decided she'd better get a solid explanation.

First, she leaned over the console and gave her handsome firefighter boyfriend a kiss.

"All right," she told him. "Rocky's Rescues is in the capable hands of my assistant, Ashley, and she's ready for our new boarder, a Dalmatian named Dot, if you can even stand that."

Surprised she didn't get a laugh on that, Chloe settled in to pull on her seatbelt.

"I've let down my mother and sisters by canceling the meeting to plan Tori and Raina's wedding-palooza," she continued. "No one seems to want to disown me for that, which is a relief."

Still no smile.

"I said goodbye to Lady Bug and Buttercup and got very sad eyes in response, since you said we couldn't bring them and..."

He shifted the truck into reverse, spitting driveway gravel as he backed out.

"Hey, hey," she teased, giving him a shoulder poke. "It's not a run-down animal rescue anymore, thanks to you and your bros who did all the renovations to make this my home, but...until we asphalt the driveway, go easy, okay?"

He simply nodded.

"Travis, are you even going to say hello?" she pressed when she didn't get more than that. "Or tell me why we have to go to Jacksonville?"

On a deep inhale, he finally looked right at her, his green eyes somber. "Apparently, my dad died."

She gasped, pressing both hands to her lips. "Travis! I'm so sorry! Oh, I'm yammering on about...ah. Travis. I'm sad for you."

"Please don't be," he said, but she heard the heavy note in his voice. "As you know, I haven't had contact with him since the day he blew out of my mother's house when I was in second grade. He's been dead to me for a long time."

"Still." She fell back against the headrest with a grunt of pity. "It's very sad. When did it happen? And how did he die? How old was he and...why do we have to go to Jacksonville?"

He took a moment, turning onto the street before answering.

"He died about four months ago of a heart attack, and he was...I don't know how old, exactly. My mom would have been sixty-four, so maybe a few years older. And we have to go to Jacksonville because one of his neighbors called me last night and asked me to come down to talk to her about something he left behind."

"Wait. *What?*" She leaned forward. "Your dad *lived* in Jacksonville? An hour away? How did I not know that? Did you know that?'"

"Yes, I did but I don't talk about him. What else was in that litany of questions? What do you need to know?"

Everything, she thought, but knew full well that his father was a sore subject. This had to hurt, no matter how much he said he didn't care.

She just shook her head and reached for him. "I'm so, so sorry, hon. What are you feeling?"

He shot her a look. "Like, we pass a Cracker Barrel on I-95. Let's stop there for lunch on our way back. Those mashed taters are..." He chef-kissed the air. "Perfection."

"Travis." She squeezed his arm. "Don't bottle up your grief or make jokes. Your father died and you're thinking about mashed taters? Also, who calls them that?"

He gave her a conciliatory smile. "My mom did. And, babe, believe me, she was the only parent who mattered, and I cried plenty when that great lady went to heaven. Her death changed my life, as you know."

"'No regrets, coyote,'" Chloe said, quoting the phrase Travis told her his mother always used.

That philosophy had taken this amazing man from a corporate job in New York to become a firefighter on Amelia Island—he had seized the day and had no regrets.

"Well, you might regret not even feeling slightly bad about your father's death," she said softly. "Can you tell me what you remember about him?"

He didn't answer for a long, long time and she stayed quiet while he no doubt meandered down memory lane.

"Not much," he eventually said. "Can we talk about something else? Was Suze mad that I yanked you away from Wingate business?"

She didn't see how they could talk about anything else, but she understood that grief was different for everyone, and his was still raw. She obliged him by changing the subject, telling him about how much she loved the "cat room" he'd finished making for her last week.

But no matter how much she talked about the animal rescue that he'd helped her transform into a comfortable home and business, she could feel her usually bright and funny man was hurting and emotionally absent.

She waited until they'd turned onto 295 and headed west before she slyly took the subject back to his father.

"So, can you remember the last time you saw him?" she asked softly, hoping that would help him open up about the man. "I mean, I know it might be hard to recall, since you were seven—"

"I was thirty."

She drew back, surprised. "You saw him four years ago? Here? In Jax...or..."

"Three and change years ago, but, yeah," he said, the response nearly inaudible.

"And you didn't tell me?"

"I hadn't met you yet," he said.

But the news stung. "Why wouldn't you tell me that, Travis? Or that he lived so close?"

He took his eyes off the road long enough to pin his emerald gaze on her. "Chloe, I don't know how to explain the broken mess of my family to someone who has six stick-to-your-side sisters and the greatest parents who ever lived."

Actually, she kind of understood that, and nodded, but she was still thinking about the timeline. He'd only moved to Amelia Island a little over a year ago.

"So, you knew he lived here before you picked the Fernandina Beach Fire Department when you decided to chase your dreams?"

"Yes."

She distinctly remembered their first conversation when he made it sound like the FBFD was the only department that wanted to train a thirty-three-year-old MBA with a closet full of suits and ties.

"So you picked this location to be near him?"

He stabbed his hand into his close-cropped hair, threading his fingers through it with enough force that it looked like he might pull a few chestnut-brown hairs out by their roots.

"Not exactly but it probably had something to do with it." He gave her a sincere look. "This is all hard to talk about."

"Okay," she whispered. "Take your time."

He nodded, but it took a good half-mile on the highway before he cleared his throat and started to speak.

"I found his address a couple years before my mom died," he started. "Then, when I was moving up in the corporate world, I got sent to a finance conference at the Ritz on Amelia Island. I was close, so I decided to look him up. I wanted to...*connect*." He scoffed the last word, telling her that the connection never happened.

"Anyway, I got to his house, parked across the street, and sat there for a while. Then the door opened and three people came out. It was a youngish dude, in his twenties, and a woman, also young, with long braids, a beautiful Black girl. And my dad, who was, you know, twenty-five years older than I remembered, but I recognized him. I just sat and watched. They all laughed and talked and hugged." He shook his head and gave a dry snort. "So much *hugging*."

"Then what happened?" Chloe asked when he didn't seem to want to finish.

"My dad went back inside and the couple walked down the driveway. I got out of my rental car and stared at the house. The guy kind of checked me out and asked if I was looking for someone. I said Dale McCall and he said..." Travis swallowed. "'Oh, that's my dad. He's in the house.'"

"You didn't know he'd had another son?"

"No. And it just...got me. Like a dagger in the heart. Here's this dude, maybe five years younger than me, with what I assume was his girlfriend, hanging out and... hugging." He swallowed hard. "In my whole life, I have no memory of hugging my dad."

"Oh, Travis." She reached for him again. "That had to hurt."

He rolled his eyes at the understatement. "It gutted me. I had this dream of walking up to the front door and shaking his hand, having him all proud of what I'd become and saying he was sorry and...hugging *me*."

"What happened?" she asked softly, already knowing it hadn't been any of that.

"I left. Never even knocked on the door. I got in the rental car, drove back to the conference, and forgot about him."

"Why?" she asked. "Why didn't you talk to him?"

"I just couldn't," he said. "I can't explain it, but I was consumed with jealousy. Gripping, ugly, dark jealousy. I hated that kid who said he was his son. And my dad. Hated them both with everything I had. Still do, if I'm being honest." He gave a whisper of a smile. "Which, apparently, I finally am."

And she so appreciated that. "But you came back to Amelia Island a few years later," she said.

"I did," he admitted. "The department was on a list of about ten places looking for trainees and I remembered that it was beautiful and warm and..."

"Close to your father."

"That might have played a role, but I never, ever

went back to his house." He let out a sigh, his broad shoulders relaxing as they rolled onto the Buckman Bridge. "Until today, that is."

"Oh, so we're going to that same house?"

"The address the neighbor gave me is on the same street, so yeah." He squeezed her hand.

"How did the neighbor find you?"

"I've had the same cell phone number forever, and I suspect my mother might have given it to him years ago. I don't know." He huffed out a breath. "Listen, Chloe, I don't miss my dad. I didn't need my dad. My mother was awesome and now I have..." He slid into that slow grin that curled her toes and touched her heart. "Wingates. And you, my home girl."

"And, boy, do we hug."

"Seriously." He had to break their hands apart to turn the wheel, glancing down at his GPS. "I've probably hugged your dad more than any other man alive."

"He adores you. Ever since you built that fence around their little guest house, you've been tops in Rex Wingate's book."

"Then he won't say no when I ask for"—he reached for her hand again and lifted it over the console—"this."

It certainly wasn't the first time he'd danced around the subject of marriage. Not even danced. He hadn't proposed, but only because they hadn't even been together for a year. And her last engagement had ended so...horrifically.

But Travis was so different from Hunter Landry. She wouldn't be running away from the altar this time.

On the contrary, she couldn't wait to be married to Travis.

"Do you think he'll, you know, give the old Rex blessing?" he asked when she hadn't responded after a few beats. "You do, don't you?"

He actually sounded nervous, which was adorable. "I guess there's only one way to find out, Probie."

"Hey, not a probie anymore." He shot her a smile and checked his GPS. "Two miles. And, man, I really hope it is a neighbor and not some...trap."

"A trap?" She sat up a little straighter. "What do you mean?"

"You know, his son. Maybe this is just a ploy to get me here, acting like there's some kind of inheritance for me."

She fluttered the seatbelt against her chest, considering that. "Well, if he left you money, then—"

He held up his hand to stop her. "I don't care if he left me a billion dollars and a yacht, Chloe. I won't take one thing of his, not now, not ever."

"Really? Even if he left you a ton of cash?"

He turned onto a side street and took a breath, visibly pulling himself together.

"I don't want his money," he said. "If he left me anything—and I don't know why he would, since he has a real son—it can go to a firefighter charity, every penny."

"You're his real son, too, you know. And if this is a way for your brother to meet you, then—"

"Chloe, no," he said, his tone serious. "I've lived this long without any ties to him and I don't want them now.

Whatever this is about? I don't know. Don't talk me into taking anything of his or getting all...emotional. We'll shake hands, say nice things, and if my dad left anything, I'll instruct him to send it to the Fallen Firefighters Foundation. Promise?"

"I promise," she whispered, squeezing his hand. "Is that why you wanted me to come?"

He leaned across the console. "You make me feel better, Chloe Wingate. When you're with me, I can handle anything. I love you."

"Aw." She kissed him lightly. "I love you, too, Travis McCall."

THE NEIGHBORHOOD in the town of Orange Park was typical of a million like it in Florida—quiet streets, lots of trees, and lined with one-story homes built in the seventies.

On the last turn, Chloe noticed that Travis looked long and hard at a small brick house on a corner, but they parked two doors away.

Holding hands, they walked together to the front door, which was opened by an older woman, easily in her eighties. She greeted them with a yellowed smile and patted her gray hair self-consciously.

"You must be Dale's boy," she said as she pulled the door wider and welcomed them closer.

Next to her, she felt Travis stiffen, but he covered with a handshake. "Mrs. Hanrahan?"

"That's me. Everyone calls me Gramma Kay. Hello, dear." She beamed at Chloe while she shook Travis's hand. "Aren't you a beauty?"

"Hello, Gramma Kay," she said, smiling, and somehow knowing it would help Travis if she handled the social niceties. "This is Travis, and I'm Chloe, his girlfriend."

She gave Chloe her hand to shake, which was knotted from arthritis but soft as silk and surprisingly strong.

"Come in, you two," she said, gesturing them toward a dimly lit living room that smelled like talcum powder and whatever she'd had for breakfast. It was neat, but dated and well-lived in.

At her invitation, Chloe and Travis sat side by side on an orange crushed velvet sofa that might have been around as long as its owner.

"Now, let me look at you," the woman said, sitting in a recliner across from Travis and leaning into the light. "Oh, I can see the resemblance. Yes, sir. You got a lot of your daddy in you."

He shifted with palpable discomfort. "How can we help you, Mrs. Hanrahan?"

She let out a sigh, as if the question disappointed her. "You can let me offer my deepest sympathies on the passing of your father."

Travis nodded silent thanks.

"He didn't talk much about you, but I know he loved you," she added, as if she could read minds.

"We, um, weren't really in touch," Travis said.

"Oh, I know. I'm likely the only person on Earth who

knew about you, and that was just because he gave me your name and that cell phone number. And he told me to call you if I ever needed you, but only if it was an emergency."

Since the man was dead, Chloe figured that emergency had come and gone, but she waited for the woman to continue, fascinated.

"And this, young man," she said, lifting a brow the color and consistency of a Q-Tip, "is one big, fat emergency."

Travis glanced at Chloe, then back at the other woman. "How so?"

"Well, you're the next of kin."

"Oh, no, I'm not. He has—er, had—another son."

Her eyes widened and then she took a slow breath. "You mean Connor?"

"I don't know his name."

She dropped back into the recliner, her gray eyes misty. "Oh, Dale," she muttered to the air. "Why'd you do this to your kids?"

"Pardon?" Travis asked.

She groaned as if what she was about to say would hurt. "Connor and his wife, Aliyah, were killed in an accident two years ago. And none of us, including your daddy, were ever the same."

Travis blanched and automatically reached for Chloe's hand, no doubt getting a punch of guilt for the feelings he'd harbored toward the half-brother he'd never met.

"I...I didn't know that."

"No, of course, you were...not in contact. Because of your stubborn old man. So you are next of kin, son, and this is an emergency." She leaned forward, staring at him. "Connor and Aliyah had a little boy, Judah. And through the grace of our good Lord, that child survived the accident in his car seat."

Chloe sucked in a breath. "There's a child?"

"Dale took him the day they died. And for two years, those two were inseparable, Pops and Judah. Always outside on the street, playing ball, or Dale jogging after that little yellow toy car. I had the great privilege of babysitting that boy many, many times. In fact, he came down the street, all alone and crying when...he found... his Pops on the kitchen floor."

Chloe whimpered and glanced at Travis, who looked like he might pass out.

"He's about to be five now and..."

"Is he here?" Chloe asked, looking around as if this little orphan might appear in the doorway.

"Oh, no, they won't let me keep him," she said. "You see, I'm too old. He's at a temporary foster home. But there he is."

She gestured toward a framed five-by-seven photo on a crowded bookshelf.

"Oh, my gosh," Chloe whispered, nearly melting at the sweet and tiny face of a mixed-race toddler with fat curls and a huge smile and a pair of eyeglasses held in place by an elastic band. "He's precious!"

Travis glanced at the picture, still ashen, maybe shaking, then looked at the woman. "Why are you telling us this?"

She gave a soft laugh of disbelief. "Because he's in a temporary group home over in Mandarin right now. There's just enough money to start him a little savings after the house is sold, but that won't last long. Especially if the wrong people get their hands on it."

"The wrong..." Chloe pressed her hand to her chest. "Will he be a foster child?"

"Soon as they shove him into something they call 'the system,'" Mrs. Hanrahan said, gripping the armrests of the recliner.

"He's so cute," Chloe said, studying the picture.

"Oh, honey, I prayed hard about what to do," the old woman confessed to Travis. "You see, I'm the only person on God's good Earth who knew about you, so I figured that was for a reason. I had to call you. Before little Judah gets shuffled from house to house and waits for a family, I thought I should tell you. Next of kin could take him, no problem. You just sign some papers and he's yours, I think."

Travis's jaw loosened. "I...I can't do that."

Chloe gasped. "Travis! He's an orphan!"

His shoulders dropped and she instantly remembered her promise. But this wasn't money or a house or a *thing*. This was a beautiful, darling, adorable *child*.

"What about his mother's family?" Travis asked. "Doesn't—didn't—she have parents? Siblings?"

"Oh, talk about irony!" she exclaimed. "That angel

was raised in foster homes herself, which is why I'm so certain this isn't what she'd want for her precious baby. She was a go-getter, just like Connor. They met in college—she was bright and put herself through, worked every day—then the two of them got married and started a small business together. They were terrific. Until...that sad, sad day."

"And my...Dale's wife? Connor's mother? Where's she?" Travis asked.

She shook her head. "Oh, honey, she died of cancer when Con was about Judah's age. Dale raised that boy all by himself, then was ready to do it again with Judah. There's nothin' he wouldn't do—"

Travis held up his hand as if he couldn't take any more. "Got it."

"You are Judah's only living relative," the woman continued. "And I just know that boy should have a better chance than foster homes."

"I'm sorry, but I'm in no position to raise a child," he said.

He *wasn't*? Chloe blinked at the statement, forcing herself to stay quiet.

"I'm a firefighter and I frequently do long, long shifts," he said quickly, as if his excuse needed explanation. *Which it did.* "I'm really sorry, Mrs. Hanrahan. I can't help you or...no, I can't."

Was he really going to say no to this child? A shiver rolled over Chloe, along with a crushing blow of disappointment. He wouldn't even meet the kid? She'd jump in heart and soul to take care of that child.

"So, um, we better get out of your hair." Travis stood,

awkwardly muttering his goodbye and thanks, taking a step toward the door. "Best of luck to you. And him," Travis added. "You ready, Chloe?"

She was ready to go get that child. But she just stayed seated with tears stinging her eyes.

"Just one minute," the old woman said, taking two, no, three tries to push up out of the recliner. "I have some information for you about him, in case you change your mind. Stay right there."

She disappeared down the hall, and the minute they were alone, Chloe popped up.

"Travis, you can't possibly—"

"You *promised*, Chloe."

"I promised not to take money. I didn't promise to let that beautiful child, who is your *nephew*, be raised in foster homes! You heard her. You're his only living relative!"

Only then did she see Travis's tears. Unshed and threatening, they filled his green eyes and reflected deep, deep pain.

"Chloe, I can't do it. My father loved his other son so much more than he loved me. He had nothing to do with me. Nothing! Then he raises another son and takes in his kid and...and...*plays in the street* with him. All without acknowledging my existence. I'm sorry, but I cannot look at that kid every day and be reminded of that."

"Do you see him?" she demanded, pointing to the picture and refusing to give credence to that excuse. This wasn't about his father or his half-brother. This was the life of a child.

With trembling hands, she took the frame off the shelf and held it out. "Look at that angel! Look at that sweet face!"

He didn't look. "He's not a puppy you rescue from the side of the road, Chloe. You can't put him in a kennel and find him a good home. He's a *child*."

"Exactly! And I don't want to *find* him a good home. I want to give him one. *Ours*." The idea clutched at her heart, and she pressed the picture against her chest. "We could raise this boy and give him a wonderful life. His parents were killed. His grandparents are dead. His mother was raised in foster homes! Don't you have a heart?"

Tears rolled down Travis's cheeks. "I do. And it was broken by my father. I just...I can't. If you don't mind, I'll be in the truck. Say goodbye for me. I don't want her to... see me."

He walked out, leaving her in shock and fighting her own tears.

"This is the address of the group home," Mrs. Hanrahan called as she came down the hall, then stopped short in the living room. "He left?"

"I'm so sorry," Chloe said, still clutching the photo. "This is hard for him, as you can imagine."

"I know, I know. Dale was...a tough nut to crack." She groaned on her next breath. "I don't really know the history, I'm afraid, and I knew this was a long shot, but I had to ask. Judah is such a dear, dear baby. I'd give anything to take him myself, and I'm sure some nice family will want him."

"That makes me feel better."

"Here." She stuffed a piece of notebook paper in Chloe's hand. "You can go to this address, but call the social worker first. Her name is Mae Ling. I met her. She'll make sure it's okay for you to meet him. Talk to your man and pray about it. Please."

Chloe glanced at the door, pretty sure *her man* wasn't going to talk about anything. "I'll try and thank you... Gramma Kay."

That made her smile.

"Oh, here." Chloe handed her the framed picture.

"You keep it," she said.

"I can't keep your—"

"Let me." She took the picture and turned the frame over, flipping the back off with crinkly but capable old hands. She slid the picture out and handed it to Chloe. "I have a hundred more. You look at him and...well, you know."

She knew. Who could look at that face and say no? Well, Travis, apparently.

"I'm so sorry," she whispered again, sliding the picture and paper into her bag. "It's a complicated, emotional situation."

"There's nothin' complicated about that child," she said. "He loves dogs, but only the little ones."

"Oh," she let out a whimper, thinking of eleven-pound Lady Bug, her precious puppy who loved children.

"And plays T-ball and loves tractors. Oh, that kid goes nuts for a big yellow tractor. And he'll be five on the eighth! For months he's been talking about a Spider-Man party. You think that'll happen at a group home? Oh, and what about his eyes? He needs those glasses! Who'll take him to an eye doctor?"

Chloe held up both hands, her heart cracking so hard she could feel it. "Please. I can't want him any more than I do. But it's not my call. Travis is…"

"A good man who's been hurt by his stubborn, dumb dad. I know." She lifted a narrow shoulder. "I'll pray for him. And you."

"Thank you."

They said goodbye and Chloe walked out to the truck, seeing Travis sitting in the driver's seat with his head back, his eyes closed, in visible agony over what just happened.

She opened the passenger-side door and hoisted herself up to the seat, tucking her bag and the picture it held under her feet.

Travis turned to her, his tears dry but his eyes red-rimmed.

"I know I'm a big, fat disappointment to you," he said on a rasp.

"No, no." She tried to make that sound genuine, but she couldn't argue the point. A real man, a good man would take that child, wouldn't he?

"Well, I'm a disappointment to myself. But that's my dad's legacy, don't you see? He made me look in the mirror and see a kid Dale McCall didn't want. Then, everything I did—from high school to college to business school to following *his* dream that I be a firefighter—

everything was so I could stop disappointing him and he'd magically care about me. But he didn't even know! Not one of those accomplishments hit his radar while he raised another kid by himself and was willing to do it again for a grandson. But me? He never knew a thing about me."

"But your mother knew. I know." She reached for his hand, realizing she'd never known he'd become a firefighter for his father.

"And now?" Travis scoffed. "Now, I get to be yet another disappointment by not being *man* enough to take on the responsibility of that kid." He groaned in agony. "I wish I could say yes, Chloe, I do."

"Then let's use the address she gave me and go see him."

"No!" He barked the word.

"Why not?"

"Because every single time I look at that kid, all I'd feel is...this pain." He banged his fist on his chest. "I can't bear a life full of that. Sorry."

He turned away and stabbed the ignition, rumbling the truck down the street without a word.

They drove all the way home in a sad and confused silence, no stop at Cracker Barrel, no change of heart.

Chapter Four

Sadie

The sun had dipped behind the Amelia River when Sadie walked to the front door to lock up her chocolate shop. There weren't many tourists strolling Wingate Way on a weeknight, and tonight she was grateful. All she wanted to do was close Charmed by Chocolate and spend the evening...charmed by Scout.

The thought made her smile. Everything about Scout Jacobson, the man she'd been dating for several months, put her in a good mood. Did that mean...

Oh, she didn't know. Should she know if she was in love with him or not? Some days, she was certain she was. Deeply. Others, the very idea of ever loving anyone again gave her a shiver of fear.

Today must have been a love day, since she'd been thinking about him from dawn to dusk, and couldn't wait to shower, dress, and head over to his house on the outskirts of Fernandina Beach. He'd promised to make her dinner and let her play with sweet little Rhett Butler, his "ward" for the summer.

Not that the orange tabby he'd been cat-sitting was

much of a cuddler, but Scout had sent lots of cute pictures. She wasn't a crazy cat person, but she loved how nurturing and caring Scout was. He'd have to be for Kitty Worthington, the busiest of town busybodies, to trust him with her beloved Rhett while she spent the summer in Europe.

His cat skills told Sadie that Scout would make a wonderful father, but didn't she already know that? And was she ready for it? Well, she was thirty-six, so...tick-tock went the baby clock.

Scout was certainly ready. In fact, they'd agreed that tonight would be the perfect time to have that serious discussion about...the future. Their next step. A life together. A family.

All of that made her wandering heart clench a bit.

Was that out of anticipation—or fear?

Just as she turned the lock, Sadie caught sight of a familiar blonde walking two dogs across the street.

What was Chloe doing in Fernandina Beach instead of her rescue refuge a few miles south of town?

She pushed the door open and stepped out on the street. "Hey, sister!"

Both dogs barked at her, one a pocket-sized furball affectionately known as Lady Bug, and the other, her pit bull of a maidservant, Buttercup. The two dogs were never far apart, though they made an unlikely pair, and they were never far from Chloe, wherever she was.

But why was she here?

Chloe waved, checked the street, which was empty of

traffic, and jaywalked over to greet Sadie with the two dogs leading on their leashes.

"What brings you to town this time of night?" Sadie asked, giving her sister a hug when she arrived, then a quick pet to each of the dogs.

"I dropped off a dog I'd been boarding for a client, and decided to take a walk down Wingate Way, hoping one of my sisters' businesses would still be open."

"You are in luck," Sadie said, regarding her youngest sibling carefully, noticing she didn't look as bright and bubbly as usual. "Everything okay?"

"Yeah. No. I don't know."

"And on that definitive note, you want to come inside?"

"It's so beautiful tonight and the dogs are way too tempted by all that chocolate," Chloe said. "Walk with me? Or are you busy?"

As much as Sadie wanted to start her night with Scout, it could wait. In the months since she'd moved back from Brussels, she'd learned that when one of her six sisters showed up for "no reason," there was always a reason.

And she wasn't about to say no to the baby of the bunch.

"Let me ditch my apron and grab my keys and phone. I'll be right back."

She shot a quick text to Scout announcing a brief delay and, a few minutes later, the two sisters were strolling along the banks of the river and past the long wharf, led by Lady Bug. Buttercup stayed close to Chloe, stopping to sniff wherever she could.

"Sometimes this part of Wingate Way reminds me of Europe," Sadie mused when Chloe seemed unusually quiet. "The river, the small town, the little shops and pedestrian traffic."

"Mmm." Chloe nodded, but her gaze was distant, locked on the lights across the river on the mainland, making Sadie wonder if she'd even heard the comment.

"So how did the big planning sesh go?" Sadie asked.

Chloe shot her a look of confusion. "The planning— Oh. With Mom and the brides. I, um, canceled."

"Why?"

Blowing out a breath that puffed out her cheeks, Chloe slowed her step. "I had to go to Jacksonville with Travis."

"Oh?" The trip wasn't that odd, but the note in Chloe's voice was.

"Yeah. There's the small matter of a four-year-old orphan boy who happens to be the son of Travis's late half-brother and has no other living relatives."

Sadie nearly tripped on her next step. "*Excuse me?*"

"Travis's dad passed away—"

"Oh, Chloe! They didn't have a relationship, though, right?"

"Zero. Travis hadn't seen him since he was a child, but he had another family, a son, and that young man and his wife were killed in an accident and left behind a little boy. Dale, Travis's father, had been taking care of him, but he died suddenly. A neighbor called Travis to see if he could take the child and keep him out of the foster system."

Sadie could only shake her head, trying to process this bomb her sister just dropped. "Is he going to?"

"No," she whispered, the single syllable packed with pain. "And that's every kind of wrong, if you ask me. Which, for the record, Travis did not do, since this is his decision, not mine."

"Come over here," Sadie said, motioning toward a bench that faced the river. "We need to be sitting down for this."

On the bench, Chloe slid a photograph from her bag, handing it to Sadie. "Look at Judah McCall and tell me that isn't the single most adorable little man you've ever seen."

Sadie angled the five-by-seven print in the dim light and, yes, she had to smile. The child's face was tipped to the side, wearing glasses that looked slightly crooked, under a mop of dark curls. He had a button nose, an endearing baby-toothed smile, and sweet, soft skin the color of fine cacao powder.

While she studied him and the dogs settled to snooze, Chloe relayed the details of her morning, focusing mostly on Travis's abject refusal to even discuss the possibility of taking in this poor child.

"I want to be understanding of Travis's position," Chloe finished with a soft grunt. "But I am not. Who says no to a child?"

Sadie lifted a brow. "Well, lots of people. Especially a single man who didn't know the kid existed and still harbors deep and real psychological pain from being abandoned by his father. Oh, and he frequently works forty-eight-hour shifts at the fire station. That's who."

Her eyes shuttered. "I guess, but...look at that sweet, sweet baby boy."

"That's just it, Chloe. He's a *boy*, not a puppy."

"That's what Travis said." She leaned over and gave Buttercup's big head a scratch. "This from the same guy who brought this dog to me—and she was pregnant! We found all her puppies a home and kept her. No foster homes for Buttercup or her pups."

"Buttercup's a dog," Sadie said, easily able to see Travis's side. "She won't need to be groomed into adulthood, provided with food, clothing, and shelter, given an education, raised to be a fine man, and worried about forever."

Chloe slid her a side-eye. "Yes, Judah will need all that, which is what families do. That is what this child deserves, not to be shuffled around foster homes, a victim of the system."

And Sadie could see that side, too. "It's a massive decision, Chloe. You have to at least give him time to think about it."

"I don't think he is thinking about it," she said. "He has this unbelievable ability to wipe his mind clear of anything and focus on other things."

"Like saving lives, putting out fires, and generally being a hero."

Chloe sighed, staring out at the water.

"It's his decision, Chloe, not yours."

"I know," she said glumly. "I have a weak spot for strays and rescues. And I know nothing about this kid, or even the first thing about being a mother."

"A *mother*? Did they ask you to take the child?"

"No, but we're talking about getting married—"

"You are?"

"Are you surprised?" Chloe asked. "Travis and I love each other, we're perfectly compatible, and we both want the same things in life. Or at least I thought we did."

"Is that all that's necessary to get married?" Sadie asked, an image of Scout flashing in her mind.

They loved each other, were perfectly compatible, and wanted the same things in life.

"Well, I mean, there's that indefinable...thing," Chloe said. "But we have that, too. Always have, since the day I bumped into him on the street and my phone went flying."

Sadie frowned. "What is that...thing?"

"Indefinable," she repeated.

"No, no," Sadie insisted. "Define it."

Chloe angled her head, thinking. "I guess it's that magical, chemical, wonderful...connection. Like no one else is in the world when we're together. We have that in spades and I do think we're going to stay together forever. So I simply do not see a problem becoming parents to a child that is related to him and is currently about to be dropped into the foster system."

Sadie nodded, knowing that was a real and immediate problem worth discussing, but she was stuck on the *thing*.

"Did you feel it from the very beginning?" Sadie asked. "The thing, I mean."

Chloe threw her a look, like she was surprised Sadie had stayed on that topic. "Yeah, I guess."

"Both of you felt it? Or did one of you grow into it?"

Chloe regarded Sadie closely, inching in to narrow her eyes in question. "Are you having issues with Scout?"

Sadie opened her mouth to answer, then shut it again. She'd forgotten how difficult it was to keep anything from her sisters.

"Let's not go there," she said. "Keep talking about Judah. What are you going to do?"

Chloe took the picture back and slid it in her bag. "I'm not going to do anything about Judah. I gave my opinion, but as you said, it's not my decision. What are you going to do about Scout? Because a blind man can see that man feels *all* the things for you."

Sadie sighed. "And I feel them for him, but I'm a slow burn, Chloe."

"And Scout's ready for a bonfire," Chloe joked.

"We're friends before anything else, but I can feel that shifting every time we're together." Sadie let her head drop back, closing her eyes.

"Do you love him?" Chloe asked.

"I...don't know. It's hard to have perspective," she admitted. "I was destroyed by my last relationship, as you know. Eloped and dumped all in the blink of an eye. Then betrayed for my chocolate recipe and bought off by the man's family, who erased our marriage from history."

Sadie gave a derisive snort. "Is it any wonder I'm petrified to fall in love again?"

"Hey, you're talking to the original runaway bride," Chloe said.

"Then you understand," Sadie said. "Don't get me wrong. I'm crazy about Scout. He's solid as a rock, sweet as pie, and looks at me kind of like Buttercup is looking at you right now."

Chloe chuckled and leaned down to nuzzle the dog's big tan face. "But you want to take it slow."

"Not forever slow," Sadie said. "Scout's forty. And he wants kids. That's why he's practicing with Rhett Butler."

"Excuse me?"

"Kitty Worthington's cat, Rhett Butler."

Chloe cackled. "Who would name—never mind, it's Kitty. Wait, she's in Europe with Raina's former mother-in-law, isn't she?"

"Exactly. Kitty and Val headed overseas and Mr. Worthington went to Maine for the whole summer, so Scout is watching her cat, Rhett Butler. He's taking the responsibility very seriously and I believe this is his practice for parenthood."

"Gee, she could have boarded ol' Rhett at Rocky's Rescues," Chloe said, sounding a little miffed. "Travis helped me redo a whole room just for the cats, with climbing trees and private sleeping areas. We get lots of cats for boarding."

"Don't take it personally," Sadie told her. "Kitty is

super weird about Rhett. Her last cat, Scarlett O'Hara, ran away and never came back, so she is paranoid."

"Aww," Chloe cooed. "Maybe she should try Elizabeth and Mr. Darcy next time. Happy-ending books only. But, seriously, any man who could get Kitty Worthington to trust him is a keeper, Sadie."

"I know that," she said, reaching into her back pocket for her vibrating phone. "I bet that's Scout now," she said. "I told him..." She frowned at the screen. "Uh-oh."

"What's wrong?"

"Rhett Butler emergency. Scout needs me now."

"Oh, I'm sorry for keeping you, Sadie." Chloe pushed up. "But thanks for talking to me."

"Any time," Sadie said, and meant it. "I liked learning about 'the thing.' Assuming Rhett is okay, we did agree that tonight is the night for talking about...our next step in this relationship."

"My advice, big sister?" Chloe took Sadie's hands and pulled her closer. "Take the next step. He's a good man, he puts a light in your eyes, and you need to let down your walls so you can see that."

"Aw, Chloe." She gave her little sister an impulsive kiss and they turned to walk back to the chocolate shop. In that short time, Sadie got three more texts that just said, "Please come now," with way too many exclamation points.

"Gotta run! Keep me posted on the Judah sitch!" she called, rushing toward her car. As she hurried to his house, she was a little surprised—and pleased—that she wanted to drop everything and help him. Was that...the *thing*?

She hoped so, but deep inside, she just wanted to feel...love.

Scout shot out of his three-bedroom ranch-style home with a look of sheer panic on his face. He rushed to Sadie's car and pulled the driver's-side door open before she had her seatbelt off.

"Gonzo," he announced. "Absolutely disappeared into thin air."

Sadie gasped, somehow able to understand even though he didn't say who, what, when or how. Rhett Butler was missing.

She climbed out and put her hands on his shoulders. He wasn't much more than five-foot-ten and his body was more "soft" than muscular, but she'd hugged him enough to know she'd never felt him so tense before.

"It's okay. We'll find him. I promise. How long ago did he get out?" She looked around, suddenly seeing the dozens of forty-foot pines and oak trees—many of them draped with Spanish moss—in a completely different way.

Instead of natural beauties that provided shade and increased the value of every property in this residential section, the trees were actually...a place a cat could hide and never, ever be found.

"I have no idea how he got out, Sadie." His voice was

just about broken with frustration as he followed her gaze up. "I was here around lunchtime to check on him and he was fine. Hiding under my bed, but I could see him. Then I came home from work a couple hours later and I couldn't find him anywhere."

"Open door or window?"

"I found a tear in the screen on the back porch," he said, true pain in his voice. "It doesn't look big enough for him to get through, but he's not in the house."

"Well, we're going to look everywhere," she assured him. "Every inch of the house. Oh, do you have an attic? My mom found cats in the Wingate House attic a few months ago. A pregnant one with kittens."

"I checked the attic. Everywhere. Inside, outside, all around the yard, and..." He let out a moan. "Kitty will never forgive me. She may ruin my life. If I even live to tell the tale."

"We'll find him," she assured him on a laugh.

Scout finger-combed his hair, making the thick brown waves messier. "Seriously, I gave her my word nothing would happen to that cat. Sadie, I am nothing if not a man of my word."

She couldn't argue with that, looking around—and up—again. A cat could leap from branch to branch and find his way a mile down the road and never touch the ground.

"But they always come home, don't they?" she asked.

"One would hope, but they're not boomerangs. Cats get lost all the time."

She snapped her fingers. "Home! Have you checked Kitty's house? She's not far, right? Just off Ash Street?"

"Oh, you are a genius!" he exclaimed. "Maybe he sniffed his way back to his real home."

"Come on." She gestured toward the passenger side. "Let's go over now."

"First, let me leave some food at the front door and get Kitty's house key. You look around out here."

"Okay, and Scout?" She took his hands and pulled him closer. "We'll find him."

"And if we don't?" he scoffed. "Me...*owwww*." He made claw fingers and a mean face, which made her laugh, even though it was a serious situation.

While he went into the house, she looked around his yard, which, sadly, wasn't fenced in. Not that a six-foot fence would stop a cat, but maybe. She found the tear in his back screen that couldn't have been five inches long, but Rhett Butler was long, lean...and bright orange.

Surely they'd find him.

"There's food on the front porch," Scout said as he hustled to the car.

"Won't he just eat it and leave?" Sadie asked.

"But if he knows it's always out there, maybe he'll show up again and again."

They were quiet as she drove very slowly—looking between every house, peering at every bush and around every corner. She wove the car through a warren of side streets, then along Central Park until they reached a cheery yellow turn-of-the-century home with meticulous gardens and more trees.

Night was falling fast and the only real light came from some spotlights on the front shrubbery, making her heart fall at the thought of how difficult this would be.

"Don't call too loud," he said as they got out. "I don't want a neighbor to hear us and send a text over to Kitty in Paris. She'll be on the next flight home."

And that would break Valerie Wallace's heart, Sadie thought. Raina's former mother-in-law had escaped a treacherous health scare and she and her new buddy, Kitty, had decided to celebrate with a long-dreamed-about tour of Europe.

She had no doubt Kitty would come home for her cat —and make Scout's life miserable for losing him.

They combed the property, looked up every tree, and searched every bush. Sadie even crawled under the tiny space below the front porch—Scout couldn't fit—but there was no sign of the orange cat.

They used the house key to go inside to check every window on the off-chance Rhett had found an open one. They searched high and low, to no avail.

Frustrated and disappointed—and starving—they headed back to Scout's house.

"I'm going to make us some dinner," he said as they climbed out of her car.

"I'm going to do one more walk around the property," Sadie replied.

With two flashlights, a pocket full of kitty treats, and a whole lot of determination, she combed the acre or so of his lot, calling for Rhett Butler until her throat hurt. When she heard a rustling in one of the oak trees, she put the flashlights on the ground—pointed up—and started to climb.

She'd made it six feet off the ground when she spotted Scout walking across the grass toward her lights.

"I'm up here," she called with a laugh.

He slowed and looked up at her. "Look at you, Sadie Wingate."

"I know, I know. But I heard a noise..."

He reached the bottom of the tree. "Come on down."

"Did you find him?" she asked hopefully.

He just shook his head. "No, but I found you climbing a tree looking for him, which is...really cute. Please come down."

She gave up and shimmied down the trunk, hopping to the grass, tumbling onto her backside.

She looked up at him, her heart folding at the expression on his face as he offered her his hand. Despite his frustration and worry, he gazed at her...well, yes, like Buttercup looked at Chloe.

He helped her up, and right then, in the reflection of two flashlights and a full moon, she felt...something. Something real and strong and tender and...yes. Was this...the *thing*?

"We were supposed to have that talk tonight," she reminded him on a whisper. "About...us."

His features softened, really smiling for the first time since she'd arrived so many hours ago.

"I don't need to talk, Sadie. I know how I feel about a woman who'll drop everything, crawl under a porch, and climb a tree for me."

"For you and Rhett Butler. And please let me make a 'frankly, my dear, I do give a damn' joke."

He snorted. "Come on in. I made chicken and vegetables and there's wine."

"Mmm. Wine." But she didn't move, except to slide her arms around his waist and look up at him. "You sure you don't want to talk?"

"Do you?"

She gazed at him, her whole being feeling tender and warm and trusting. She wanted to...know. Was this love? Friendship? Something in between or a little of both? Was that how she defined the *thing*?

Without a word, she lifted her face toward his and invited a kiss. Their lips met for a long, long time as they melted into each other.

"If this were a movie," she murmured into his lips, "Rhett Butler would jump down from the tree, land at our feet, and meow a happy ending."

"If this were a movie," he replied, twirling one of her long curls in his fingers, "I'd swoop you into my arms, carry you into my bedroom, and...have a different happy ending."

"I like yours better."

With a smile, he tugged her toward the house. "Me, too. But let's just walk together. No swooping. Who do you think I am? Superman?"

She dropped her head on his shoulder, chuckling at his easy, self-deprecating humor. "Consider me swooped, Martin Jacobson."

Chapter Five

Susannah

Twenty-four hours after her run-in with Ivy Button, Susannah was still a wreck. Somehow, she'd managed to hide it from Rex, but only because he'd been wrapped up in doing a Wingate Properties deal with Chase.

When he was home, she pretended to be too busy to talk. So she spent hours in the tiny office space she'd set up in the smaller guest room, pretending to be consumed with the business of running Wingate House as a wedding venue.

She was consumed, all right.

With grief and fear and worry. But not doubt. Not for one split second did she doubt her husband. That woman —and possibly Doreen—had lied about him. Rex Wingate was not capable of hurting someone like that, period, full stop.

Her faith in him did not, however, erase the echo of the ugly, unthinkable words.

It wasn't enough to rape a poor lovestruck woman who had the IQ of a dust mop—Rex got her pregnant, too!

Absolutely wretched slander, that's what that was. The only person who knew the truth, Doreen, had been dead for more than a year. How could Rex possibly defend himself from such awful allegations?

This would wreck him. Goodness, it could implode their family, their businesses, their lives. And it could bring on a heart attack or seizure or...another stroke.

She couldn't let herself go there.

But what if Ivy Button really did have some kind of contract or claim on the property? True or false, it gave her the power and the upper hand. Worst-case scenario? They could lose the glorious house that had been in their family for more than one hundred years.

Best case? There wasn't one except for Ivy Button to disappear into the shadows as quickly as she'd arrived.

Susannah's first instinct had been to run to the problem-solver of the family, Raina. But one look at Raina and Tori, and she realized that she simply couldn't dump this in the laps of any of her daughters.

She couldn't bear to plant that dark and despicable seed, giving them a mental image that would physically hurt no matter how much they'd know it was a lie.

Especially when everyone was finally so happy! Every single one of her daughters was in a solid, steady, stable place in their lives, all of them living right here on Amelia Island.

And one of the biggest reasons for their happiness? Rex had survived a stroke well over a year ago, reminding all of them just how much they adored their loving father.

Madeline, the oldest, had recently married for the first time at fifty, and spent every day on a cloud with the only man she'd ever loved. Tori and Raina were both about to exchange vows with wonderful men—and on the same day! Rose was blooming, as always, in a loving marriage with four delightful kids.

And the youngest three, Sadie, Grace, and Chloe, were all at lovely new places in their lives. Chloe had launched her animal rescue—of course, with the help of her father—and Sadie had opened Charmed by Chocolate.

Moreover, both of them were on the precipice of falling in love with terrific guys.

And Grace! Married to a man of great faith, and she finally had her darling daughter in a special program to address her autism.

The last word put another hitch in Susannah's heart. Doreen had died suddenly on the heels of Nikki Lou's diagnosis and, at the time, Susannah and Grace talked about the possibility that Doreen had suffered from the same disorder.

The older woman's lack of social skills, her inability to have emotional connections, her outbursts and sometimes inexplicable behavior...all of it made them realize they'd been wrong in calling her "Dor-mean." They should have recognized the signs that she was somewhere on the spectrum of autism.

Did Rex have any inkling of that on the day they—

"Please don't tell me this Wingate House business has you that miserable."

She spun around at the sound of her husband's voice, stunned, yanked from her thoughts, and surely looking as guilty as she did miserable.

"Oh, hello. I'm sorry—just thinking."

"And hard," Rex said. "Anything I can help with?"

Yes, she thought. All she had to do was tell him, and he'd start the process of fixing this problem. But how would it feel to face such an unfair accusation? It could... kill him.

And that wasn't hyperbole.

"Suze?" He came into the room, searching her face. As soon as he did, the tiny gray cat sleeping between two oversized pillows on the daybed made a happy noise and stretched, her eyes on Rex. Susannah may have rescued Cora and her kittens from the inn's attic, but this cat loved Rex more than anyone else.

She didn't answer as he sat on the edge of the comforter, stroking Cora's head, but looking at Susannah.

"This is more than scheduling problems at your wedding mecca," he observed.

"Yeah, no. I just..." She had no idea what to say.

Maybe if she got him to talk about it. Maybe if they circled the subject of Doreen Parrish, she'd find out what happened, get a clue as to how to defend him. Could she do that?

"What are you working on?" he asked, absently pressing the heel of his free hand against his chest as he looked over her shoulder at the darkened computer screen and the empty desk surface under it.

"I'm just...thinking."

"About the double wedding?" He shook his head with a wry smile. "I had a feeling nothing about that would be easy, but the girls have it in their heads now. Don't tell me, Tori wants to cater it and Raina wants to make all the decisions."

"No, they..." She fisted her hands and said a silent prayer for help before asking her next question. "Rex, do you ever think about Doreen Parrish?"

He inched back, his dark brows drawing together. "Not too often. Why?"

"Because I...I came across something that made me think of her and I, um, wondered."

"If it has sentimental value, I suppose you could give it to Blake," he said. "He's asked me a few questions, knowing that she was his biological grandmother. I've tried to paint her in a not-too-negative light, but, hey, there was a reason the girls called her Dor-mean."

She flinched at that.

"Which I suppose is deeply unkind," he added, reading her reaction. "What brought that on?"

"I guess I've been thinking about...you and her. You know, you had a...a thing? What would you call it?"

He didn't answer right away, then said, "I'd call it a mistake. Well, ultimately, it gave us Blake, and I love him as much as any of my grandchildren, but that..." He shook his head. "That encounter was not my finest moment. I should have said no, and it couldn't have been easy for her to have a kid and give him up for adoption."

"And you absolutely didn't know?" she pressed. "She never told you she was pregnant?"

He tipped his head, a frown forming. "You know that, Suze. I had no idea until my biological son showed up and needed money."

"Then you talked to her, right?"

"Of course. Like I told you, I was furious she'd never told me about Bradley, but she just dismissed me and looked past me."

"But you did pay Brad," she said, wondering if there was something in that exchange that could prove Rex's innocence.

"I helped a man who was losing his family farm, but that's all he wanted. No relationship." Rex searched her face, clearly flummoxed by the conversation. "Why, Suze? What was it you found?"

"Nothing, really." How could she tell him...*it was Ivy Button and she found me*. She took a deep breath, and... couldn't do it. "Did your father know what happened?"

"From what I've been able to piece together, she and my dad had an...arrangement that gave her a secure job for life. Did he know she had a baby? Maybe. He certainly never told me, but he was a fair man and wanted to help her when she came back."

"So he offered her a lifetime job at the inn," Susannah said, familiar with that version of history. "Nothing more?"

"What else could he offer her?"

She shook her head, dangerously close to the truth. "Is there any...paperwork?" At his look, she added, "Of that arrangement, I mean."

"Oh, no. It was unspoken. As long as he was alive, she

had a job, and after he died, well..." He lifted a shoulder. "We didn't have the heart to let her go, and by then you did the heavy lifting on the inn management and she basically cooked breakfast and ticked off housekeepers."

She stared at him, thinking. "You're sure he never wrote anything down to confirm that arrangement?"

"I don't think so. Why?"

Because it would go a long way to keeping Ivy's grubby hands off the Inn. "I don't know," she said instead, purposefully vague. "It feels like a loose end."

"To what?" he asked on a laugh, turning his attention to the cat trying to knead his legs. "All parties involved are long gone and I don't have anything terrible to say about Doreen. She was...a sad case."

"Did you know that when you"—she lifted a brow—"were with her?"

"I knew that I was a dumb kid and she was...determined." He looked down at Cora, petting her small head. "Look, the poor woman's dead and I don't need to besmirch her reputation."

But her niece was about to besmirch Rex's.

"Why didn't you...turn her down?" she asked, shifting a little uncomfortably.

"'Cause I was, what, nineteen? Not the age of, uh, reason when it comes to things like that. When a girl says..." He shook his head and looked up from Cora, agony in his eyes. "Don't make me relive the sins of my past, Suze. It's embarrassing. Are Raina and Chase on their way over with—"

"Can you tell me about what happened?" she asked.

He screwed up his face. "Why?"

"I'm curious."

He grunted and looked skyward, a typical man who didn't want to talk about things like this.

"Suze, it was the late sixties. I know you were only a kid then, but for teenagers and college kids, like I was? It was...free love, no boundaries, and...and...she was *dead set* on sex. I'm sorry, it's not something I'm proud of, but it happened." He leaned forward, easing the cat to the side to pin his tortured expression on Suze. "Don't judge me for that. Or her, for that matter."

Someone was going to judge him if this got out. All seven of his daughters, a town full of people who loved him, and every client he'd ever had.

And if she told him that, it would break him. Even if it wouldn't, she couldn't bear to see how he'd react—from anger to sorrow to helplessness.

"I'd really like to drop the subject," he said, with nothing but pain and remorse in his voice, a world of pain in his eyes. In fact, he winced, and pressed his chest again.

"Rex." She stood, alarmed. "Is it your heart? A chest pain?"

"No, it's nothing," he insisted. "I don't like talking about this, even with Blake. I'm sorry it happened, and I think I paid the price for one really dumb teenage mistake."

"You have," she said, walking to him and putting her hand on his chest. "Does it hurt?"

He searched her face, agony still making his dark eyes

even darker. "What hurts is that I disappointed you. I know, I know. I was young, but it's no excuse. I should have looked at that girl and been the one to say no. I just took advantage of her willingness."

"No, no," she insisted. "You didn't take advantage of her. Don't say that. Don't ever say that. If anything, it was the other way around."

He lifted a shoulder, as if to say the semantics didn't matter. "I'm still not proud of my past, Suze. So let's keep it buried like poor Doreen."

The doorbell rang and ended the conversation for them, and made Cora leap off the daybed and scoot under it.

"That's probably Raina and Chase dropping off the babies," Rex said, standing to leave the room and looking very happy for the distraction.

She nodded, following him to the front door with a sickening sense that this wasn't going to stay buried. Not for very long.

Chapter Six

Raina

"How did we get here?" Raina mused, perching her elbows on the gleaming wood of the conference room table of Cooper and Broderick, a family law practice on the south end of Amelia Island.

Next to her, Chase gave her a bemused look, his dark eyes glinting, his handsome smile warm but a little wry. "I assume you mean that rhetorically, or were you really not paying attention after we left your parents' house and I drove us here?"

"I meant, how did this happen so fast? I was talking to Tori about it yesterday. It feels like a week ago that I got the call that my dad had a stroke and my ex-husband was showing all the signs of cheating—that I missed, thank you very much—and then I moved to Amelia Island, bought a house, fell for the owner, had two babies, and wham. We're at a family law office arranging for you to legally adopt two baby girls. Oh, and we're getting married." She looked skyward. "One of these days, anyway."

"Do not delay our wedding, Rain," he said, taking her

hand. "And do not reduce this amazing time together to a bullet-point presentation."

"Some habits die hard," she joked.

"You miss work?"

She snorted. "Not even a little. Especially when I heard about how you and Blake already have two offers on the new development down on Juniper."

"Hey, that was all your nephew. He's a natural, you know, and he's teaching me the Wingate Properties ropes as much as I'm mentoring him."

She smiled, thinking of how easily Chase had slid into her role to manage the business.

"I'm disappointed that your father wasn't more excited about that deal when I mentioned it today," Chase said, a frown pulling. "He seemed a bit preoccupied."

She'd noticed that as well. "Do you think whatever is bothering my mother is working on him, too?"

"I don't know, but you're right about Suze. She's tense."

Raina shuttered her eyes, worried when her mother did the whole "fake happy" thing again and managed not to whisper a word about what was really on her mind. She still seemed distracted, no matter how much she pretended otherwise.

"I'll make sure you get time with her when we pick up the babies," Chase said, always so in tune with Raina's thoughts. "Maybe you can find out what's going on. Or tell her your surprise."

"Then it wouldn't be a surprise," she said. "Anyway,

we'll have to see what the lawyer says. It's probably the dumbest thing he's ever heard—the totally unnecessary adoption of four adult women."

Chase gave an amused look. "Truth? It's so Wingate, it kind of hurts."

"I know, right?" She gave a happy clap, clinging to the idea no matter how dumb it was.

They both looked up at the sound of footsteps, peering through the glass wall at a young man who looked fresh out of law school, and a woman with short auburn hair, her face deep into a legal file, flipping pages like a speed reader.

Coming into the conference room, the man introduced himself as Timothy Sherwood, the newest attorney in the firm, who'd be handling the adoption process. Yes, he was definitely still in his twenties, but he seemed enthusiastic and bright, and how hard could it be to shepherd this adoption through the legal loopholes? Raina greeted him, and turned toward the woman who waited her turn.

"Helen Lensky-Fallon," she said, shaking Raina's hand. "I'm an adoption specialist that legal firms bring on as a consultant and a representative. My job will be to conduct the interviews, visits, and investigation that will uncover anything that could delay or impair the process."

"Nice to meet you," Chase said, getting a raised eyebrow from behind the woman's reading glasses.

"We'll see about that," she muttered as they took seats. At their surprised look, she shrugged. "I'm a stickler for rules and regs, and I assure you that not one T will go uncrossed and no I will be undotted. If you're hiding something nefarious, I will find it."

Raina and Chase exchanged a quick look.

"Nothing that I know of," Raina said, giving him a playful elbow. "Unless you have a secret wife in the attic you forgot to mention."

They both laughed, but Helen with the hyphenated last name didn't even crack a smile.

"From a legal standpoint, this is an easy process," Tim said, flipping a legal pad to a page with some notes on it. "We file for a hearing and before that happens, Helen will do the interview and site visits, conduct the research, and basically ensure that when we stand in front of the judge, there are no surprises. Then you, Mr. Madison, will be named the legal father of..." He glanced down at his legal pad. "Charlotte and Lillian Wingate."

Chase nodded, but shifted his attention to the woman. "How many interviews and visits?" he asked. "We were under the impression this was a fairly quick process."

"We're talking about two children who are too young to speak and have two living biological parents," she replied. "You and Ms. Wingate aren't married, have known each other for less than a year, and have three divorces between you." She flicked her brows. "That I know of."

They both managed not to react, but under the table, Chase squeezed Raina's hand in solidarity.

"The living biological father has relinquished all

parental rights," Raina said, glancing at the attorney. "You've shared the documents from my divorce decree?"

"Oh, he has," Helen answered for him. "But look at Tiny Tim." She pointed a pen in the lawyer's direction and the poor guy turned bright red. "Do you think he has the experience I do?"

The lawyer gave a nervous laugh. "Well, I—"

"This is not an open-and-shut adoption process," Helen said, steamrolling right over young Tim. "So you two will need to exercise patience, restraint, and be ready to offer up your lives and families to scrutiny."

"That's fine," Chase said. "But we want this done as quickly as possible."

She regarded him over half-moon reading glasses. "What's your hurry, Mr. Madison?"

"My hurry is a powerful desire to be legally, financially, emotionally, spiritually, and morally responsible for two tiny babies I already love like my own," he said without a nanosecond of hesitation. "You are welcome to scrutinize anything you like, ma'am. We're just asking that it be done expeditiously."

She shuttered her eyes and shifted her attention back to the file.

"As I said, legally, it's rather easy," Tim said, trying to recover from the insult to his age. "While Helen does her part, I will submit a motion to get on the judge's calendar. Once we have that date fixed, we'll take it from there."

"Do you have any other children?" Helen asked Chase.

"I don't."

"Are you sure?"

He gave an uneasy laugh. "As sure as I can be."

She flipped a page. "I see you have family in Italy."

He lifted a brow. "The only family I have is in Palermo," he acknowledged. "My parents, an American mother and Italian father, have passed. I have no siblings. Will you need to go to Italy and interview my cousins?"

"As much as I'd like to, we can probably do that by video conference," she said. "And you, Ms. Wingate? Do you have family close by?"

She almost laughed. "I'm one of seven sisters, and we're all on Amelia Island."

"Then I'll meet every one of them. Parents?"

"Yes, both living and currently watching the babies." She considered the special favor she'd wanted to ask, but thought better of it. Helen would not be the right person to coordinate a "surprise" adult adoption. In fact, she might be the most wrong person in the world.

Maybe Tim could help.

The woman asked a few more questions, making random notes as the attorney looked through a calendar, and they discussed various dates that were blacked out or unavailable.

After that, they signed some papers and then Tim closed the files to end the meeting. When he said he'd walk them to the elevator, Raina decided to take the chance.

As they headed into the hall, she shot a look at Chase, who nodded, of course knowing what she was thinking.

How wonderful it was to have a partner in life who could read your mind.

"Mr. Sherwood," she began. "I have one other request, and it's, uh, a little unorthodox."

"You can call me Tim," he said. "Just not Tiny Tim," he added with a dry laugh. "And ask me anything."

"Thank you. I wanted to know if you think it would be possible to arrange to adopt an adult stepchild without letting the adopter know until the hearing."

Tim gave a soft laugh of confusion. "I'm not sure I follow."

"My mother, who is technically stepmother to three of my sisters and me, never finalized our adoption when she married my father," she told him. "She went on to have three more daughters, and we're all very close. But I recently learned that my mother didn't legally adopt us and I would like to make that happen."

"We can set up a meeting with her and—"

"I want to surprise her," Raina interjected. "I'd like her to find out the adoption is happening at the same hearing when Chase adopts my daughters."

He inched back, a frown pulling on his face. "I doubt that is something that could be—"

"Oh, yes, it can." Helen popped into the conversation from around the corner, not even trying to hide that she'd been eavesdropping.

Raina turned to her, stunned by that, and her response, not sure how to react.

"I assume I'm interviewing all the same family members," she said when all three of the others stared at her. "Well, then, I can ask a few questions. How many years back are we going?"

"They just celebrated their fortieth anniversary," Raina said. "And Suze—that's my stepmother—has been in my life since I was three."

Helen the hard-hearted looked like she might melt, putting a hand to her chest. "Then I want to be in that courtroom when she gets the good news."

"But I'll need signatures—"

Helen wiped away Tim's argument with the sweep of her hand. "You just fill out the motion for this family, get the hearing on the calendar with this one, and the adoptees and new mother can sign everything that day."

"Oh!" Raina gasped, suddenly overwhelmed by the support from such an unexpected corner, and warmed by the words *adoptees* and *new mother*. Susannah would love that! "That would be so wonderful!"

"I'm not making any promises," she said, "but it shouldn't be that hard."

"Thank you," Chase said. "I admit I'm surprised by this, considering your love of crossed T's and dotted I's."

"I had a stepmother I loved very much," she said. "She's the reason I chose this business." She gave a tight smile. "She tried to adopt me but couldn't for long and complicated reasons, and eventually, we let it go. But at the end of her life, I wasn't allowed to go into the ICU when she was dying because of a legal technicality."

"Oh," Raina muttered. "That's beyond wrong."

"I don't want anyone to go through that," she said. "And I love your idea of surprising her."

"Thank you," Raina said, seeing the woman in an entirely different light. "I'm sorry you lost your mother."

She nodded and turned, and they all stood in a moment of awkward surprise.

"I'll call you, Raina," Tim said. "And you can email me the names of the adoptees and your mother's information. I'll add them to the hearing schedule when I file."

When they said goodbye, Raina and Chase floated out to the car on a cloud of laughter and anticipation. They were certain the hearing would be one of the best days of their lives.

"WHAT IS GOING ON HERE?" Raina asked as they pulled into her parents' driveway. "Was there a Wingate party I didn't know about?"

With a quick scan of the cars, it looked like a lot, if not all, of her sisters were here. Had something happened to her parents? The babies? She slipped her phone out to check to see if there'd been an emergency text on the 7 *Sis* group chat.

Nope. Nothing.

"Let's see what's going on," she said, shooting a worried look to Chase.

They hustled to the front door, which was unlocked, and when they opened it, they heard chatter and laughter, which was a relief.

"Hey, who had a party and didn't invite me?" Raina

asked as she came up the stairs to the main-floor living area.

There, she saw a group of familiar faces all hovering around one—no, two—babies. Charlie was in Madeline's arms, and Lily was tucked as close as she could get to her Aunt Rose.

"Here's your mama!" Madeline, Raina's oldest sister said, as she turned the baby to see her. "Charlie's refusing a bottle. Can you feed her?"

Raina brushed her hand over her swollen breasts. "Happily. Where are Suze and Dad? And what are you all doing here?"

"The bat signal," Chloe joked. "Out it went and here we are."

"What bat signal?" She walked toward Madeline, not surprised that Charlie's little arms extended toward her.

"Well, first, I was at Chloe's," Sadie said. "Because of a cat emergency."

"A what?" Raina asked, taking Charlie.

"But Chloe was whining because of a...kid emergency," Sadie added.

Raina whipped around to Chloe, who did indeed have red rims around her blue eyes. "Who's kid? What's wrong?"

Chloe raised her hand. "Long story, but we came here to see Mom, because she called to say Dad had a work emergency and had to go to Wingate Properties to help Blake. She wanted help with the babies, and since Sadie and I were together, we came as a BOGO."

Chase glanced at his phone for the first time in hours.

"Oh, yes, there's an issue with the Juniper property. I should run over there. Can you stay here for a while, Raina, and I'll pick you and the babies up later?"

"Absolutely. I have all the help I need and the fridge is stocked with pumped bottles."

He gave her a kiss and a wave to the group, leaving them with a promise to call as soon as he knew what time he'd be back.

"Where's Suze?" Raina asked as they migrated to the living area, where she grabbed a blanket and tucked Charlie under it to nurse.

"Right after Chloe and I got here," Sadie said, "she got a call from a client who was waiting for her at Wingate House. She said she'd totally forgotten that meeting."

"And how did the rest of you get here?" she asked, looking from Rose to Grace to Madeline.

"The babies fussed," Rose said, "so Chloe called in for experienced backup." She patted Lily. "On my way out, I bumped into Grace and she decided to come over with me."

Raina laughed softly. "How many Wingates does it take to babysit two infants?"

"Any excuse for a party," Rose joked.

Raina shifted her attention to Madeline. "And you?"

"I came to see Suze, separate from all of this, because..." She made a face, her dark eyes clouded with concern. "I called her earlier and she seemed kind of preoccupied and I sensed something was wrong."

"Yes! Tori and I noticed the same thing," Raina exclaimed.

She shared the whole story about Susannah's puzzling drop-in visit the day before, letting all of them take turns at theorizing what might be wrong. Was she working too many hours at Wingate House? Was Dad sick again? Was planning Tori and Raina's wedding too much for her?

They didn't know, but all agreed they'd be on the lookout and help Susannah any way they could.

As the topic slowed, Raina leaned back and turned to Chloe and Sadie, who were side by side on the floor. "And now for the cat and kid emergencies?" she asked.

The two of them looked at each other with a question in their eyes.

"You go first," Chloe whispered. "The cat's...easier."

"Not for Scout," Sadie murmured, then looked around. "Rhett Butler's missing."

Raina sucked in a breath, knowing full well how serious that was. Kitty's biggest concern about taking the trip had been leaving her cat, since her husband had headed up north for the summer.

"Kitty will freak out," Raina said. "Sorry for stating the obvious."

"I know!" Sadie moaned, dropping her head back so her curls fell over her shoulders. "Scout didn't even go to work today, and he's still looking. But I thought I had a good idea to fix the problem."

"A ridiculous idea." Chloe rolled her eyes. "You can't just exchange one orange tabby for another, Sadie."

"You want to try and fool Kitty with a substitute cat?" Madeline asked on a strangled laugh. "Are you crazy?"

"No, I'm not crazy, I'm desperate," Sadie said. "But orange cats look…kind of alike, right? If we got one about the same size and weight, would Kitty really know?"

Raina snorted. "Oh, where is Tori when we need her to do her classic Kitty meow?"

"She's at the café," Grace said. "But, Sadie, I'm pretty sure if someone tried to replace Slinky with another short-haired brown dachshund, Nikki and I would know instantly. Have you put up signs around town?"

"Scout is making discreet inquiries," Sadie said. "We don't want it to get back to Kitty, who is at the top of the Eiffel Tower today."

"If Kitty finds out Rhett Butler's lost?" Raina looked skyward. "She'll cancel the rest of the trip and come home immediately, and Val will be back in the house."

"You've made peace with her," Rose pointed out.

"I have, and she's going to start looking for a condo, but…" Raina shrugged. "Not going to lie. I adore having just Chase and the babies and me."

"I know she'll come back," Sadie said. "But Scout is wrecked. He hardly slept last…" Her voice faded out as she realized what she'd just admitted to. "And, hey," she added quickly, poking Chloe, "this is the sister who needs advice from the Wingate brain trust. I only have a missing cat. Chloe's trying to bring home an actual child."

"What?" Several of them posed the question in unison, the attention shifting to the youngest sibling.

By the time Chloe finished her story about Travis's

orphaned half-nephew, everything else had been forgotten and the sisters were slack-jawed at the news.

The response was loud, heartfelt, and, whoa, everyone had an opinion.

Raina knew that was a big ask. Likewise, Madeline seemed extremely cautious about whether it could work, and Sadie seemed to agree with them.

Rose and Grace, the softest hearts in the family, were ready to add the child to the family that minute.

"Chloe, you know it would change your life completely," Raina pointed out. "You'd end up taking care of little Judah for long stretches while Travis is at the fire station."

"And those stretches can be endless and frequent," Rose chimed in, the voice of experience as a firefighter's wife. "But we'll all help you."

"It has to be Travis's call," Madeline said. "The financial responsibility would fall on his shoulders."

"It's funny, I just came from a family law office," Raina added after they all shared their feelings and advice. "Maybe we could add yet another adoption to the hearing day. I'm pushing for six at the moment."

"Six?" several of her sisters asked in unison.

She waited, feeling a smile pull. "I really wanted Tori here for this, but—"

"I'm here!" Tori called out from downstairs. "Grace texted me and FOMO hit hard."

Raina waited until Tori jogged up the stairs, through the flurry of greetings and explanations, bringing the one missing sister up to speed on all their discussions.

While they talked, the babies were fed and taken away by various aunts dying to hold sleeping little angels. With her arms empty again, Raina reached out for Tori, got a hug, and brought her next to her on the sofa.

"I got the Big Plan underway," Raina said in a stage whisper. "Shall we share?"

"Yes!"

"So, guess who never adopted us?" Raina asked the group with a sly smile.

"Susannah," Madeline said with no question in her voice. "It's a sore spot for her, too, so don't rub it in."

Raina wasn't surprised that Madeline knew what they didn't in this regard—at about twelve years apart in age, she and Suze were more like best friends than mother-daughter.

"But we can heal that sore spot," Tori said. "She can still adopt the four of us who are technically stepchildren."

"And we can make it a surprise," Raina added, which pleased them all. After she answered their questions and told them what the adoption specialist had said, she leaned back, her arms feeling oddly empty not to be holding either baby.

"But what do you think is bothering Suze?" Madeline asked.

"Maybe we should do an intervention?" Raina suggested. "We can all wait here until she's back and ask."

"No, no," Rose said. "Let's not gang up on her. She'd hate that, plus, I have to go."

"So do I." Madeline stood. "I don't think we should intervene. Whatever is bothering her will come out organically, like I thought it might today. And I bet it will disappear if you can really make the adoption surprise happen, Raina."

Raina nodded, aching to talk to her mother, but suspected they were right. When Susannah was ready to share what was on her heart, she would. In the meantime, she was comforted knowing her sisters shared her concerns and approved of her secret plans.

"I'm going to stay and tell her about Judah," Chloe said. "I need a tie-breaking vote on what to do."

"Travis's is really the only vote that counts," Raina said softly.

Chloe nodded and sighed. "I know."

Feeling her baby sister's consternation, Raina ached to solve the problem for her. Good heavens, they already had two babies and four grown women on the adoption docket. Could they add little Judah and make it their lucky number of *seven* adoptions at one hearing?

Like Chase said, it would be the most Wingate thing ever. And nothing would make Raina happier.

Chapter Seven

Chloe

Rocky's Rescues was officially full. Chloe had four dogs boarding, two strays that would surely be adopted soon, two new feline guests in the cat room, and a bunny living in a cage she'd found in the garage.

But no orange tabby cats, sadly.

And that made Sadie look like she might cry.

"It's been a week," Sadie moaned, standing up from the kitchen table where she and Chloe had shared coffee and combed the local social media for any announcement of someone finding a lost cat. "And no one has seen him."

"I've put out an APB in the rescue and stray world," Chloe told her, closing the laptop. "I've had those two false alarms and—"

"One looked exactly like him," Sadie said.

"Yeah, except...not." Chloe shook her head. "I can't be party to the cat switch, but I'll keep trying to find him, I promise."

"Oh, I hope we do." Sadie rinsed out her coffee cup, but her attention seemed to be on Chloe. "Any news on the Judah front?"

Chloe leaned against the counter, looking outside at the dog kennels, her mind feeling a million miles away.

"He's turning five today," she said, hearing the sad note in her voice.

"Oh, really?"

"I mentioned it to Travis last night and he just shut down the conversation, which is so disappointing. He won't talk about it, he won't consider it, he won't explore his feelings."

"In other words, he's a guy," Sadie mused.

"Sure, but this has to be talked about, considered, and explored."

"Give him time, Chloe," Sadie said. "I'd bet everything I have that he's thinking about it and he's going to take baby steps to get there."

"But that boy is—" She frowned at the sound of someone pulling into the driveway. "I don't have someone bringing in a boarder today. Who could that be?"

"I don't know, but pray they found an orange tabby and are looking for the owner."

"I certainly will," Chloe said as she breezed through to the front of the house to open the door and see a familiar truck. "Oh, it's Travis. I thought he had a shift today."

She stepped outside, vaguely aware of the dogs in the front yard pen barking at her as she looked up into the driver's seat where Travis sat.

"Hey," she said, reaching the door just as he opened it.

"You busy?" he asked.

"Just the usual. Why?"

He swallowed and stabbed his fingers into his hair. "I want to, um..."

"Go see Judah," she whispered, just knowing from the look on his face that's what this was about.

"For his birthday."

She managed not to do a little jig right there in the driveway. "Yes, I'll go," she said, staying remarkably calm. "On one condition."

"I'm not taking him for good, Chloe, I just—"

"We have to stop at a Walmart on the way."

His brow flicked with curiosity, then he nodded. "Okay, Walmart it is. But you have to come, Chloe. I need you."

"Let me ask Sadie if she'll stay until my assistant gets here, and I want to put the dogs in the kennels so they don't get too hot." She didn't wait for him to change his mind, but flew into the house with the second-best news she could give her sister.

No tabby cat, but hope for Judah.

As she excitedly grabbed her bag, she gave Sadie an impulsive kiss. "Thank you for staying for a few minutes. Ashley will be here soon."

"It's fine. I only want one form of payment—the ability to say, 'I told you so.'"

"You did tell me," she admitted.

"Give him time, Chloe. He'll come around."

She sure hoped so.

After the trip to Walmart, Chloe called the social worker who seemed very excited to arrange for them to meet Judah. It took everything Chloe had not to warn the woman that she couldn't get her hopes up, but she did her best to make it clear that Travis simply wanted to meet his half-nephew and bring him a birthday gift.

A birthday *gift*?

While she talked, she glanced in the backseat and smiled, pretty sure there wasn't a truck or piece of toy construction equipment left in the kids' section of that store. They couldn't find a Spider-Man costume, but Travis got a T-shirt with the image in his size and one in a kids' small.

He also got a Spidey mask, a Lego set of the character, and a Spider-Man floor puzzle for toddlers. They'd lost at least forty-five minutes trying to decide if a puzzle for three-year-olds was appropriate for a five-year-old, but Chloe finally called Rose, who gave them a green light. And a squeal of delight.

"I will be there to meet you," Mae, the social worker, said. "You aren't allowed to be alone with Judah, but once we meet and talk, everything should be fine. Should I bring release paperwork?"

Chloe made a face, happy she'd decided to make the call without putting it on speaker phone. But how to answer that?

"It doesn't mean you can take him permanently," the woman added. "But I can let you leave the premises if you stay within one mile. Assuming that goes well and I can make a quick visit to your home, we can allow him to come for a weekend. Then—"

"Uh, just the most basic paperwork," she said with a glance at Travis, forcing herself to hold back. "And we'll be there in..." She squinted at Travis's GPS. "Thirty-three minutes."

"But who's counting?" Travis murmured with a smile. A genuine smile, Chloe thought as she said goodbye to the social worker and turned to him.

"I'm counting," she said. "I'm not going to try and pretend I'm not excited to meet him."

He sighed and nodded.

"Are you?"

"I'm going, aren't I?"

"But are you excited?" she pressed.

"I'm...curious."

She studied his profile, one of her favorite sights to linger on. He had strong features, the tiniest smattering of freckles when he'd been in the sun a lot, and unfairly long lashes. But once again, she noticed that his jaw wasn't set so tight, and that vein in his neck didn't seem to throb like it had anytime she'd tried to bring up the subject of Judah.

"What changed?" she asked on a soft whisper.

He threw a sideways look. "Wingates," he muttered. "Even if they go by another name, they still...influence."

"Gabe?" she guessed, knowing how close Travis was to Rose's husband, Gabriel D'Angelo. He was another firefighter—the one who'd trained Travis—and, as a father of four, he was a family man down to his last strand of DNA.

"Of course Gabe." He shook his head with a soft laugh. "But really, it was Rose, who came at me via Gabe."

She felt a smile pull, thinking about her sister, who would help anyone, anywhere, any time. No doubt she and Gabe stayed up late discussing Chloe and Travis's situation, and then Gabe had swooped in and...said something.

But what?

"You gonna tell me what he said, or is it covered under the secret firefighters code of silence?"

He smiled at the tease. "Nothing like that. He just got me to talk, and got me to think, and made me realize that..." He huffed out a breath. "It's not the kid's fault that my dad cared about him. And it wasn't Connor's fault that he was motherless and managed to stay close to the old man."

"And it wasn't your fault your father left."

He shuttered his eyes. "If it wasn't my fault, then it was my mother's, and you know that woman is a saint to me."

"How about it was Dale's fault?" she suggested. "How about you let your father take the blame for making the decision to leave, divorce your mom, and start a new life? He's not here to do that, but there's no reason you can't shift some of that responsibility from your shoulders to his."

"That's kind of what Gabe said," he told her. "He suggested I act like a grown man, not the five-year-old in this situation, and at least meet the kid and...and..."

Her heart hitched. "And what?"

"Just meet him."

One step at a time, she thought. One baby step at a

time. Well, one five-year-old who loved Spider-Man and tractors step at a time.

A WOMAN WAS WAITING in the driveway when they arrived at a two-story stucco house in a residential area called Mandarin, south of Jacksonville.

Travis glanced at the woman, then the house, which was in need of lawn work, love, and a fresh coat of paint. There were a few bikes on the grass, a dirty soccer ball, and a fenced-in backyard that looked spacious enough.

Travis took a slow, deep breath and turned to her. "Chloe, please promise me—"

"No," she said. "I'm not making any more promises. Let's just meet the child and see what happens."

"Nothing is going to happen," he said. "'Cept, you know..." He tipped his head to the back seat. "Big present time."

She smiled at that as they climbed out of the truck and a woman she assumed was Mae Ling, the social worker, walked over to greet them warmly.

"Does he know who I am?" Travis asked after a quick introduction. "Do I, like, have to explain it to him?"

Mae smiled. "I've told him that you knew his Pops, and that you wanted to stop by and wish him a happy birthday. He's very young, Mr. McCall, and scared and shy. Don't expect sparkling conversation, but he should like that you brought him gifts."

Chloe lifted the Walmart bags, handing two of the four to Travis. "We sure did."

"Just be warned," Mae said. "This isn't his ultimate home. A group home is a temporary holding place for boys—only boys in this house—who haven't yet been placed. They try to keep it ten and under, but recently two teenagers were placed here. Kelly and Ron Headrick run this house and they're both saints. Overworked and underpaid, but saints."

"How long will he be at this house?" Chloe asked.

Mae's brows furrowed. "Hard to say. He was in two other places before this, and I'm new on his case. He'll be in this kind of situation until he's placed into a foster home, or adopted. That could be months or...more."

Chloe's heart dropped at the very thought of that much upheaval in a child's life, but she just nodded and followed Mae to the front door, which opened before they even knocked. A woman who was probably in her mid-forties stood there with a smile that looked hopeful as she greeted them and Mae made the introductions.

Kelly hesitated before opening the screen door, letting out a sigh that deepened creases of exhaustion around her eyes.

"It's kind of a mess," she said. "I do my best to keep up, but all these boys..." She threw a look over her shoulder as if she expected one to come bounding out any second. "Can I just bring him out here to you?"

"Of course," Chloe said. "If that's okay."

"More than okay," the woman answered. "I'd offer

you some iced tea, but if I make it, it's gone in five seconds."

"It's fine," Travis told her. "We just want to—"

"See Judah, of course. They should all be as easy as that little angel. Never asks for a thing. Hang on."

She turned and left them standing there in the blazing sun, the Walmart bag with construction toys in it cutting lines in Chloe's hands.

"Come on now, Judah," she heard Kelly call. "Just say hello."

A tiny shadow appeared in the doorway, not three feet tall, wearing a baggy tank top and shorts, a pair of worn sneakers on his feet. He stayed back, a thumb in his mouth, giant brown eyes looking at them from behind his glasses.

"Come on, then." Kelly gave his narrow shoulder a gentle nudge. "Talk to them."

He slinked further back, refusing to come all the way to the door.

"Judah," Chloe said, reaching into the bag she held. "We brought you a front-loader."

His eyes flashed.

"And a..." She rooted around in the bag. "A dump truck. This one's big enough to roll on the ground with real dirt."

He took one step forward.

"We heard it's your birthday," she added. "And I, um..." She closed her fingers around the Spider-Man mask, the only other thing in her bag, and pulled it out, shoving it in Travis's hand. "We brought Spidey himself to sing 'Happy Birthday.'"

That got the child a little closer, but he still stayed protected by the screen door, looking up at Travis with nothing but wonder in his eyes.

"Didn't we just pass a park?" Travis asked under his breath, stepping away from the door.

"Right down the block, that way," Mae said.

Travis backed away completely. "Take him there." With that, he jogged to the truck and jumped in.

Chloe felt her jaw drop. Was he *chickening out*? Really? One glance at the kid and he ran off—and took some of the bags?

The screen door popped open and tiny Judah stepped out into the sunshine, looking up at Chloe like, well, yes, like a lost puppy who craved love and a home and food and a blanket and more love.

"Hello." Chloe crouched down to get to his height, vaguely aware of the truck rumbling off down the road. She'd let Travis have it later, but first...Judah.

"Happy birthday, Judah," she said gently, having to force herself to keep from giving him a hug. "I heard you are five years old today. You're a big boy, aren't you?"

He nodded, his dark gaze stuck on her face, then moving down...to the front-loader.

"Would you like to take this to the park?" she asked, looking up at Mae. "I don't know where... Can we take him?"

"Yes, let's walk him down there."

"Would you carry this?" Chloe placed the front-loader in his tiny hands, getting a hint of a smile in return. Just enough to make her want to see it full and bright.

"Let's go!" Without thinking, she put a hand on his shoulder.

"Um, no touching," Mae said. "Just walk with him."

Of all the things she hated about this, that might be the worst. But Chloe just gave him a smile and tipped her head. "To the park, then, birthday boy!"

She chattered about nothing—the trees, the toys, the weather, being five—as they walked two blocks to a small outdoor park that had two swings—one was broken—a plastic slide and just enough dirt for a front-loader to...do whatever a front-loader did.

Move dirt, Chloe learned, as the little boy sat down and started pushing the toy. She brought out the rest of the construction toys and sat next to him, while Mae found a slice of shade under a palm tree and sat there to observe.

While he played, the only sound some "vroom-vroom" of a pretend engine, Chloe tried to imagine what to talk to him about...and where the heck Travis went.

How could he just bolt like that?

"Oh, look, Judah, this one has a little man inside." She pulled out the simple toy and handed it to him, looking around again for another man in a truck. *Her* man.

No, not her man. No man of hers would just bail on a kid like that out of, what, fear? Resentment? Jealousy? Ancient hurts and immature reactions? She would never—

She whipped around at the familiar sound of a truck engine.

"Oh, he's back," she murmured, and Judah looked up and followed her gaze to the truck, stopped right next to the entrance of the park. "Uncle Travis has returned."

"Uncah..." Judah blinked and forgot the toys, staring as Travis got out of the truck and walked around to the back, dropping the tailgate.

"And what the heck is he doing?" she asked on a whisper, not really expecting an answer from the child.

Travis disappeared around the passenger side of the truck. Maybe opening a door to reach inside? She couldn't tell. She waited, watching him go back to the tailgate.

Then he put both hands up to his mouth and hollered, "If it's anyone's birthday today, you better get over here now!"

Judah's eyes widened and he looked up at her, a question on his dear little face.

"I think Uncle Travis means you, buddy." She pushed up, her heart kicking with guilt for doubting Travis. "Can we go over there?" she called to Mae.

"Sure, let's go." She wasn't about to let them kidnap the kid.

The three of them crossed the grass, easily able to see Travis pull on the Spider-Man mask and step out, wearing the matching red and blue T-shirt.

Chloe let out a little moan of delight.

As they got closer, he beckoned them to the back of the truck, where a round chocolate cake sat open in a

Publix bakery box, a blue number "5" candle unlit on top.

Judah's mouth dropped open.

"You know, Judah, when I was a kid..." Travis said, adjusting the face mask. "And, yes, Spidey was a kid. Well, back then, the birthday was all about the cake."

A slow smile pulled on the little boy's face.

"Can you climb up like a real Spider-Man?" Travis asked him.

Judah tried to scramble up on the tailgate, and with one masked look at Mae, Travis reached down and hoisted the child into the truck, ignoring the woman's soft admonishment.

"Should we sing?" Travis asked.

"We must sing," Chloe said, perching her hip on the tailgate.

"No lighting the candles," Mae added with an apologetic smile, knowing full well she was a killjoy but just doing her job.

"Then we'll pretend they're lit," Chloe announced, clapping her hands. "Ready, set...*Happy Birthday to you...*"

With each line of the song, Judah's face brightened. Chloe's heart soared. Travis's smile grew, and even Mae looked moved.

"Pretend blow out," Travis said, pointing to the candle. "But a real wish. Go for it."

Judah sucked in a breath, puffed out his cheeks, and blew out a candle that was never lit. They all clapped like it was the best candle-blowing ever, even Judah.

Then he looked up at Travis and grew very serious. "Thank you, Uncah...Man," he whispered, barely audible.

"Yeah," Chloe said, fighting tears. "Thank you, Uncah Man."

Travis just sighed and closed his eyes, and right that moment? Chloe had never loved him more and would marry him this afternoon if he asked.

Chapter Eight

Sadie

Sitting outside the Humane Society of Camden County, Georgia, a full forty minutes away from Amelia Island, Sadie took a deep breath and prayed that Wiggles, an eleven-pound orange tabby with a white chest, was really Rhett Butler.

Two hours earlier, Sadie—nothing if not resourceful—had easily tapped into Chloe's computer and found the database of local cats recently logged with the county as strays or lost. She instantly zeroed in on Wiggles, a new arrival overnight, just brought into a shelter on the other side of the Florida-Georgia line.

The minute Chloe's part-time assistant showed to run Rocky's Rescues, Sadie had jumped into her car. She'd been up early making chocolate, so she was able to turn the shop over to the new front clerk she'd hired. Free for the rest of the day, she zipped up to the small town of Kingsland, arriving at a dreary fenced-in animal shelter on a county road.

She hadn't told anyone—and by anyone, she meant

Scout—where she was going, but with every mile, she got more excited that this cat might be Rhett Butler.

Or a close match.

They'd been to all the humane society shelters, animal refuges, and pet adoption places in Nassau County this past week. Not only had they not found Rhett Butler, but they hadn't seen any orange cats, which were apparently pretty rare. But they were almost always male, so that helped the cause.

The cause that Sadie refused to lose just yet.

Parking, she tapped her phone to look again at the shelter's website. She peered at a grainy image of Wiggles, who really was the spitting image of Rhett Butler.

She'd only seen Kitty's cat a few times and remembered that he was skittish and preferred to hide under a bed rather than be held, so she couldn't be *sure* if the match was perfect, but it couldn't hurt to check the little guy out, right?

Please, God, please. Let it be Rhett Butler that some kind soul found on the side of the road and brought here.

An old man at the front desk didn't seem to care who she was, if she had ID, or...anything. When she asked about Wiggles and showed him the picture on her phone, he thumbed down a dimly lit hall, and said, "Cat holding tank is the last door on the left."

She followed the directions, her heart skidding around with each step. It was clean...enough. The place smelled, though, and echoed with distant barks from the canine prisoners—er, dogs.

Not a person was in sight, so when she reached "the last door on the left"—even that sounded like a horror movie—she turned the rusted knob with great trepidation. Was she stepping into the "cat holding tank" or the lion's den?

She inched the door open, cringing as if she could be attacked any minute, and heard...nothing. Well, some snoring and a few soft mews.

The room was lit by an unforgiving fluorescent light in the ceiling, shining milky yellow over a wall of small cages.

"Oh, they really are in prison, the poor babies," she whispered, tiptoeing inside.

She scanned the half-dozen or so residents, most sleeping, one pawing at its cage, and there, at the end, found an orange ball of fur.

"Are you the answer to my prayers?" She took a few steps and huffed out a breath of the stinky air. Definitely not for the faint of heart or nostril in here. "Are you... Rhett Butler?"

She put her hand on the cage door and gave it a little shake, instantly waking the cat.

He stood, turned, and stretched up and down like a well-trained yoga instructor. Then he took one step closer to stare at Sadie with a curious gaze that was, oddly enough, the exact green-gold-hazel of her own eyes.

Then he pressed on the metal of the cage, sticking his little nose closer to her, with a quick flick of a pink tongue that practically pleaded, "Take me out!"

Instantly, she felt a connection.

And hope. She leaned closer and got a better look, almost swaying with shock. This *had* to be Rhett Butler! He looked exactly like she remembered the cat.

"Rhett? Is that you?"

"Excuse me. Can I help you?"

Sadie spun around at the sound of a female voice, finding a tall, tattooed, twenty-something girl staring back at her in the doorway.

"Oh, hi. I think...I'm not sure, but I think this is my cat." She turned back to the cage and looked into those eyes again.

"You don't know?"

"I'm not sure. And he's not exactly mine. He's, um, my boyfriend's. Actually, my boyfriend's late mother's best friend who is in Europe and he's cat-sitting, but Rhett Butler ran away and we can't find him, but I think..."

As the young woman's face shifted from accusation to amusement, Sadie's voice faded out.

"I suspected he was a stray when some guy brought him in," she said, coming into the room. "Do you live nearby?"

"Down on Amelia Island."

Her eyes flashed with disbelief. "And you think this is your cat? That he could walk, what, twenty-some miles?"

"You just said someone brought him in. Maybe they found him on the road."

"It was a local guy," she said. "At least, that's what he said. We don't always deal with the most honest folks in this business."

"That's a shame," Sadie said, turning back to the cat. "Well, I'm being straight with you. I think this could be the cat my boyfriend is sitting."

"You have a picture?" she asked.

She nodded, reaching for her phone to slide through Scout's texts. He'd sent her a bunch of pictures he had taken the night he picked up Rhett Butler. Flipping to them, she looked from the screen to the cage and back again.

"See? It's him!"

The other woman looked at the phone, then the cat, then the phone. Then looked a little skeptical. "The white bib looks different," she said. "And Wiggles is skinnier."

"You would be, too, if you walked twenty miles. And the bib? That's just the angle. I'm sure this is Rhett Butler. Right?" She turned to the cage and put her finger inside. "Is that you, Rhett?"

He meowed and licked her finger.

"Huh." The woman came closer and pulled a card from the side of the crate, reading it. "Yeah, this dude picks up strays, brings them here with fake names, and hopes they have a shot at finding a home. So he wasn't just somebody dumping a cat they didn't want."

Sadie cringed at the thought.

"I'll take him," she said, her lifelong instinct for impulsiveness rising to meet the occasion. But this was the right thing to do, she was sure. And if she called Scout...well, he might try and talk her out of this madness or want to wait. Or drive up here to see Wiggles and if he wasn't Rhett?

He'd talk her out of what sure seemed like a great solution.

"Can I?" she urged. "Can I take him home?"

"Let's see how he reacts to you." She slid the bar of the door up, slowly opening the cage. The cat purred and took a step closer, a curious look in his eyes.

"Hello, Rhett Butler," Sadie cooed, holding her hand to his lips for a sniff. "Remember me? I hang around with Scout."

He licked her knuckles and nuzzled her hand, which would make him...not Rhett Butler. But maybe the trauma of his trip and imprisonment had changed his personality.

"See?" Sadie said, turning to the younger woman. "He knows and trusts me."

She still looked dubious. "I'm not supposed to let you take him without a background check and a mountain of paperwork, but..." She watched the cat rub his back against Sadie's hand, a look of rapture on his face. "Okay," she relented. "I have been dying to get some of these cats out of here before our next inspection."

"Great, I'll take—"

"And you can't bring him back," she interjected. "If he's not your friend's cat, that's your problem. You take him, you own him. And you can't hurt him."

Sadie nodded enthusiastically, tunneling her fingers into maybe-Rhett's soft fur. "I wouldn't dream of it."

It didn't take long for Sadie to fill out some paperwork and pay a fee. She threw in an extra fifty bucks as a shelter donation, which got her a free temporary carrier to safely transport the cat home.

With very little fuss, she was back on the road to Amelia Island.

"I don't know if you're Kitty's cat or not," she said to the cat curled inside the flimsy carrier on the passenger seat, staring at Sadie like she'd hung the moon. "But if you fool Scout, you've got the job. If you don't, then I hope you like living above a chocolate shop, 'cause I got a feeling you're mine...Wiggles Butler."

"Come home. I have a surprise."

Scout didn't respond at first, and all Sadie could hear on the other end of the phone was a soft intake of breath. "You found him."

She laughed. "How do you know I'm not wearing something skimpy just waiting for you?"

"Because— Wait. Are you?" There was a cute little hitch in his voice.

"Which of those two things would be a better surprise?" she asked.

He just laughed. "I'm at the cookie shop. Gimme ten minutes. If it's the cat, don't let him run away again. If it's...skimpy? Um, don't you run away."

She decided not to take Wiggles-Might-Be-Rhett out of the carrier for fear he'd bolt, so she waited on the front porch swing listening to him purr. Before long, Scout pulled in, probably having driven faster than at any other time in his life.

Watching him climb out of the front seat, she squinted into the afternoon sun, knowing he didn't see her tucked away on the covered front porch. He smoothed his T-shirt, finger-combed his always unruly hair, and coughed into his hand to check his breath.

Goodness, she adored him. The man was so unassuming, so unpretentious, so very real. His heart was gold, his soul was pure, and she could look all over the world—and had—and not find a better guy. Was that love? Was that...the *thing*?

Now all he had to do was...believe this was Rhett Butler and they could celebrate.

"Sadie!" He spotted her and jogged closer, his face bright with anticipation. She stood up to greet him, and he slowed his step, his gaze slipping over her torn jeans and the Coming Up Roses T-shirt she once borrowed from Rose and never gave back, because she loved it.

Nothing about her outfit was skimpy, but his smile got even bigger.

"You found Rhett Butler!" He broke into a run up the stairs, coming full stop at the sight of the cat carrier. "It's a miracle!"

All she could do was laugh—and hope—when he threw his arms around her and lifted her off the ground with a bear hug.

"Where? How? Why didn't you call? And what is he doing in that thing? Sadie!" He planted a kiss on her lips. "How much do I love you?"

Love? Her heart tripped. Did he love her? He'd never said that before. He'd implied it, he'd danced around it, he showed it every day, but he never came right out and said it.

She swayed a little.

"Come and see him," she said, assuming how much he loved her was a rhetorical question that didn't need a response. She guided him closer, watching him as he peeked into the carrier.

"Well, hello there you little..." His shoulders fell. "Stranger." He looked at her with a hint of hurt in his eyes. "You can't be serious."

"It's not him?" she asked, disappointment biting at her.

"Sadie."

"Are you sure?" She got closer and unzipped the corner of the carrier. "He was a stray that got brought into the Humane Society up in Kingsland and—"

"Georgia?" His voice rose. "You went to another state for him?"

"Because...couldn't it be him?" She eased the flap open. "If not, it's his twin brother."

Scout let out a grunt of defeat, but his smile didn't completely disappear when he looked at her. "You're so sweet, Sadie."

"But dumb."

He laughed and opened the cat carrier a little more to test the waters with his hand. "Not the least bit dumb. You're well-meaning and good and— Oh!" Laughing, he looked in the carrier. "He licked me."

"Yeah, probably not the move of *the* Rhett Butler, also known as Ice Man. Has he ever licked anyone?"

Very slowly, he opened the carrier zipper all the way. Instantly, the cat meowed and took a few cautious steps, then climbed right into Scout's lap, looked up with adoring eyes, and starting kneading his khaki pants.

"Whoa, you're a lover, aren't you?" Scout exclaimed with a laugh. "What's his name?"

"Not Rhett Butler," Sadie said with a sad sigh, moving the carrier to the floor to sit next to him. "But he does look like him, doesn't he?"

"He does," he agreed.

"Enough that we could fool Kitty?"

Scout studied the cat, placing his hand palm up and letting him lick it again. "Well, hello there, Mr. Not Rhett Butler and Kitty Will Know It In Two Seconds."

"Wiggles," she said glumly. "His name is Wiggles."

The cat turned at the sound of her voice, gazing at Sadie with grateful, soulful eyes, then crawled closer, nuzzling her, making them both laugh.

"You picked a good one, Sadie."

"I picked the wrong one." She shook her head. "And he's non-returnable."

"Well, that's okay." He leaned back and scrutinized the cat. "I'll hang on to him."

"Or I will," she said. "He's really hard not to like."

The cat meowed loudly, as if to underscore that point, and made them laugh.

"Well, let's get him some food," Scout said. "And let him get used to the place. But not the patio, because I'm sure Rhett got out through the screen." He dropped his head in defeat. "Never to return."

"Never say never," she insisted.

"You're right. We have more than a month before Kitty gets back. Anything could happen."

She reached a hand toward him. "Thank you for not getting mad at me for this. You know I can be a little impulsive."

"And I've discovered how wonderful that is," he said, bringing her hand to his lips to kiss it. "It's one of the things I love most about you."

She tried to breathe, but just held his gaze. "That's twice in the space of about five minutes, Martin Jacobson."

He smiled. "I love when you use my real name."

"And that's three times."

"Sadie." He put both hands around Wiggles, lifting him into the air so they were face to face. "Why is she so surprised, Wiggie?" he whispered into the cat's ear. "Doesn't she know I love her?"

"Oh, Scout." She leaned closer, her cheek brushing the orange fur as she came in for a kiss. "I..."

He smiled, expectation in his eyes.

"I...I..."

"You don't have to say something you don't feel."

"I do feel it," she whispered. "Every time I look at you. Or think about you. Every single time."

"But you can't say it," he said, giving her another kiss as the cat squirmed between them, so happy he couldn't pick a lap. "I don't care, Sadie. I mean, I do, but I can wait. In the meantime, let's bring Wiggles inside and... and..." He kissed her again, longer this time.

"Keep looking on the local pages for found cats."

He just laughed. "Not exactly what I was thinking, but that, too."

Chapter Nine

Susannah

In the nearly two weeks that had passed since Ivy Button appeared on her doorstep, Susannah had lulled herself into a sense of complacency. Not a false one, she hoped. But perhaps the stranger had been lying. Maybe it had been a bluff, or a bet, or a mistake.

Not that any of those options seemed likely, but since Susannah hadn't seen the woman or heard from her, it had become easier to forget that it ever happened.

Was it possible she'd never lay eyes on Ivy Button again? She hoped so.

Her afternoon appointment with a bride-to-be was coming to an end, and Susannah was sorry to lose the distraction.

Kara Cheswick closed her tablet and stood, taking another satisfied look around Wingate House's spacious dining room.

"I can't wait to bring my fiancé back here and finalize the date, Susannah," she said. "Please don't let that weekend in September get snagged."

"It won't last long," Susannah said, forcing herself to

pay attention, something she'd had to do constantly these past few weeks. It had taken a physical effort and a busy schedule not to let her mind roam to the dark place of worry.

She'd kept herself so busy that she and the girls had yet to have more than the most cursory discussion about the double wedding.

They'd picked a date, smack in the middle of July, the only possibility, because July was *hot*. That meant it had to be an evening wedding, and it frequently rained on summer afternoons, so the weather was iffy at best. However, all the choice dates in the fall were taken.

"I mean, look at this room!" Kara gushed as they walked into the adjoining sitting rooms in the front of the house. She stopped, looking up at the needlepoint sampler of a stitched replica of Wingate House with a poem sewn into the canvas. "This is just adorable."

"That was handmade by Coraline Wingate, my husband's grandmother," Susannah said, her voice rich with pride. "We found it in the attic not long after I decided to transform Wingate House into a wedding venue, and it was perfect."

"'Come live with me and be my love,'" Kara read from the top line. "Why, yes, it is perfect. Everything about this setting is ideal for my small but mighty list of family and friends." She impulsively hugged Susannah as they stood in the vestibule to say goodbye.

"Kevin and I will be back next week, as planned. We'll bring a deposit."

Susannah thanked her and said goodbye, lingering in

the late afternoon shadows cast by the tall oaks in the front yard. There, she let her gaze travel over Wingate Way like a periscope coming up from the water to observe the seas.

Instead of hoping for a glimpse of one of her daughters or a familiar face from town, she was watching for...Ivy.

The street was empty but for a few tourists taking pictures of the Victorians and a teenage boy walking a dog.

Maybe Ivy was gone. Maybe the nightmare was over. Maybe Susannah could get away with not ever telling a soul she'd had the conversation.

With the exception of the discussion she'd had with Rex, the subject of Doreen never came up again. They'd slid right back into the rhythm of life, and she tried to put it out of her mind.

He was back in the office a few hours every other day or so, which was just the perfect amount of work for a man his age. He obviously enjoyed working with Chase, so spending some time at Wingate Properties was as much fun as it was work for Rex.

When she heard her cell phone ring, she rushed back toward the dining area so she didn't miss a call. Throwing a passing glance out the mullioned windows that lined one wall into the garden, she caught a movement that brought her to a standstill.

Was that...a person? A bird or stray dog? Goodness, could it be Sadie's missing cat? If not...who was on the property?

Ignoring the ringing phone, she walked to the window for a better look, easily able to see the paver-covered patio and small pool, the pergola with the vineyard lights, and the round gazebo. Everything was visible now that they'd removed the hundred-year-old live oak that had grown so big it dominated the yard and blocked the guest room water views.

Her jaw locked with nerves, she scanned the whole area, north to south and clear to the side yard and river. She squinted into the gazebo and bent down to look under the large table that had been made from the old oak tree.

Finally, she stared at the guest cottage, which now served as the dressing room and gathering place for groomsmen on a wedding day.

Wait—was that a flash inside? Had she left the light on when she and Kara toured the small house an hour or so ago? No, because the bride-to-be had commented several times on how bright and cheery it was, and Susannah had told her about the tree.

But she could have left it unlocked, so...anyone could be out there.

Not that Fernandina Beach was a hotbed of crime, but still. Should she call for help? She grabbed her phone and held tight, peering outside.

And then she saw someone move from behind the guest house window, sending a sliver of ice through her veins. Was it...a worker? One of her daughters? Could Grace's husband, Isaiah, be out there? He'd have a key, since he'd lived in that guest house when he managed the inn.

Oh, come on, Suze. Get real.

She *knew* who was out there. She knew who'd come back. Walking toward the outside door, she stepped into the sunshine and steeled herself, determined not to let one beady-eyed blackmailer scare the life out of—

The cottage door popped open and Susannah gasped noisily.

"Hey, Suze." Raina stepped out and squinted in the sunshine. "Did the client leave?"

For a moment, Susannah couldn't breathe, the relief was so palpable. It actually hurt her chest to *not* be looking at Ivy Button.

"What...why..."

"I saw the car and figured that your appointment was still here, so I just..." She thumbed at the guest house, a slight frown pulling as she regarded Susannah, who no doubt looked like she'd feared Jack the Ripper—or worse—had been hiding in the little house. "It was open."

"Oh...okay."

Raina gave a dry laugh. "I've been calling you to tell you I was out here. But I figured you remembered that I was going to come over today to take some pictures of the cottage. Chase and Justin wanted to see the layout. Rose and her girls asked to babysit because it was a half...day...at school...." Raina's brow lifted as her words trailed off. "Am I ringing any bells from the conversation we had, um, two days ago?"

Not a one.

The adrenaline dump made Susannah weak and she walked to the gazebo to step out of the sun and sit, setting the phone on the table face down.

"Susannah Wingate, what is going on with you?" Raina demanded, following her into the shade.

"Nothing, you just...I saw someone and, yes, I forgot and..." She huffed out a breath.

"You're shaking," Raina said, sitting next to her and taking her hand. "And I'm not going to take one more brush-off from you. Something is up and if you don't tell me, I'm going to assume the worst."

"What would that be?" Susannah asked.

"That you're sick or dying, or Dad is. That someone is in trouble or some tragedy is about to strike or something...awful. I don't know, but you are acting Weird with a capital W, and you have to tell me what's going on."

Susannah swallowed, her whole body aching to tell Raina everything. Raina's purpose in life was to solve problems. Honestly, no one in the family did that better than this woman right in front of her. And this particular problem was even "real estate" related, which was Raina's specialty.

She desperately needed a second opinion, and Raina's voice was one of reason and love. Should she carry this burden alone? Or was sharing it with one of her daughters somehow stealing their joy and planting an ugly seed?

"Susannah." Raina leaned in, underscoring the rare use of the formal name with narrowed blue eyes that demanded the truth.

"I had a visitor a few weeks ago," she began, speaking softly. "A woman who claimed to be Doreen Parrish's niece."

Raina inched back. "She had...family? I mean, other than the one from the child she gave up for adoption."

"A different family. This woman is named Ivy Button."

"Ivy..." Raina's brow shot up with a judgmental arch at the cutesy name. "Okay."

"And she says that Doreen's sister is her mother. And she, the mother, whose name I don't think she gave me, is Doreen's heir."

Raina nodded, following the bread crumbs. "And she's furious we gave away all of her belongings," she guessed. "Well, we didn't know she had a sister. She never said a word to anyone—about that, or anything, to be honest. And there was nothing valuable in that apartment."

Susannah let out a shuddering breath. "Ivy claimed that Rex's father, Grandfather Regis, left her...well, he left her..."

Raina leaned in when Susannah didn't finish.

"Wingate House," she said on a quick breath.

Raina stared, then gave her head a shake as if she didn't quite get the last two words. "Pardon me?"

"She claims she has the paperwork—a contract and letters, but she never showed me anything—that prove Rex's father essentially promised her ownership of Wingate House."

"Why would he do that?" Raina asked on a disbelieving laugh. "It's ludicrous to even think about it, and why wouldn't Doreen mention it? Please, Suze. This is such a scam it hurts to think about it. Someone who read about her death and where she worked, and...I don't know. This screams of a swindle, and we will not fall for it."

Was it? Susannah closed her eyes. "Maybe, but..."

"But what?"

God, she hated this. Yes, the girls knew that Rex had a teenage indiscretion; that truth had come out when they found a photograph of Doreen holding a baby named Bradley Wingate.

That baby had become Bradley Young, adopted in Iowa. No, it was not easy for Rex's adoring daughters to think of him being quite so...human. And with someone they called "Dor-mean," too.

"Suze?" Raina pressed.

"She knew that Rex and Doreen...you know."

Her eyes widened. "Oh. That's a twist. But maybe Doreen confided in her sister. They found out there was a baby and she wants to meet Blake? But she certainly can't have Wingate House." She scoffed again at how preposterous that was. "If she wants to meet Blake, I'm sure we can..." Her words faded out. "Why are you crying, Suze?"

"I thought all that, too." She swiped a tear and sniffed. "This woman, this Ivy person...she...said that Doreen claims it...wasn't...consensual."

Raina jerked like she'd been slapped. "*What?*" She breathed the word, blanching.

"And that if we don't honor this alleged 'contract,' she will smear Rex's reputation and go to the press with a story that he, um, took advantage of a mentally disabled woman."

The color returned to Raina's cheeks. In fact, they deepened with a flush of fury. She opened her mouth to speak, but took a breath as if she couldn't quite seize the words.

"First of all," she finally ground out. "My father would no sooner assault a woman than he would jump off the Empire State Building and try to fly. He doesn't have a violent, mean, hurtful bone in his body and he would never, ever do that."

"I know, but she—"

"No but!" Raina barked. "It's not possible and I'll... I'll..." She pounded her chest with a tight fist. "I'll take on *anyone* who tries to say otherwise."

"I agree!" Susannah exclaimed. "But how do we prove that?"

"Well, what does Dad say?" Raina asked.

Susannah stared at her, silent.

"You didn't tell him?"

"No," Susannah sighed. "I always feel he's one measure of bad news away from a heart attack or another stroke or seizure."

"I get that," Raina agreed gently. "It's hard not to want to protect him after the stroke."

"I know he's healthy and taking good care of himself now, but..." She sighed and looked out at the garden, seeing only the sight of the man she loved crumpled on the floor. "I have some post-traumatic shock from that day he had the stroke. I thought I was saying...goodbye..."

When her voice cracked, Raina reached to hug her. "He didn't die, Suze. He didn't."

"By some miracle of God," Susannah said.

"No kidding," Raina replied. "I'm not much for taking the time to read the Bible, but you have to consider that someone incredible had a hand in what's happened the past year or so. Yes, Dad had to endure the stroke, but it brought unexpected surprises, didn't it?"

Susannah nodded. "It did. You came home, took over the business, bought a house, fell in love..."

Raina pointed to her. "And had two babies, which I honestly believe were conceived when I left here for that desperate act to save my marriage."

"Tori came back."

"And found Hottypants—"

Susannah snorted at Justin Verona's unfortunate—but forever—nickname.

"Seriously, Suze. He was Dad's *neurologist*. She'd have never met him if he hadn't gotten sick."

"And Sadie came home," Susannah said on a smile.

"Your chickens are all in the coop." Raina gave her hand a squeeze. "So no post-stroke trauma. It was all part of the Wingate plan, as they say."

"The grand Wingate plan," Susannah repeated. "You know, in my whole life, nothing has ever made me prouder than to be a Wingate and become the mother of you girls. Nothing. The greatest pride..." Choked up, she couldn't finish.

Raina wrapped both hands around Susannah's shaky one, holding tight. "Sometimes, in gooey moments like this, I want to call you Mom."

"You can."

"Can I?"

Susannah drew back at the question. "Raina! Of course. You can call me anything."

"It's just..." Raina inched back. "I was surprised that you so casually mentioned that you'd never remembered to, you know, adopt us." She gave a dry laugh. "Not something you forget."

"I've never forgotten it," Susannah said. "And it wasn't that I didn't 'remember' to get it done, I merely put it off out of respect to Charlotte. It wasn't like she was a horrible ex lurking on the sidelines. I wanted to honor her memory as your...*real*...mom."

Raina smiled. "You are my real mom."

"Thanks." She blinked back a tear. "What are we going to do about...the situation?"

"Please." She rolled her eyes. "It's a fat scam, I'm certain of it. All we need is to threaten to report her to the authorities. No, no, better yet—let's let Madeline's ex-FBI agent husband take her down. She'll disappear so fast we won't remember what she looked like. No, Suze. I'm not afraid of some nitwit named Ivy Button."

"Oh, Raina. I wish I had your—" Susannah looked at the phone when it hummed and vibrated. She turned it over and stared at the screen. "Unknown caller. Should I answer?"

"Yes. It's probably a bride-to-be wanting our mid-July

date. Do not give it away," she said, trying to lighten the mood.

"Or it could be..."

"Slimy Button. Good. Answer and I will make it my mission to ruin her. Go." She flicked her fingers at the phone. "Pick up."

Susannah touched the screen and tapped the speaker button so Raina could hear. "Hello?"

"Suze? Ivy Button here."

She inhaled sharply and shared a long look with Raina. "How did you—"

"It's on the internet. So's a lot of stuff about your family and businesses. Anyhoo, when can we meet so I can get the keys to my house? I imagine there's some paperwork to sign, so let's get this show on the road."

Susannah tried to swallow. "Um, Miss—"

"When and where?" she demanded, her voice harsh over Susannah's more gentle approach.

Raina leaned in and mouthed, "Tomorrow."

Suze's eyes widened, but Raina just kept silently saying the word.

"Tomorrow," Suze repeated.

"At the inn?"

Raina shook her head hard. "At Wingate Properties," she whispered.

At Wingate? What about Rex? But Raina pointed to the phone, nodding insistently.

Wasn't Raina afraid?

No, she realized. She was fearless. Suze had no idea if she'd learned that or had been born that way, but she'd always been fearless. Reaching out her other hand, she took Raina's and squeezed, so deeply grateful for this daughter.

"We will meet at Wingate Properties," Susannah said, channeling her inner fearless Raina.

"Should I bring my lawyer?" Ivy asked.

At Susannah's question, Raina give a "who cares" shrug.

"Bring whatever and whoever you want," Susannah said. "Be there at..."

Raina held up one finger.

"At one o'clock."

"Will Rex be there?" Ivy asked. It was the very first time Susannah sniffed a little fear from the woman. She looked at Raina, who shook her head slowly.

"No. I'll be there," Susannah said.

"Alone?"

She looked at Raina, who lifted a brow and said the unspoken family motto with just one glint of her deep blue eyes.

"A Wingate is never alone," Susannah said, squeezing Raina's hand.

For a few beats, Ivy was silent. Then she huffed out a breath. "Whatever. I got this in the bag, so you can pack the room with people, if you want. That inn still belongs to me and my mother."

We'll see about that, Susannah thought as she looked at the steely expression on her daughter's face.

"Goodbye, Miss Button."

With that, they both hung up and Susannah quietly

placed the phone on the table, staring at it for a beat before looking up at Raina.

She'd never in her life seen such fierce determination, pride, or...yes, fearlessness on a woman's face.

"I might not have legally adopted you, Raina Wingate," she whispered. "But I couldn't love you more."

Chapter Ten

Raina

The "need to know" list was short, Raina decided. This was not a family situation that had to be spread, shared, and supported by the entire Wingate clan. At least, not yet. And as tempting as it was to bring Madeline and Adam into the mix, Raina decided she could probably nip this in the bud without upsetting anyone's apple cart.

She told Chase, of course, and they'd talked about it late into the night. The claim was outrageous and absurd, but Raina needed far more information and proof before she got really worried. As far as she was concerned, Ivy Button was a classic con artist who would need to show her cards and have them closely scrutinized.

No doubt she thought Susannah was easy prey with an older husband who'd been sick, never taking into consideration the power of the Wingate family. She couldn't possibly dream of getting Wingate House, but money? Oh, she most likely dreamed of that. But all that would be clearer after the meeting that would start in... less than half an hour.

Chase wanted to be here, but in the end, they agreed that he could help the most by making one hundred percent certain Rex was away from Wingate Properties all afternoon. He'd brilliantly arranged a meeting with a client selling a multimillion-dollar estate on St. Simons Island in Georgia.

With two hours of driving, a long lunch, and an important negotiation, Chase would have Rex gone for the better part of the day. Raina had hired her favorite local sitter who wasn't a sister, because she didn't require an explanation of why Raina was having a meeting in town.

Even Raina's former assistant, who now worked for Blake and Chase, had unknowingly helped her out by taking the day off. That meant one less person who'd be curious about Ivy Button and her meeting with Susannah and Raina.

But Blake was here, zipping by her office, busy as ever.

"Just like old times, huh, Aunt Raina?" Blake called out on one of his trips. "What is the special occasion?" he asked, pausing at the door.

For a moment, Raina seriously considered bringing him in on everything. After all, as Doreen Parrish's biological grandson, Blake had skin in the game. That meant Ivy Button, if she really was Doreen's niece, which Raina doubted, was Blake's cousin.

But the kid had enough family issues. He'd basically been disowned by his father, an Iowa farmer who deeply disapproved when Blake decided to come out of the closet to his family and friends. His mother followed his father's lead, and that left Blake alone in the world.

He was resourceful, though, and had done the research to discover the names of his father's birth parents.

That led him to Amelia Island well over a year ago. After Doreen died and the sisters discovered they had a half-brother who'd been adopted, Raina put the puzzle pieces together that showed Blake was their nephew.

It took some work, but she'd brought him into the fold and now he was a treasured member of the Wingate clan.

Did he need to know there were more broken branches on his gnarled family tree? Not yet, she decided.

"Suze and I have a meeting and it seemed easier to have it here than at the inn," she explained.

The truth was, she didn't want Ivy Button anywhere near the inn where her alleged aunt's life was lived. Here, Raina had all the power, not to mention the files, the computers, and the psychological advantage of letting Ivy know she was up against Wingate Properties. And that was a formidable opponent.

"Ah, the joys of a double wedding," Blake said, going exactly where she'd hoped he'd go without forcing her into a lie. "And where are the dumplings?"

"With a sitter," she said.

He made a face. "I could have watched them while you discuss...what is this meeting for again? I don't—" He turned and his face brightened. "Hello, Mrs. Wingate!"

Saved by Susannah, Raina stood and came around

her desk. "Suze." She reached out and hugged her mother a little tighter than necessary.

"She's downstairs," Suze muttered in her ear. "I saw her on the street. She was on the phone and didn't see me."

Raina leaned back. "I'll go get her."

"Do you want me to get your guest?" Blake asked brightly. "I'm happy to—"

"I'll go, Blake. We'll just need some, uh, privacy with her."

"Of course," he said, far too classy to press for more information. "I'm actually going to be downstairs in the copy room working on a pile of contracts for clients. Just buzz me if you need me, Raina. For anything."

"Thank you, Blake." She gave him a smile, led Suze into the office to take a seat in one of the swivel chairs surrounding a small table, and pointed to her. "How will I know her?"

"Beady eyes. Black hair. Skinny to the point of unhealthy. And filthy sneakers."

Smiling at her mother's description, she jogged down the wide curved stairs that once were the centerpiece of her great-grandfather's bank building and crossed the marble floor to the front entrance.

Just as she reached it, a woman who matched Susannah's description right down to the scuffed Nikes pulled open the door.

"Hello, Raina."

She startled slightly, not expecting to be recognized. "Ms. Button?"

"How many are here?" she demanded.

"Just my mother and me. You?" She looked over her shoulder. "Did you bring Doreen's 'sister' so we could meet her, too?" She knew how the question sounded—like she didn't believe a thing that would come out of this woman's mouth.

Ivy just flicked a brow and tapped a cheap tote bag on her arm. "I brought all I needed to get you out of my Victorian mansion and my life. You can read it and weep or let me walk down the street to the local newspaper. I'm sure they'll publish Doreen's account of what your saintly father did to her."

Bile rose but Raina refused to even blink in response.

"We're upstairs," she said, gesturing in that direction as she started to walk. After a few steps, she turned to see that Ivy hadn't moved. "Are you coming?"

"Why would I?" She reached into the bag. "Read these and—"

"Upstairs, Ms. Button," Raina ground out. "We don't conduct business in the lobby at Wingate Properties."

Her eyes fluttered with a disgusted sigh as she clomped her dirty sneakers up the stairs behind Raina, who ushered her across the admin area where Blake and Dani usually sat at their desks, and into the big office, the picture window offering sunlight and a view of Wingate Way.

"We meet again," Ivy said to Susannah, who didn't stand when they walked in.

Her mother gave a tight smile, either unable or unwilling to talk. That was fine. Raina would handle this meeting and it wouldn't—unlike every other meeting—start with small-talk or an offer of something to drink.

"Show me what you have," Raina said as the woman plopped into one of the swivel chairs.

She reached into the tote bag and pulled out a manila envelope, slapping it on the table. "It's all there. Just hand me the keys."

Raina snorted in response. "I'm sorry you're so delusional, Ms. Button, but that is not the way real estate transactions work. It's not the way obscure and highly questionable legal claims work. It is not the way estate law and inheritance works. And..." Raina finally sat down next to her and leaned in. "It is certainly not the way the Wingate family works."

The other woman angled her head, too tough to show she was intimidated, but Raina knew her personal power.

"Read the letters she wrote to my mother, and then you can tell me what will work. In the meantime..." Ivy looked around. "Can a person get a cup of coffee in this place?"

"No." Raina lifted the dreaded envelope.

Peeking inside, she saw a bunch of handwritten... things. Loose-leaf paper, mismatched stationery, and one very crinkled paper napkin. Without reading a word, she tossed it back on the desk. "What do you really want? Money?"

"I want the inn." She picked up the envelope, opened it, and pulled out a folded and paper-clipped piece of paper. "The one that says it goes to Doreen Parrish—or her heirs—on the day that Reggie Wingate Jr. passes away. That's your dead grandfather, right?"

"Stop it!" Susannah barked, startling both of them. She leaned forward, putting her face closer to Ivy's. "You will *not* enter this building, which was built by the blood, sweat, and honor of the Wingate family, and disrespect a single member of it." She literally seethed, the words hissing through gritted teeth. "Is that clear?"

The other woman had the decency to lean back and shut up while Raina read a document that looked like it had been typed on an IBM Selectric sometime in the 1970s.

Well, not sometime. Specifically, on November 17, 1971. That was the date at the top of the document, which didn't look like a legal filing, but was notarized in Nassau County, Florida.

That would help to track down the veracity of this thing.

She skimmed the words...*I, Reginald Wingate II, do hereby swear that upon my passing, ownership of the property known as Wingate House of 109 Wingate Way in Fernandina Beach will be gifted to Miss Doreen Joy Parrish, or her living heirs.*

Her first thought was...Doreen's middle name was Joy? Oh, the irony. Her second?

This was a fraud and all she had to do was figure out a way to prove that.

"I'm sorry, but there is no way in heaven or hell or anywhere in between that any man named Reginald Wingate would make this decision, sign this paper, or give that house away to anyone for any reason." She tossed the paper. "Nope. Not a man with Wingate blood in his body and I will bet a gallon of my own that's the truth."

"You want the truth? Read the letters." Ivy stuffed her hand in the envelope and whipped one out, shoving it into Raina's hand. "Just read them, Raina. Or would you like me to read them out loud for your mother's benefit?" She whipped open a folded piece of loose leaf. "'No matter how much I told him no, he insisted—'"

"Stop it." Raina wrenched the paper away and balled it in her fist. "Do you think we don't know Rex Wingate better than you, you little scam artist? This is a lie!"

"You have to prove that," Ivy said, calm and cool.

"No." Raina stood up, digging for her own composure. "*You* have to prove that."

"Then I'm going to drag your father through so much mud, he'll choke on it and his big, fat house. The newspapers don't fact-check, anyway. They love dirt and, baby, this story is filthy."

"So are you," Raina muttered out through clenched teeth, glancing again at the letters, a plan formulating.

Somewhere in this office, there had to be something written or signed by Doreen Parrish. She had to compare the handwriting, for starters. And there had to be some record of this bizarre promise her grandfather had made.

"I need to hit the bathroom," Ivy announced, pushing up. "Where is it?"

She considered telling her to go down to the public bathroom on Centre Street, but she wasn't done with this woman. She had questions and needed to find her weakness. But before that, she needed to find something Doreen had written, because that might nip this in the bud.

"Down the hall on your left." When Ivy left, Raina turned to Susannah. "I need to dig through some files. Can you stand to be in here alone with her? I don't want her poking around or talking to anyone."

"I can manage her," Susannah said.

"Find her weak spots," Raina added as she gathered the envelope to take it all with her, including the balled-up paper. "But don't let her upset you. She's lying, and I am certain we can prove it."

With that, she shot out and jogged down the stairs, knowing exactly where in the file room—the bowels of the building that all administrative assistants called the dungeon—she might be able to find employee files. Surely Doreen had signed something.

The file room was empty and dark, with air-conditioning blasting to make it cold, too. She couldn't remember the last time she was down here. Maybe one summer in college when Dad told her if she couldn't file, she couldn't be a real estate agent.

Taking a deep breath, Raina turned, tried to orient herself, and only realized then that she was trembling.

Okay, this was serious. This woman could make enough trouble to bring real harm to the family. Would she win in court? Unlikely. But she could destroy the Wingate name, and truly, deeply hurt Rex in the process.

And she couldn't—

"Raina?"

She spun at the sound of Blake's voice, startled by it.

"What are you doing in the file dungeon?" he asked, coming closer. "You can ask me to find something. I reorganized every inch of this place a few months ago because I couldn't find a thing."

"I...I...need something."

"No kidding." He reached for her hand. "Aunt Raina, I haven't seen you this upset since the day you nearly lost those babies."

"You saved them and me," she whispered, the memory dear to her.

"And I can again," he said simply. "Why don't you tell me what you're looking for, why that snotty woman has you so upset—she was rude and couldn't find the bathroom—and let me help you again."

She leaned against a filing cabinet, overwhelmed by the support. "You really are a Wingate."

"No greater compliment, considering my own father has disowned me."

And Rex—all of them, really—loved and accepted him. Blake needed to know what was going on.

"Okay, you can help me," she said. "But brace yourself, Blake."

To HIS CREDIT, not much fazed Blake Youngblood. He listened, reacted, and recognized that the moment called for action, not a deep dive into the topic of his biological grandmother. That could come later.

With Raina, he made a quick game plan to attack the files. She rushed back upstairs to the office, worried to have left Susannah alone with that monster for so long. In the office, it was dead silent and colder than the file dungeon.

Ivy was sprawled on one of the swivel chairs, flipping through her phone, and Susannah stood near the window.

With her arms wrapped around her waist and her gaze locked on Madeline's salon across the street, Susannah looked wound tight and ready to spiral out of control.

"I need some time," Raina announced as she walked in.

"Enough time for me to walk down to the local newspaper office?" Ivy asked. "And get these Instagram and Facebook stories tagging all things Wingate ready to roll?"

Raina shot her a death glare. "Time to talk to you, Ivy."

The other woman looked dubious. "Chat away." She put her phone down and crossed her arms. "What do you want to know?"

"You background, for starters," Raina said, perching on the edge of the chair across from her. "And more about your mother, Doreen's sister."

"What do you want to know about her?"

"Her name."

"Felicity," she said. "Felicity Button."

"You hesitated. Is Button your real name?"

"Her married name, and, yes. It's mine now that I divorced and went back to my maiden name. Many Buttons in the world, starting with Benjamin."

"Where do you live, Ms. Button?"

"Minnesota."

"Oh? That's far away."

"Planes fly," she said drolly.

"Do you live with your mother?" Raina asked.

"She's in an assisted-living facility."

"But you want to move her here, to the inn? Will you care for her yourself?"

Dark eyes narrowed. "I'll get a nurse, but honestly? I don't see how that's any of your business."

"You swoop in here and demand ownership of one of our family's most valuable assets?" Raina fired back. "*Everything* about you is my business."

She picked up the phone. "I'm posting this on Instagram. I have all you Wingates tagged."

Raina leaned forward. "Don't threaten me, lady. I have every right to know everything, to have the documents you showed me verified by a professional, and to drag your sorry self into court and prove that my grandfather did not sign away Wingate House to Doreen Parrish. Now, how may I speak with Felicity?"

"You can't. She's deaf and half blind and doesn't know her name half the time."

"I don't care. I'll take her phone number."

"It's all in that envelope. Which is…" She looked around. "Where is it?"

"I have it," Raina said, knowing that the envelope was downstairs with Blake, who she hoped was comparing handwriting samples.

"Fine. I made copies of everything."

"Good, because I'm keeping that. And I'm checking with the county to see if that document was filed."

"Make it fast, Raina, because—"

Blake tapped on the door and poked his head in, sparing a quick glance in Ivy's direction, then gesturing for Raina to come out.

She pushed up and walked outside, closing the door behind her. "Please tell me—"

"It's a perfect match." He held out a piece of paper that looked like some sort of form. "This is a survey of all employees that was conducted fifteen years ago by Rex. He must have been in his touchy-feely stage, because he explains that he hired a consultant to make sure—"

"The employees were not under too much stress," Raina said. "I remember this. It was right after I left the company, married Jack, and moved to Miami. There was quite a bit of turnover and he was worried." She made a face as she read Doreen's scratched responses to the questions. "A match?"

"Look at the capital W in Wingate, and compare it to this one." In his other hand, he held a loose-leaf paper that had come from the envelope. "See that little curlicue? Oh, and look at the way she writes little capital E's in her name. It's not only a match, it's perfect."

She studied the writing on the form.

I am the manager of Wingate House and it is a very important job.

It read—and looked—like a ten-year-old wrote it, reminding Raina that Doreen was slightly mentally challenged, but functional.

She shifted her gaze to the letter he'd pulled out of the manila envelope.

Rex Wingate is a spoiled rich kid who takes what he wants. And what he wanted was Doreen. Nothing would stop him from taking what he wanted by force.

She winced, disgusted and dismayed by the words, and the fact that the handwriting on both was identical.

"Have you read these letters?" he asked her.

"Glanced," she said. "They read like an old romance novel from the 1970s. And she only speaks of herself in third-person."

She looked up at him. "In other words, fiction. This is nothing but Doreen's imagination."

"Did she read a lot of that stuff?" Blake asked.

She nodded, remembering the hefty paperback collection they'd found when they cleaned out her apartment. "So now I have to prove that this whole thing was... her imagination?"

"Except she had a baby, and Rex admits it happened, so...at least one aspect of it was true. They did the deed. No imagining that."

She exhaled, even more worried now. "What about the Wingate House files?" she asked, searching for another solution. There *had* to be one. "Anything from my grandfather about giving that house away?"

"Not a word, but I did see his signature and..."

"It matches this?"

"Pretty close, but not exact. Close enough that it might hold up in court, but I'm no lawyer."

Raina shut her eyes and grunted. "Now what?"

"I have one other avenue to pursue." Blake said. "My father."

"Your father didn't have contact with her," Raina said. "At least, as far as I know, when he came to town to meet my dad—"

"And demand money," Blake interjected, sounding as disgusted as she knew he was.

"He told my father he didn't want to meet Doreen," she said. "So I don't know what contacting him will do, except make you miserable."

His expression fell. "It's been over a year since I even spoke to him, Raina."

"Oh, Blake." She put a hand on his arm. "I am sorry this is stirring up old and dark feelings for you. And you've done plenty. I can't wave a sample of Doreen's handwriting in front of that witch's face and send her home, but I'm far from defeated."

He gave her a sad smile. "Nothing defeats Aunt Raina."

"You got that right, kiddo. Let me take it from here. Thanks for this. Oh, do you want to formally meet your alleged cousin? I'm not sure she realizes who you are. My mother mentioned your father's name to her, and she claimed she had no idea there was a child. I think the less information we give her, the better."

"Agreed, and I did have one interaction on her way to the bathroom, but let me walk her down when you're finished. I'll look with a more discerning eye and won't reveal a thing."

With a quick nod, she gathered herself, then turned and walked back into the chilly atmosphere of the office.

"A month," Raina announced. "I need one full month to do my due diligence."

"Two weeks," Ivy volleyed back.

At least she was negotiating.

Raina shook her head. "One month. Leave contact information for your mother and I do not want to see your face anywhere near Wingate Way from this day until that one."

She gave a smug smile. "I'll be back in three weeks. Make this easy on your family, Raina. Tell them you sold Wingate House because it didn't make enough money as a wedding venue."

Raina could feel Susannah bristle from the other side of the room.

"And it won't," Ivy continued, either not aware of or not caring that Raina was taking slow steps toward her. "Because once I reach out to all those wedding websites and let them know the place is owned by a rap—"

"Get out of here," Raina practically spat the words in her face, through tightly clenched teeth. "Get your disgusting, lying, libelous self out of my office and my company and my town. I mean it, Ivy." Her eyes narrowed as she leaned in, inches from Ivy's rough skin and cheap hair dye. "You have no idea what will happen if I unleash the full power of the Wingate family and, trust me, you don't want to find out."

With one withering look, Ivy left and Raina dropped on the sofa, wiped out from the encounter. In an instant, Susannah was next to her, wrapping Raina in a hug and love and all the affection she could muster—which was a lot.

Raina just closed her eyes and put her head on her mother's shoulder. "Don't worry, Suze. Don't worry."

But she knew they both were worried sick.

Chapter Eleven

Chloe

Chloe looked up from her phone, kind of hating what she had to say to Tori, Raina, and her mother after just twenty minutes of wedding planning. They'd moved heaven and Earth—and two babies—to get this time together and even sat outside on the inn's porch because the cleaning crew was working inside.

But it just wasn't meant to be.

"You're not going to believe this." She winced, expecting them to be furious. "Travis just texted that he went down to Jax and was allowed to get Judah for the whole day. Only twelve hours—which is so sad, it hurts—but he said Judah's very quiet and he wanted to bring him to the refuge to see the dogs and...and..."

"Go," Tori said when the other two were silent.

But they'd been nearly catatonic this whole meeting. Raina threw out a few ideas and Mom? Susannah was in another zone.

"Are you sure?" Chloe directed the question to her mother, who was the one who'd needed help with this event.

Susannah blinked, yanking herself from wherever she was. "Go...where?"

Chloe snorted softly. "Mom, are you sure you're up for this? For this wedding?"

"Yes. Yes, she is," Raina answered for her. "It's just so hot out here and it's not even the middle of June. In a month, we'll have to hand out battery-powered fans as wedding favors."

"I like that idea," Tori said, pointing at Chloe. "Add it to your list."

The list was woefully short, to be honest. "This is all so much easier than when I did—or didn't, to be more accurate—the wedding planning thing. Basically, we're having a family gathering at the inn. Rose has the flowers covered and—" She glanced down at her phone to see a call from Travis. "Sorry. Now he's calling."

"Go!" This time Tori stood. "I'm taking off, too. My line cook just texted that the café is swamped, and they need me. Can we regroup on the wedding planning at some point?"

Raina and their mother agreed and, in less than a minute, Tori and Chloe were walking to the street where they'd both parked.

"Honestly? I'm glad you broke up this meeting," Tori said softly. "Raina and Suze are frustrating me. I mean, for a stay-at-home mom, Raina was reading and writing texts like she was back at the helm of Wingate Properties, and Suze seems a million miles away."

"I noticed that, too, but..." Chloe glanced at her

phone, realizing how close Travis was. "I gotta run, Tori. They'll be fine."

Tori answered with a sigh of frustration, but Chloe couldn't stay and discuss the issue. Yes, Raina seemed preoccupied. And Mom? She hadn't been herself for a few weeks.

Maybe it was the pressure of this wedding.

Making a promise to herself to pay more attention and take the reins on this one, Chloe hustled home as fast as she could, unable to ignore the fact that Judah and Travis had all of her heart right now.

Using the dashboard, she called Travis back.

"I'm on my way to the refuge," she said the second he answered. "How's Judah?"

"He's good, but I told him we're going to see dogs and he has made it clear he only likes 'wittle wittle' dogs."

She cooed at the baby talk. "Tell him he's in luck! Not only is there Lady Bug, but I got a Yorkie named Cupcake yesterday and he's going to love her!"

Travis chuckled, sounding so relaxed, considering how big this one-on-one day was.

"Are you on speaker?" she asked. "Can you tell me what changed your mind?"

"Not speaker, he can't hear. And, I don't know. Mae called to check on us and mentioned there are a few couples who might..." He lowered to a soft whisper. "Foster Judah—"

She gasped softly, hating the thought of him going to live with a forever family that wasn't them.

"Chloe, come on," he murmured, no doubt picking up on her worries.

"I know, I know. It's fine. Let's just focus on today and making it amazing for him, okay?"

"Yes, I love that. See you in a bit."

Chloe pulled into the refuge and did a quick handoff with Ashley, who filled her in on more boarding reservations that had come in over the last few hours. They quickly reviewed the kennel management checklist—everything had been cleaned, dogs were fed, and the kitty litter was disposed of.

With everything under control, Chloe zipped through the place, trying to see it through Judah's little eyes. He probably wasn't passing judgment, but the small house had undergone a lot of renovation in the past few months, and she was proud of what it had become.

No longer the ramshackle house with some kennels in the back for boarding and taking in dogs for rescue, Chloe had managed to make the house a home for people and animals. Travis had gutted and rebuilt her a beautiful kitchen at the heart of the place, and she'd turned the larger spare bedroom into the cat house. The smaller one functioned as her office, and the main bedroom had been transformed into a bright, cozy sanctuary of her own.

The screened-in back porch was comfortable and, like the kitchen, looked out into the spacious yard where she'd upgraded four kennels that were nearly always filled.

But was this a *family* house?

Not with only one functioning bedroom. Could she

move her office somewhere—the hall or the back porch—and turn that smaller room into one suitable for a little boy? Possibly. Or maybe Travis could really build that addition they'd casually talked about. That could be a beautiful master suite and her current room could work perfectly for a little guy.

Whoa, talk about getting ahead of herself.

Just then, Travis's truck rolled over the gravel, so Chloe snagged little Cupcake and hustled to the front with the Yorkie in her arms and Lady Bug at her side. With the more intimidating Buttercup in the back, Judah should be very comfortable.

Travis got out first and she went right to him for a hug and kiss, looking into the back seat of the large truck to see a sweet little boy in a car seat, sucking his thumb, eyes wide, glasses just a bit crooked.

"He's really shy," Travis said. "Or scared. He honestly hasn't said ten words since I got him."

"It has to be hard, Travis. Of course he's scared. Let me talk to him."

When he opened the back door, she gave Judah a smile and held up tiny little Cupcake, who curled into a ball and tried to basically squirm out of Chloe's grip.

"This is one of my guests at Rocky's Rescues," she said. "Would you like to meet Cupcake?"

His dark eyes flashed but he shook his head hard, and Cupcake looked equally disinterested.

But Lady Bug was jumping, trying to get into the truck. She barked a few times, and Judah looked down at her. Lady Bug barked and whipped her fluffy tail furiously, scratching her little nails on the running boards, desperate to make a new friend.

Far more interested, Chloe had to admit, than Cupcake.

She turned and put the little Yorkie in Travis's hands. "Can you put her back in the house? She's happiest in my office and her bed's in there.

"I think we'll have better luck with Bugaboo."

"Bug-boo," Judah repeated, making Chloe laugh as Travis disappeared into the house.

"Yes, that's what I call this little munchkin." She bent over and gave Lady Bug a hand, which was all it took for her to leap up and scramble right into the car seat with Judah.

She barked, loud and high-pitched.

"She's saying hello, Judah."

He giggled, inching back at the dog's insistence, but he took his thumb out and tapped her head carefully, as if he didn't know if she might bite him or not.

"She's very friendly," Chloe said. "I've had her since she was a puppy and she's never bitten anyone."

He looked up at her, the first glimmer of real trust in his eyes. "Bug-boo?"

"You can call her anything and she'll answer. Her official name is Lady Bug. And I'm Chloe. Do you remember me?"

He nodded and looked down at his chest. Behind Lady Bug's little body—already nestled against him—she saw the Spider-Man T-shirt they'd given him.

"Yes, I was there for your Spidey birthday party. You

want to get out and see my animal refuge? I live here, but so do lots of doggies and a few cats. But don't worry—you don't have to play with them if you don't want to."

Lady Bug looked up and licked his chin, getting another giggle.

"Well, you've made one friend, Judah."

He stroked her head with such a gentle touch that Chloe's heart clutched.

"Bug-boo."

"Bug-boo," she agreed. "And she obviously loves you."

He looked up, through the windshield. "Uncah Man?"

She fought a smile at the name. "He went to take Cupcake for a nap. Do you want—"

"No nap," he said with more urgency than she'd ever heard from him.

"No, no nap," she promised, reaching in to unlatch his seatbelt. "But I sure hope ol' Uncle Man remembered to pack some of your trucks. Because if we have anything around here, it's dirt. And that dirt needs to be moved."

He gave a slow smile and nodded, pointing to a few plastic grocery bags that held what looked like some clothes and toys. His suitcases, she presumed, with another hitch of her heart.

"Well, let's get moving some dirt, my friend. Bug-boo will certainly help. And by help, I mean bark in your face and lick the dirt off your hands."

Again, he smiled, his whole face brighter as they unloaded. He was barely out of the truck when he grabbed one of the yellow plastic trucks and ran to a patch of dirt, Lady Bug jogging along with him.

In an instant, he was on the ground, making "vroom-vroom" sounds not much louder than Lady Bug's happy barks.

"Can you make me a great big mountain of dirt, Judah?" Chloe asked.

"Dirt!" he exclaimed as he got to work.

Just then, she turned to see Travis standing on the front step, watching, an unreadable expression on his face.

With a quick check of Judah, she walked across the driveway, holding out her arms, unable to wipe the smile from her face.

"He's happy," she announced.

He didn't answer, but gave her a funny look, then pulled her in for a hug. "Oh, Chloe, what am I gonna do?"

She inched back, looking up at him. "You want him, don't you?"

"I don't...I do...I have no idea. It's such a massive, life-altering, world-shaking decision."

"I know," she agreed, turning to look at the child pushing a pile of dirt and saying something softly to the little dog skittering in excited circles around him. "I don't know who loves who more. I had no idea Bug was longing for a kid."

"I wasn't."

"I know," she said, sliding her arm around him. "Certainly not a five-year-old who is technically your half-nephew."

His eyes shuttered.

"Travis, just enjoy the day. Let him play. You don't have to make a decision now."

"But the more time I spend with him..." He gave her a look. "Mae said there are two couples seriously considering him. And not just for fostering."

"For adoption?" she asked, punched by that news. "Like, we could get squeezed out completely if we wait too long?"

"Babe, I am not ready to say yes to this."

"I know, I know," she agreed. "I mean, the living situation alone is daunting. Unless we..." She squished her nose. "Did the addition of a new main bedroom suite and—"

"Not yet, Chloe," he said gruffly. "One day at a time."

"Okay. But if someone..." Her voice trailed off when a car turned into her driveway. "Might be a customer, but no one called. Can you stay with Judah?"

He nodded, heading over to the little boy while she walked closer to the car, spying a much older man behind the wheel, with snow-white hair and a weathered face. Slowly, he turned off the ignition and finally opened the car door.

He looked up at Chloe with watery blue eyes, blinking as if the sunlight or seeing a person surprised him.

"Hello," Chloe said, resisting the urge to give the man a hand. "Can I help you?"

He finally got out of the car, standing to maybe five-

five, a little old man with a cardigan, brown pants, and white sneakers.

"Where's Rocky?" he asked. "Rocky Zotter? The owner of this place?"

"She retired and moved away," Chloe explained. "I'm Chloe Wingate, the new owner, but I didn't change the name. It's still Rocky's Rescues. What can I do for you?"

"Do you board cats like Rocky did?"

"Absolutely." She beamed. "In fact, I have a just-completed cat room, with wonderful climbers, spacious individual kennels, all air-conditioned. Would you like to see it?" When he nodded, Chloe called to Travis and Judah, "Be right back, you two. Quick tour." Then she turned to her guest. "What's your name, sir?"

"I'm Henry," he said. "But everyone calls me Hank. Except my dear late wife, who called me 'Old Hank,' which I never thought was very funny. But I guess I got the last laugh, 'cause I'm old and she's..." He pointed to the sky and made a sad face.

"I'm sorry, Hank," she said, guiding him inside.

"Oh, this is all different," Hank said, pausing to look around. "Brighter and newer than when Rocky was here. I'm glad I drove all the way up from Long Point to come here."

"I've spent the last few months and a whole lot of dollars fixing it up," Chloe said. "Let me show you the new cat room."

Which could have been a little boy's bedroom, but she had no idea she'd need one, and the cats brought forty bucks a night.

She opened the door to see her two current boarders, one asleep, one climbing a cloth-covered stairway to nowhere.

"Very nice," Hank said. "Can I make a reservation? I have to go into the hospital for a procedure in a few weeks and I have to feel like my little man Elvis is safe and sound."

"Elvis will be very happy here, but I'm sorry you have to go to the hospital, Hank."

"Oh, it's fine. I'll be ninety this year. I didn't think they bothered with them medical things on old guys like me, but my doc says this'll give me at least five more years." He gave a yellowed grin. "And I want to have my Elvis next to me for all of them."

She smiled back. "I understand that, sir. Let's go make your reservation."

As she took him into the room she used as an office, they passed the kitchen bulletin board where she allowed clients to post pictures of dogs and cats or advertise adoptions. At the board, he stopped and stared at the colored printout of Rhett Butler's "Missing" poster.

"Well, I'll be. Why do you have a picture of my Elvis right there?"

She did a double-take. "Oh, no, that's not your cat. He's been missing for a few weeks. Is Elvis an orange tabby? They're so cute."

"He's...missing?" The old man seemed to turn pale. "From here? You lost him from here?"

"No, near Fernandina Beach. My sister's boyfriend was cat-sitting and—"

"That's Elvis," he croaked.

"Excuse me?"

"I haven't had him three weeks."

"Really?" Her heart jumped. Could she have found Rhett Butler?

"My lady who comes and cleans my place for me brought him to me. Said she picked him up on the street at one of the houses she cleans."

Chloe stared at him, then the flyer. "You have Rhett Butler?"

"I...I..." He looked closer. "Oh, dear. Yes. That's my little boy, Elvis." He grabbed onto the edge of the desk like he might faint. "I never imagined he belonged to someone—"

"He belongs to a woman who's in Europe right now, and a frantic cat-sitter who'll be overjoyed to hear this."

He stared at the flyer, fighting to take a breath.

"Are you all right?" Chloe asked.

"I'm...I'm...no. No, I can't give him up!"

"Maybe it's not the same cat," she said quickly, worried he was about to keel over.

"Oh, it's the same cat. But I...I..." He closed his eyes and a tear dribbled down his wrinkled face. "I love him."

"I'm sure you do, Mr.—Hank. But..." But he couldn't keep Rhett Butler, and Chloe sure didn't want to be responsible for the poor man getting that news.

"I think I'll just go now," he said, turning away. "I'll call you if I want to make a reservation."

"Please, please wait." It wasn't hard to catch up with

him. "Can't they just come and see him? Maybe it's not Rhett Butler."

He kept walking, silent, right out the door and to the driveway.

"But...but...can I give you her number, in case you change your mind?" Chloe asked, feeling desperate that this might slip away. All she knew about him was that his name was Henry, went by Hank, and he lived in Long Point, which was a large area on the island that included townhouses, a hotel, and many, many homes.

He reached the car door and turned, shocking Chloe with full tears spilling. "I can't give him up. I can't."

"And maybe you won't have to, but they should be able to know."

A storm of emotions played over his weathered features, with his eyes registering grief and fury and fear and, finally, resignation. "I suppose it would be wrong to keep him. That's what my Margie would say."

"I don't know what it would be," Chloe said softly. "But someone does already love Rhett Butler very much and I'm sure she'd be grateful that you've taken care of him so well for these past few weeks."

Very slowly, he pulled open the car door. "I live at the Driftwood Villas," he said gruffly. "Unit 2A. I'll be home tonight."

"Thank you," Chloe whispered, helping him into the driver's seat right before he closed the door and broke into a visible sob.

Poor Sadie and Scout. This wasn't going to be an easy rescue, but at least they'd found Rhett Butler.

When Hank left, Chloe turned to the boys—one large, one small— and one dog, all playing in the dirt.

"Who likes chocolate?" she called.

Judah looked up, his face and hands covered in dirt, but his eyes told the story. He loved chocolate.

"Let's clean up and make a trip to town," she said. "I'm going to take you to the best chocolate shop in the world."

His eyes widened, but he instantly put a hand on Lady Bug's head, not having to say what he was thinking.

"No worries, darling," she assured him. "Bug-boo goes where I go. Uncle Man, we have a mission."

Travis popped up into action, like the great firefighter he was, and reached for Judah's hand—like the great father he could be.

Chapter Twelve

Sadie

With her clerk working the front of Charmed by Chocolate, Sadie was free to spend the day in the shop's kitchen, which was definitely her happy place. There, she could create new recipes and stock her display shelves with fresh delights that the locals and tourists on Amelia Island seemed to love.

When she was this busy, she only glanced through the glass that allowed customers in the retail area to see the candies being made. But something caught her eye as she poured out a batch of silky cocoa nibs, refined to perfection in the *melangeur*.

Turning to look, she had to laugh at the sight of Chloe, waving wildly to get her attention.

Wait a minute. Was that a child with her? Was that... *Judah?*

Without a second's hesitation, she wiped her hands on her apron and abandoned her slab of chocolate, rushing out to greet them.

"Hello!" She grinned at the little boy who stood with his face pressed so hard against the display glass, it made his glasses crooked. "You must be the proverbial kid in a candy store!"

Chloe chuckled, her caring hand resting so naturally on the child's shoulder it kind of took Sadie's breath away. She'd never thought of her youngest sister as the maternal type, though she was fantastic with their nieces and nephews.

Sadie always thought it was because Chloe was young—at heart and in life. But standing there with a mother's touch and more than a little pride in her eyes? Sadie saw her thirty-year-old baby sister differently.

"What brings—"

"I have great, amazing news," Chloe told her, bouncing on her sneakers to meet Sadie halfway around the counter for a hug. "But first, chocolate. Judah, this is my sister, Sadie, and she made all of these beautiful treats."

Judah looked up with a gaze Sadie suspected Santa Claus saw on the face of every child at a mall—a little wonder, a lot of respect, and a whisper of fear.

"It's nice to meet you," Sadie said, lowering to his tiny height. "I know there's a lot to pick from but I bet you'd like a cake pop."

He stared at her, the slightest shake of his head.

"You don't like cake pops?" she asked, turning to the display. "It's that thing right there that looks like a chocolate-covered lollipop with cake inside."

"Well, I know he likes cake," Chloe said, that protective hand patting his narrow shoulder.

"And lollies," he whispered, so soft Sadie wasn't sure she'd heard him.

"Then this is perfect." She looked up at Chloe, aching to ooh and ahh and fuss over how cute he was, but she didn't want to terrify the poor child, who seemed overwhelmed. "Can I give him one?"

"Yes, and one for Travis, who is outside with Lady Bug. Then I want to talk to you. It's urgent."

Sadie gave her a curious look, but handled the business of the cake pops, chatted with the shy but incredibly adorable child, and set two coffees at a small side table while Chloe walked Judah and the cake pops outside.

What could her great news be? Well, that they would be adopting Judah, of course. She wasn't sure why that wouldn't merit an all-fam meeting and a huge party, or why Chloe would tell Sadie first or alone, but it didn't matter.

Whatever Chloe's news was, she seemed happy when she flew back into the shop and practically threw herself into the café chair across from Sadie, her blue eyes bright with her news.

"Thank me now, because I have found Rhett Butler!"

"What?" Sadie gasped, the words not even computing and so not what she was expecting. "You have him?"

"No, but I know who does. I think. An old man came into the rescue today to tour so he could arrange to board his cat, then he went crazy when he saw the flyer. He said he just got the cat from his cleaning lady, who found him in the street a few weeks ago! I'm pretty sure he has Rhett Butler."

With each word, Sadie sat up straighter, flabbergasted. "No! That's amazing, Chloe. Thank you!"

"Well, don't thank me yet. He has him, but he doesn't want to let him go."

"Too darn bad. That cat's not his."

"He cried," Chloe added with a grimace.

Sadie inched back. "But if it's Rhett, then he can't keep him. Are you sure it's not another cat?"

"Not entirely, obviously, but he told me where he lives and said he'd be home tonight, so you and Scout can go down there and see."

Sadie let out a sigh and her excitement dropped a notch. "Well, he can't be *that* attached if it's really Rhett and he's only had the cat for a few weeks."

"You have to go see him."

"Oh, we will. Scout will be over the moon. He's been miserable trying to decide if he should tell Kitty and ruin her vacation. Hopefully, this is Rhett, the old man is sensible, and we can put this behind us. Thank you, Chloe! Great sleuth work."

"I didn't do a thing. It was serendipity that Ol' Hank came into Rocky's Rescue to board his cat." Chloe sipped the coffee, her eyes widening with appreciation. "There's chocolate in this brew."

"You expected anything different?" Sadie asked with a laugh. "It's good, huh?"

"Fabulous." She turned and glanced through the window, frowning. "Where did those two go?"

Sadie leaned in and looked hard at her sister. "You know what I thought the good news was, don't you?"

"Yeah," Chloe replied with a shrug. "He's not there yet. But today is already a huge step forward, honestly, with him going on his own to see Judah. He's thinking about it, and that's all I can ask."

Searching her sister's face, Sadie felt a hundred different questions form. "Are you sure you're ready for this, Chloe? Is he? A child is a huge responsibility and you two aren't married or living together."

"I know," Chloe said. "But those are logistical things that can be overcome. Travis needs time to come to terms with his father—and Judah's grandfather—and the pain of the past. But if he takes too much time? That little boy will be scooped up by a loving family and while that's good for him, there's something about knowing he's Travis's nephew. Well, half, but has that ever mattered in our family? He's blood and I don't want to lose him."

Sadie nodded, completely understanding that. "And marriage or living together is just...logistics?"

"No, it's more than that. But I also think that's inevitable for us."

Sadie searched her face, of course thinking of her own boyfriend. Were those things "logistics" and were they "inevitable"?

Chloe leaned in, her gaze sharp like she could read Sadie's mind. "Are you starting to feel...the thing?"

She laughed but her smile wavered.

"I don't know," she admitted. "The cat brought us closer. And all I ever feel about Scout is that he's so...nice.

Then I wonder if 'the thing' isn't just for, you know, the ones that keep you off balance."

Chloe rolled her eyes. "The ones like Tristan Saint Pierre? Did you learn nothing from your walk with a bad-to-the-bone billionaire? Life ain't a romance novel, Sadie, and the ones that 'keep you off balance,' as you say, also make you fall flat on your face into a pit of despair."

She was so right.

"I mean, look at Dad," Chloe continued. "The nicest man on Earth, and who doesn't love Rex Wingate?"

"Amen to that," Sadie said, pushing up, already anxious to see Scout and test out Chloe's theory, hoping to feel...the thing. "I better finish my truffles and clean up so we can go get Rhett. Text me the address and the guy's name."

"I will, but remember...he's very old and...tender."

"We'll be fine. I'll have the world's *nicest* guy with me." She winked and pushed her chair in. "Have fun with your boys, Chloe."

"Good luck with Rhett. And his new owner. *Big* luck with Hank."

Scout picked up Sadie outside the chocolate shop without either of them changing or having dinner at the end of the day. They were too anxious to roll down to the other end of the island and bring home Rhett Butler.

But he did take the time to pull her close and give her a kiss.

"God bless the Wingate family," he murmured against her lips. "They saved the day, the cat, my relationship with Kitty Worthington, probably my reputation, and my business. 'Cause without the chair of our Local Business Organization on my side, more than my cookies would crumble."

She had to laugh, because he was such a goofball sometimes, this dear man who got his childhood nickname because he was, through and through, a Boy Scout.

Could those traits—the very things that made him darling, different, and dependable—really be what was stopping her from just giving in and loving the man? Because Chloe was so right about the bad boys of the world.

"What?" he urged when she didn't respond for way too long. "You don't think this cat is Rhett Butler? Oh, Sadie, if this is another of your wild—"

"No, no," she assured him. "Not a wild idea like Wiggles. How is he, anyway?"

"Very much at home and so stinking affectionate, I think he believes he's a dog."

She smiled. "You're keeping him, aren't you?"

"Yes," he said without hesitation. "How'd you know?"

"Because you're so...nice."

He threw her a wistful smile, as if he knew that could be his downfall.

"I hope this really is Rhett Butler," he said. "Because if it isn't, I made a huge decision."

"You're calling Kitty?" she guessed.

"I have to. The guilt is killing me. I swear I can hear

my mother hounding me from the great beyond. 'Oy vey, Martin!'" he imitated with a classic Yiddish accent. "'Aunt Kitty is going to die of the pain!'"

Sadie chuckled. "Well, let's hope you can hear your mother blowing kisses of joy soon, because Chloe was pretty sure this was Rhett. She did warn us that the man, Hank, is not keen to part with him."

"Well, too bad." He threw her a questioning look. "I mean, how connected can he be to a cat he's had for, what, three weeks?"

"Apparently he was emotional."

"Well, I'm emotional," he fired back. "And Kitty will be at DEFCON 1. Or is it 5? I can never remember."

"I don't know, but Kitty will go ballistic if she comes home to no Rhett Butler."

"Which means, and you need to agree to this, I definitely have to call Kitty tonight if this is a false alarm."

She nodded. "As much as it pains me, I agree."

As they drove, he took her hand and gave it a squeeze. "So, good day at Charmed by Chocolate?"

"Surprising day," she told him. "When Chloe came with the news about Rhett, she brought little Judah and he is...*oof.*" She shook her head. "So cute it hurts to look at him."

He lifted a brow in her direction. "I've never heard you gush about kids, Sadie."

"This one's special."

"They all are," he said softly, and it was easy to hear the very subtle longing in his voice.

"You want kids, don't you?"

He gave her an "are you kidding" look. "But then, I want a lot of things I can't have."

"You...could have kids."

Lifting her hand to his lips, he gave her knuckles a kiss and didn't answer, and that silence hung in the car.

Finally, he sighed. "The issue of kids, assuming you and I, uh, go the distance? That would be up to you, Sadie. I would agree to anything that would make you happy."

"Oh." She let out a little sigh, so touched by that. "I guess...I honestly don't know. I just turned thirty-six, so I don't have a lot of years left to decide."

He just checked the GPS and turned at the corner. "Let's get Rhett Butler in our hands before we tackle major life issues, okay?"

"I couldn't agree more," she said on a relieved laugh. "But what are you going to do if this guy doesn't want to give him up?"

"Not give him up?" he scoffed. "He doesn't have a choice. Rhett Butler belongs to Kitty Worthington and I have the photos and all the shot records and paperwork to prove it." He narrowed his eyes in determination. "He can't give me a fight."

"I doubt he will. Chloe said he's practically a hundred but apparently he's a crier."

Scout winced at that, but shook his head. "He can be an ax murderer and he still can't have a cat that belongs to someone else."

"He's very, very old."

"I don't care if he's Moses himself and parts the Red Sea. He can't have Rhett Butler. It's not up for debate."

They parked at the condo complex, checked the unit number Chloe had texted, and climbed out of the car, holding hands in solidarity.

At Unit 2A, a man with wispy white hair and baggy slacks that looked like they could fall off his skinny body appeared behind a screen door. Chloe hadn't been exaggerating about his age—he was ancient.

"You must be Hank," Sadie said as they got closer. "My sister told you we'd be here, right?"

For a long time, he just looked through the screen, silent.

"For the cat?" Scout added after an awkward beat.

Sadie got close enough to see his blue eyes were moist, either with age...or tears. Oh, boy. This wasn't going to be easy.

"Can we see him, Hank?" she asked. "Could we see Rhett Butler?"

"His name's Elvis," he said. "Because my Margie was the biggest Elvis fan you ever met. Watched every movie he ever made about a hundred times until I wanted to scream, 'No more *Blue Hawaii!*'" He gave a smile, with more gaps than actual teeth. "But when I got this guy, I knew what my Margie would want to name him."

Next to her, Scout huffed a breath. "I'm very sorry, Mr.—"

"Jus' Hank." He pushed open the screen door. "Come on in. You don't look like you'd kill me for him."

As they stepped inside, Sadie glanced at Scout, who

exhaled a little as if to acknowledge that this wouldn't be as easy as he'd thought.

"I'm Scout Jacobson," he said, extending his hand. "This is Sadie Wingate. You met her sister today."

He nodded and shook their hands, then pulled out a handkerchief from his pocket. The yellowed cotton looked as old as he was as he used it to dab at his eyes. Very slowly, silently, he folded it into a small square and held it out.

"See my initials?" He showed them the corner of the hankie, with HMG embroidered—not very well—in blue thread. "That's the last thing my Margie made me before she passed."

"I'm so sorry." Sadie and Scout spoke in perfect unison.

"It's a mess," he said with a snort, fluttering the embroidered corner. "She couldn't see past her nose in the end, but she wanted me to have this. She knew her time was up and she worked so hard on it. See?" He held it closer. "Didn't quite finish the G for Gatling. Died that night, you see."

Sadie's heart shifted and Scout just sighed.

"That's...a nice memory of her," Scout said, the bravado from the car missing now. "Could we, um, see Rhett? It might not be him, of course," he added. "We have to be sure."

"My lady brought him here," he said, gesturing for them to follow him a few steps into a living room that looked like it had been decorated in 1955 and never touched since. "Carla's her name. Comes twice a month and tidies up for me. She thought the cat might lift my spirits since my Margie...well, the house has been pretty empty these past months."

"I'm sure it has been, sir," Scout said, voice oozing with respect and warmth. "But if this cat she found is Rhett Butler, then it will be the cat I'm watching for a friend."

"Not very closely," he muttered. "If you were on the job, son, he'd have never gotten away."

Scout tipped his head in acknowledgement of the facts, looking just the right amount of chastised. But with Scout? That wasn't fake—he *was* ashamed of losing the cat, and that touched Sadie.

"Carla was cleaning a house up there and found Elvis stuck in a tree in the backyard. She coaxed him down, God bless her, and the couple she works for said no one around them owned a cat."

That could easily have been one of Scout's neighbors. "The owner lives in town, but I was—"

"Negligent," the man interjected. "You lost him, so in my opinion, you don't love him like I do."

Scout threw a helpless look at Sadie, who was also at a loss for how to deal with Hank, who might be old, but he should have been a lawyer for how well he was making a case.

"Where is he, Hank?" she asked as gently as she could.

"I put him in a cat bag in case you showed up," Hank said. "Though I was praying you wouldn't."

Scout grimaced at that as the man pointed toward a

floral chintz sofa. "Sit. I'll get him." He shuffled down the hall, away from them.

Scout dropped to the seat with a groan of discontent. "Just what I always wanted to be," he muttered. "Someone's unanswered prayer."

Next to him, Sadie put a hand on his. "But he's the answer to ours," she reminded him.

He nodded, looking around the small townhouse. Both of their gazes stopped at a picture of an older couple standing side by side with the words "Henry and Margaret – Fifty Years" engraved on the metal frame.

They heard Hank's footfall and a very loud—and very familiar—meow.

"All righty, then. I got him in this here container, but he ain't happy."

He came in holding a canvas cat carrier with two hands, the contents squirming for freedom.

Maybe it wasn't Rhett Butler, who certainly wouldn't go into a carrier without a major fight.

"Oh, here, I'll get that for you," Scout offered, jumping up to take the carrier.

But Hank turned protectively, unwilling to give up the cat. "I just want to say goodbye," he said, taking the carrier to a worn velour recliner in the corner.

He placed it on the seat, and bent over to speak into the netting. "I have very bad news, Elvis. Very, very bad news."

Still standing, Scout sighed. "Let's see if this is the right cat, Hank." She could have sworn she heard a little hope in Scout's voice—like it would be easier to face Kitty's wrath than break old Hank's heart.

Scout stepped next to the recliner and kneeled down, looking inside. Instantly, the cat started mewing and pawing at the netting in recognition.

Scout closed his eyes with a grunt. "It's him."

"It's him?" Sadie said, her voice rising.

With a moan of bone-deep sadness, the old man practically crumpled on the sofa, looking over at the picture.

"Oh, Margie. They're taking him. My new friend. My little Elvis." His voice cracked and Scout turned, looking at him with fear and horror.

"Please don't cry," he said.

The man held up one hand and reached into his pocket for the embroidered handkerchief with the other. "I'm fine. It's fine. Go. Take him." He shuddered, fighting a sob. "I'm just...I'll be okay. Been through worse this year, I tell you."

Sadie sat next to him, Rhett forgotten. Without giving it much thought, she put an arm around his hunched and gaunt shoulders, getting a whiff of that distinctly old man smell that only made him seem more pathetic.

"You can get another cat."

"I want Elvis," he admitted, throwing a look at her. "He's been my pal."

Pity changed Scout's whole expression as he turned back to the carrier, unzipping the corner and easing the canvas down.

The cat stuck his head right out, his eyes wide, his mouth open with a meow as he stared at Scout.

"Hello, there, Rhett Butler," he whispered, lightly stroking the orange stripes on his head. He accepted it for a moment, then turned and offered his backside in a typical Rhett B move.

"You gave me quite a scare, buddy," Scout said, undaunted.

Hank sniffled and tried to push himself up, but he couldn't. Instantly, Scout moved to help him, offering a hand.

As the old man put his hand in Scout's, he looked up, tears flowing.

"He's all I got in the world now. My Margie's gone. We have a son who lives in Oregon and hasn't been here for fifteen years. Neighbors come and go. Carla comes twice a month. I see a couple of doctors." His voice cracked. "I'll be ninety in twenty-seven days," he added. "And without Elvis, I'm just gonna pray that the Lord takes me home so Margie and I can be together. I'd even watch that dadgum *Blue Hawaii* again, just to be with her."

Scout didn't let go, but eased the little old man to his feet.

"Hank, I..."

"Do you have to take him, son? Do you?" He worked to swallow, clearly ashamed of his tears but unable to fight them. "'Cause he's the whole world to me."

Scout stood with his mouth open, as if he knew what

he had to say—what he'd been prepared to say—but it all got silenced in the face of old Hank.

"I have an idea," he finally said. "His owner won't be back for about two weeks. Why don't you keep him for at least one more week? Would that help?"

"Oh, yes!" He launched toward Scout and threw his arms around him. "Yes, thank you."

"But only for..." The rest was mumbled and lost in a kiss the man gave him on the cheek.

"You're a good man," Hank announced, holding Scout tightly. "A good, good man. I'll take great care of Elvis."

Scout managed to ease out of his touch, his expression pure agony at the decision he'd just made and the one he'd have to make in a week.

But what else could he do? He was...*nice*.

And right then, Sadie loved him for that.

Chapter Thirteen

Susannah

"Did she put jalapeños in that chili?" Rex pressed his chest after the server removed his half-eaten bowl, leaning back in his chair at the Riverfront Café. "Tori knows I can't handle them anymore."

Susannah looked over her iced tea, scrutinizing her husband's face. Was he pale? A little drawn? Did a jalapeño get him or was he getting sick again?

"It's fine." He reached over the table with a reassuring hand. "A little heartburn isn't going to ruin our day together."

Susannah smiled at him, not trusting herself to respond. The day—every day that passed and they had no answers, no solutions, and no plans for how to put a stop to Ivy Button—was ruined for her.

To protect herself, and Rex, she was careful with every word she said.

She'd promised herself today would be different. He had no commitments at Wingate Properties and wanted to spend the whole day with her, running errands in town, lunch at the café, and stopping at the inn to pick something up from a planner doing a wedding there this weekend.

"Let's drive to the pharmacy to get some Tums before we go to Wingate House," he said.

She nodded, feeling her brow furrow as she searched his face, always concerned for his health.

"Or maybe you should cancel that meeting," he said, his tone cool enough that she blinked in surprise.

"Why would I do that?"

"Because it's too much," he said, letting go of her hand to prop his elbows on the table with a scowl. "And I did this. This is all my fault."

"What are you talking about?" she asked, genuinely perplexed.

"I pushed you to do...something. Months ago, when I was all better and I accused you of being a helicopter wife."

"And you were right," she said. "You encouraged me to find something else besides babysitting you, and I came up with the wedding venue. It's been amazing, Rex. Just check the bottom line."

"I don't care about the bottom line."

She lifted a dubious brow, knowing him better than that.

"I don't," he insisted. "We have enough money to last the years we have left, the business is in excellent hands with Chase and, I suspect, Blake, who's learning faster than even Raina did at his age."

"But you wanted me to find something to do with my

time, and managing a small wedding venue has been such fun for me."

"Fun?" he scoffed. "You haven't said ten words at this lunch or at dinner last night or for the past week or more. Suze. Is it the girls' wedding or just the whole business? Because I feel like I've lost you."

She stared at him, aching to tell him the truth.

She had, in her imagination, a hundred times. And every one of those times, it broke him. Or worse.

Her gaze slipped down to his chest again where the heart she loved so much beat steadily. The risk of hurting him in any way was just too high to share the truth.

"Let's go get you some antacid," she said. "We don't have to drive anywhere. Dani keeps a stock of over-the-counter meds at Wingate Properties. Let's stop on the way."

He agreed, and after they paid and said goodbye to Tori, they stepped outside into the blistering sun, the town crowded with tourists, even mid-week. The ferry to Cumberland Island was pulling out with a noisy horn, and the open-air tour bus passed them with the guide cheerily pointing out the sights.

The familiarity of her home town and the man beside her gave Susannah a much-needed boost as she put her hand in his and started to walk. But she nearly tripped at the sight of a dark-haired woman across the street, staring at them.

Was that *Ivy?*

She turned away as panic kicked her, and when she looked back, that tour bus was blocking the view.

"Welcome to the historic tour of Fernandina Beach..." The driver's voice droned on to explain the route, sounding in Susannah's head like he was underwater.

She slowed her step and forced herself to peer through the open bus windows to the other side of the street, inching left and right to see around someone's head and spot Ivy.

"After that, we'll swing past the Amelia Island Museum of History where..."

"You want to take that tour?" Rex asked with a laugh when she'd come to a complete stop.

"No, no. I was, uh, just curious where it went." She smiled up at him. "Sorry."

"No, I'm sorry," he said, putting an arm around her shoulders. "I guess I'm being selfish and demanding you be attentive to my needs when I want you to be, then leave me alone when I want that."

"It's fine, Rex," she said, distracted as she searched for Ivy.

"Nope, not fine," he said. "This is your day and we'll do whatever you want. But let's get that antacid."

The comment tore her attention back to him. "Still hurts?"

"Eh, its— Oh, look. There's Isaiah and Nikki Lou." He ushered her across the side street to reach Grace's bookstore, The Next Chapter. Their son-in-law, Isaiah, was outside with Grace's little girl, who came running toward the gate to greet her grandparents, waving a packet of flower seeds. Her dachshund, Slinky, was at her heels, as always.

"Zayah's helping me plant daisies!" she announced.

As they chatted, Susannah glanced over her shoulder, scanning the groups of tourists and individuals, not sure if she should be disappointed or elated not to see any sign of Ivy. The further they got from Centre Street, the fewer people were about, but that didn't stop her from searching for her nemesis.

"Right, Grannie Suze? Right?" Nikki Lou tugged at her arm. "Should I?"

Susannah looked down at the precious face of her little granddaughter, her heart falling because she hadn't even listened to the question. And that was wrong. This angel battled autism, and every word out of her mouth was a treasure.

Isaiah stepped in with his gentle smile. "She wants to do an all-daisy garden, but I think there are lots of flowers we could plant in that bed."

Susannah gave him a grateful smile for the save, vaguely aware that Rex was staring at her, too.

"Whatever you do, it's going to be beautiful, Nikki," she said, bending over to scoop her up for a hug. "I know I'll love it." She gave her a kiss. "As much as I love you."

Nikki grinned and dropped her head on Susannah's shoulder, scooting her legs around her waist.

"Don't get dirt on Grannie Suze," Isaiah warned, lifting her sneaker.

"It's okay," Susannah said, stinging with guilt for not giving her granddaughter her undivided attention.

"Nikki dirt is the best dirt!" She spun her in a half circle, getting rewarded with a giggle and—

A gasp. Her own, in fact, at the sight of Ivy Button not twenty feet away, taking it all in with a menacing stare.

Susannah darn near dropped Nikki Lou, but she pulled it together, gently lowering her to the ground.

"Did I hurt you, Grannie Suze?" the child asked, showing tremendous empathy, something Grace and Isaiah had been working on tirelessly with her.

Susannah's heart melted, but she was trembling when she bent over to assure Nikki Lou she hadn't hurt her at all.

When she found the nerve to straighten and look again, Ivy was gone.

"Let's go," she said to Rex, a little breathless. "We should get that medicine for you."

After a quick goodbye, they continued walking, pausing at the corner near Madeline's dressmaking shop to cross and go to the old bank building that housed Wingate Properties.

"Did Nikki upset you?" Rex asked, looking at her from behind sunglasses, but she could imagine how scrutinizing his gaze really was.

"Oh, no. It's hot and she's getting heavy for me to lift," she said, clutching his arm as they crossed after two cars passed. As they walked, she looked—everywhere.

Was Ivy following them? Why? What was her end goal?

Just as they reached the other side of the street,

Susannah got a glimpse down the side alley along the brick walls of the Wingate Properties building. No one ever walked down there, though the alley connected with the next street, but someone was in the alley now. She saw a shadow move and could have sworn she heard a noise.

Susannah knew exactly who it was.

She had to put a stop to this. She had to.

"Why don't you go in and find Dani?" she suggested. "I just remembered something I needed to tell Madeline." She gestured behind her to Madeline Wingate Designs. "I'll just be a second."

"I'll come with—"

"No. No, it's...private. I want to talk to her about...the wedding."

He lowered his sunglasses and narrowed his dark eyes over the rims. "Susannah Wingate."

"What?" she said with a laugh, hoping it sounded genuine. "It's a surprise, okay? Something I want to surprise you with and I just saw her in the window of the shop, so I'll be back. Meet you inside." She gave him a nudge. "Go. Get your Tums and I'll be right in."

Thankfully, he accepted the explanation, pulled the door handle and disappeared inside. Blake would snag him instantly and Dani would take a minute to get the antacid, so she had time to give Ivy Button a piece of her mind.

Without giving it a moment's thought, she rounded the side of the building to the narrow alleyway, marching into the shadows.

"I know you're back here!" she called, summoning more courage than she actually believed she had.

Ivy stepped out from behind a Dumpster, which was fitting.

"Are you following me?" Susannah demanded at the sight of the awful woman.

"I haven't heard from Raina," she said in her gravelly voice. "I was about to go see her when I caught you and Rex strolling along like you didn't have a care in the world."

"I didn't, until you showed up."

Ivy took a few steps closer, brushing back her dark hair, narrowing her gaze. "Look, you can't dangle me forever. Hand over the keys and the deed and we can make up some story about winning the lottery and buying it from you. No one the wiser. Wouldn't you prefer that to...destroying your family?"

"I'd prefer you disappeared the same way you came."

"You can't put me off forever." She was less than five feet away now, close enough for Susannah to see smoker's lines around her lips and a small blue tattoo on her forearm.

"Raina told you she needed time."

"Whatever Raina thinks she can do, she's wrong," Ivy fired back. "I have proof positive of what happened, letters in my aunt's own handwriting that spell out what Rex did to her, and a contract that says that inn belongs to my family, not yours. What else do you need?"

Susannah closed the rest of the space, happy that she

was taller than this woman and could look down at her, literally and figuratively.

"I'll tell you what I need," she growled. "I need you to leave my family alone. If and when we have anything to say to you, we will. Until then, stay away from all of us. And if you say one word to the media or anyone that slanders my husband, we will make your life—"

"What is going on here?"

They both whipped around to see Rex coming closer, easily able to have heard the conversation.

Susannah's heart plummeted as she moved to somehow separate him from Ivy, not wanting him to be fouled by even the sight of her.

"So you haven't told him?" she said, absolutely unfazed by his arrival.

"Told me what?" Rex scowled at the stranger. "Who are you?"

Susannah took a slow and shuddering breath, not even sure how or where to begin, and terrified what this would do to him. His heart would burn, all right, and it wouldn't be due to jalapeños.

Ivy took a tiny step backwards, no doubt intimidated by Rex, even though he wasn't the formidable man he was before his stroke.

"Tell him," she said to Susannah without taking her eyes off Rex. "Tell him we know what he did and he's going to pay for it."

"What are you talking about?" he demanded.

She crossed her arms, took a deep breath, and

Susannah held hers. How would he react? What would this do to him?

"As if you don't know, *Sexy Rexy*."

He shook his head like he was stunned by the words, then gave a dry, scoffing laugh. "Are you serious?"

"As a *heart attack*." She dragged out the words and uncrossed her arms, taking a few more steps backwards to the other side of the alley.

"Who *are* you?"

She looked like she might answer him, then she pivoted on her sneaker and took off at full speed, disappearing at the end of the alley, into the other side street.

He turned to Susannah, nothing but confusion in his eyes. "What the *hell* was that about?"

She reached for his hand, the words "heart attack" still echoing. "Let's go up to your office where it's private."

"Who was that woman?" he asked, refusing to move.

She shook her head. "Inside. Sitting down."

"She looked...familiar."

"You know her?" Susannah asked on a gasp.

"I've...maybe seen her around? I didn't get a good look."

"Come on," she said, jutting her chin toward Wingate Way. "I'll tell you everything."

He grunted as if he knew something was very wrong, wrapping an arm around her as they walked.

"Sexy Rexy?" He snorted under his breath. "Haven't been called that since my fraternity days in college."

Susannah just closed her eyes and braced for whatever was going to happen next.

For a long time after Susannah told him the story from the beginning to the last few horrible moments in the alley, Rex didn't say a word.

He didn't explode in fury or shock, weep in disbelief or sorrow, or even laugh at the ridiculous accusations.

He merely stared at Susannah, his expression unreadable, his great mind at work without revealing a single thing that was going on in it.

Maybe he was thinking back nearly sixty years, trying to remember details. Maybe he was turning over the possibility that his father had signed away Wingate House to someone outside of the family. Maybe he was cursing the day Doreen Parrish showed up at the inn looking for a part-time job.

Finally, he pressed his palms together and closed his eyes. "Do the girls know?"

Or maybe he was thinking about the impact on his family. Of course, that would be top of mind for Rex Wingate.

"Only Raina knows."

He flinched. "Does she..."

Susannah's brows shot up when he didn't finish the question. "Believe the accusations?" she asked with a laugh of disbelief. "Not for a moment. Neither do I. Good grief, Rex, you don't think we give one second of credence to that woman's claims, do you? We know you!"

His once-broad shoulders softened on a sigh of relief.

"Rex!" Susannah leaned closer from the other swivel chair in his office, putting her hand on his arm. "That is the last thing you have to worry about."

"How can I not?" he asked. "It's he-said, she-said and she's dead. And these alleged letters? Where are they?"

"Raina has them. Blake's seen them, too."

"Blake?" He choked his grandson's name. "You said only Raina knows."

"Because she's a problem-solver and she needed help finding a handwriting sample, and Blake stepped in."

He groaned. "Him, too? And we're talking about his biological grandmother."

"And a stranger named Ivy Button who doesn't have an ounce of credibility," Susannah reminded him, pushing up, fury electrifying her and making her want to pace the office and stare out the window at Wingate Way.

"Well, she has letters that match Doreen's handwriting," Rex said, reminding her of that detail she'd shared.

"I don't care," Susannah said. "I agree with Raina that she's a scam artist and we are not giving her Wingate House and we're not letting her lay one dirty fingernail on your stellar reputation."

He didn't respond to that as she watched some people cross the street, and a family walk into Sadie's chocolate shop. A couple left Rose's flower shop carrying a large bouquet, and what looked like a mother and daughter laughed as they headed into Madeline's bridal salon.

Their life was so good, she mused. Solid, steady, successful, united, with so much to lose. Still, whatever happened, the Wingates could weather—

"Thank you."

She startled as Rex's hands landed on her shoulders, not even aware he'd gotten up.

"For what?"

"Your trust." He turned her around to face him. "Your unwavering belief in me when you could very easily question if there was a shred of truth to what she's claiming."

She held his gaze, secure in everything about this man, as she'd been since the day she waited on Rex at the Riverfront Café more than forty years ago.

"Never," she whispered. "Not a chance in the world. I couldn't and wouldn't doubt you, because I know you and love—"

He quieted her with a kiss, hard on her lips, his hands gripping her. When he pulled back, the first tears were in his eyes, threatening to spill.

"I love you," she finished, placing her palm on his face. "Nothing will change that. We will get through this, unscathed and with Wingate House firmly and forever in our family. I believe that just as I believe in you."

He blinked and a tear rolled. "What did I do to deserve you?" he asked gruffly. "You and this family and your faith in me."

"You earned the faith, you created the family, and you loved me like no man has ever loved a woman."

With a whimper, he kissed her again, wrapping his arms around her and folding her closer so she could feel his heartbeat. His dear, loving heart that did not deserve to break under the accusations of one—

"Whoa."

They broke apart and turned to see Raina in the doorway, looking surprised.

"What are you doing here?" Susannah asked.

"Whatever it is, it's not as much fun as you two are having," she cracked. "Blake called me and asked if I could meet him here to discuss..." She shook her head. "Just something. Kenzie is babysitting, so I have a little time. But I don't see Blake at his desk."

"I asked him to get us coffee," Susannah said, "because I wanted to tell Dad everything and wanted complete privacy."

"Oh." Raina pressed her fingers to her lips, looking at Rex. "We weren't going to..."

"We had a run-in with Ivy Button," Susannah explained. "She was following me on the street and I..." She slid her arm around Rex. "I'm actually relieved to have it all out in the open."

"Don't worry, Dad," Raina said instantly. "We'll fix this."

"I'm not worried," he said, planting a kiss on Susannah's head. "Because I'm married to the most spectacular woman in the world, and once a man knows that, everything else will fall into place."

Raina sighed at that, walking closer with her arms outstretched to both of them.

"We're going to fix it, Dad," she repeated, bringing them in for a group hug. "In fact, Blake said he had info. I hope it's good, 'cause I just got back from hitting a dead end at the county clerk's office." She eased all the way back. "Let's figure this out."

As they hugged again, Susannah felt the weight lift from her shoulders. It would be okay. She didn't know how, but she trusted her family.

Chapter Fourteen

Raina

Her mother was right—it was a relief that Dad finally knew what they were up against. Blake came back, with coffee for all, and Raina met him outside the office to give him a heads-up that Rex had been briefed.

"Is he okay?" he asked, his first question clearly showing where his heart was. "I don't want this to throw his health."

"He's as fine as can be expected," she said, taking the decaf he'd brought for her. "Do you have news?"

"I do," he said. "But it's next-level frustrating. You?"

"Come on, I'll fill you in."

Together, they walked into the office to find Dad and Suze at the conference table, looking ready to attack the problem.

"Aw, Rex," Blake said, putting the coffee down so they could share a man hug. "I'm sorry you're dealing with this."

"I'm sorry you're involved," Rex said. "After all, this whole thing involves your biological grandmother."

Blake pulled back, emotion etched on his face. "The only family I have are Wingates. And that was just proven by my last conversation with my, uh, dad."

"You talked to him?" Raina asked, surprised and hopeful.

"I did, after more than a year." He dropped into the empty seat and ran his fingers through his close-cropped golden-brown hair, a sad shadow in his eyes. "He's not ready to, uh, move on."

"Oh, Blake." Raina put a hand on his arm, her heart tugging. It was just wrong that this wonderful young man's father simply couldn't see beyond his personal prejudices and appreciate the terrific man Blake was. "Still? After all this time?"

He nodded. "But I did talk to him, so that was progress."

"How did you think he could help?" Rex asked. "When I met your father, he indicated that he had no desire to talk to Doreen."

Blake sighed, clearly affected by it all. "When you met him, it was because I'd done all the digging and homework to discover who his biological parents were. And you know why. Because my family couldn't accept me when I came out—specifically, my father—and I hoped that somewhere, a family would love and not judge me." He gave a tight smile, looking from person to person. "And you all did, for which I'm eternally grateful. And that's one of the many reasons I'm determined to help."

He took a sip of his coffee and they all waited for him to continue.

"But, as you know, once I shared your name with my father—I guess it was my last-ditch effort to show him how important family is to me—he merely saw you as a gravy train, not a biological father ripe for a reunion."

Rex shrugged. "I would have liked to have a relationship with my only son," he said. "But I don't. His choice. For one thing, I'm blessed with the best seven daughters in the world, so there's no hole in my heart. For another, now I have you." He reached over and patted Blake's back. "And you more than make up for him."

Blake smiled at him. "Same, my dear grandfather. Same. Anyway, he used you as a bank."

Again, Rex lifted a shoulder, as if the "gift" he'd given Brad Young was nothing—even though Raina knew it was half a million dollars. "I helped him save a family farm."

"But he lied to you when he said he hadn't seen Doreen," Blake added softly. "Because he did go to see her and she…"

They all leaned forward an inch as he paused.

"She gave him a lockbox of her journals that recounted her entire experience with you. Apparently she was quite the writer, or fancied herself as one."

"What?" They all gasped and asked the question in perfect unison.

"And he…threw it away."

"No!" Raina shot forward. "Why would he do that? Did he read the journals? Can he shed any light on…"

Her voice trailed off as Blake shook his head. "He opened the box and looked for cash. He didn't say that's what he was looking for, but I know my dad. And he said he tossed the journals in the trash after a quick perusal. He said they read like a 'cheap dime store novel' and he was offended." He snorted. "My dad is easily offended, I'm afraid."

Raina fell back with a thud of disappointment.

"I can't believe that." In fact, it made no sense to her, a woman who'd lost her own biological mother at birth. She'd give anything to have journals from Charlotte Wingate, no matter how they read. "Whatever Doreen wrote," she added softly, "could have completely exonerated Dad and sent Ivy Button on her way."

Her father dropped his head into his hands, muttering softly, "The truth is, I don't know what 'experience' with me could have filled three journals."

"The one in her imagination," Raina said.

"Amen to that," Susannah agreed.

Blake turned to Raina. "And you finally got the ear of someone at the county clerk's office, right? But no luck?"

"Not yet," she said, reaching into the tote bag that carried the letters and documents she had. "But I'm not ready to quit. There is a notary name and commission number on the stamp, but no record of that name or number in the files. They even pulled out the microfiche to search."

She opened a file of notary records she'd picked up today. "And this county, unfortunately, only goes back fifty years on commission numbers, and this was fifty-five years ago."

Rex groaned. "I can't believe you've been doing all this, Raina. With two babies, and about to be married."

"Dad." She swiveled her head to gaze at him. "I'd do anything for you. We all would, and you know that."

"But this is too much."

"This has to be handled," Raina insisted. "And the next steps are a little more complicated. We'll have to hire a forensic expert to determine if the paper is really from that era and then look at similar documents from the same time. We'd need proof that would..." She made a face. "Hold up in court."

"Surely we're not going to court!" Rex exclaimed.

"Well, you're not handing her the keys and deed to Wingate House without a fight," Raina countered.

"No, I am not."

Susannah sighed. "Then she's going to ruin your reputation."

He winced at the thought.

"There has to be a way," Susannah said. "There has to be an answer."

Raina inched closer to all of them, letting her gaze move over their faces, settling on Dad before she dropped her little bomb.

"There is." She put her hand over his. "We bring in the whole family," she said softly. "All the great Wingate minds can surely come up with a way to save us."

He just stared at her, silent.

"Dad, I know you don't want to do that, but we have Adam, for one thing. He has access to FBI files, to the forensic expert I need, to law enforcement information that might help us figure out who Ivy Button really is. And we have eyes and ears all over town. Maybe someone has seen her lurking about, planning this attack. The more minds on this issue, the better. And none are better than Wingates."

He huffed out a breath. "I don't want everyone discussing it."

"Well, they sure will want to know why you handed over the jewel of your empire to that horrible stranger and her mother," Raina said. "So, one way or another, Dad, the family is going to know. But no one—absolutely no one—is going to believe her. This is your family and we all want to support and help you."

He let his head fall back, eyes closed, a wounded man, a hand to his chest. The sight made Raina bite back a whimper and Susannah reach for his hand.

"Your heart, Rex?" Susannah asked.

"There's no pain, Suze," he said. "It was just a little heartburn. But this ticker is going to break if a single one of my daughters thinks—"

"We won't," Raina insisted. "We don't. We can't. But we also can't solve this problem without using the brain trust that is our family."

After a moment, he nodded. "Get everyone to our house this evening. Well, the adults. Not Rose's kids or Tori's," he added. "Not Nikki or anyone too young to understand."

"Just the married couples?" Susannah asked.

"Or engaged," Raina said. "Because Chase already knows."

"Tell everyone," Dad agreed. "And that means Chloe can bring Travis and Sadie should include Scout. Those men are undoubtedly going to be part of the family, so they should know it's not all sunshine and rainbows for Wingates."

Raina nodded, fully agreeing with that decision.

"We'll put all the kids at my house for a party, with Zach and Kenzie in charge," she said, knowing that the two oldest cousins could easily handle the younger kids. "I'll bring the babies, if you don't mind."

"Of course," Susannah said. "You know this is the right thing to do, Rex."

He nodded, looking as though the very idea pained him.

"Dad," Raina said softly. "Your family will surround you, support you, and figure out a solution to this problem. I promise you."

His eyes brimmed with tears. "Thank you." He reached out to take Susannah and Blake's hands, his dark gaze on Raina. "I believe in you all."

"And we believe in you, Dad."

He smiled as a tear rolled down his cheek and Raina prayed she was right. Because if they didn't fix this problem, Rex might not survive the next stroke.

It didn't take long for everyone gathered at Rex and Susannah's beach house that evening to realize the subject matter was serious, the stakes were high, and their much-adored patriarch was at the center of it all.

He insisted on being the one to relate the whole story, and Raina knew that no matter how carefully he chose his words, the discussion would pain him.

A little uncertain of why they were there, her sisters and the men they loved arrived, asking questions, but somehow understanding that this wasn't a happy surprise.

No, this wasn't like the day Madeline had gathered them to announce she'd be marrying Adam that same week. Nor was this a birthday celebration, news of a new baby in the family, or something fun that would end in laughter and champagne toasts.

After greeting each other with hugs and a few whispers of, "What's going on?" they took seats in the main living area in front of the wide open French doors that let in the ocean breeze.

When Sadie came in with Scout, she greeted her mother, and then stepped over to join Raina and Chase.

"You don't look as confused as the rest of us," Sadie observed, pointing to Raina.

"I'm not, but Dad will explain everything." Raina took her hand and gave it a reassuring squeeze. "And, sadly, he's not going to announce that we've found your missing cat."

"Oh, we found him," Sadie said, looking sideways at Scout, who was still talking to Susannah. "He's been appropriated by a very sweet old man and, somehow, we have to break his heart or Kitty's. At the moment, we're letting the old man keep him, but we're going to have to steal him back."

"An old man stole him?" Chase asked on a choke. "Seriously?"

As Sadie filled them in, Raina glanced at her father, who seemed—understandably so—tense. He talked quietly with Justin, getting a comforting pat on the back from his neurologist and soon-to-be son-in-law.

After that, Dad cleared his throat and that was all they needed to get settled and pay attention. As he walked to the center of the room, he patted Blake's shoulder and took Susannah's hand, bringing her with him. Then he stood in front of them and let his gaze slide over every beloved face in the room before he spoke.

"Someone," he started, his voice soft enough that no one breathed in case they didn't hear. "Is trying to destroy our family."

Then they breathed—mostly gasps, a few grunts, and a lot of questions.

For the next few minutes, he shared the story from his perspective, including the excruciating details of how a woman they had unfairly called "Dor-mean" had offered herself to him, a nineteen-year-old college kid, and then disappeared to have a baby he didn't know about.

"I realize none of that is news to this family." He looked at Blake, who gave a tight smile. "And it ended up as something—some*one*—who enriched us and made our lives better."

"God's plan," Isaiah chimed in. "You never know what He's up to."

Rex gave a mirthless laugh at that. "Well, He's up to something, because a woman who claims to be Doreen's niece has arrived on Amelia Island and has a very different story with a very different...plan."

He told them about Ivy, her demands, her allegations, and her threats. With each bomb dropped, the room got quieter, sinking deeper into disbelief.

Not that they didn't believe Rex, because Raina had no doubt that her father wasn't capable of the allegations she'd read in those letters. But the disbelief that they could lose Wingate House and, worse, that Rex's reputation would be questioned by the neighbors, community, friends, and clients he'd spent a lifetime showering with love.

Because people did tend to believe the worst in others, didn't they?

As he finished, Chase leaned down to whisper, "I hear one of the babies crying. You stay here."

She blinked at him, so deep into the situation she hadn't heard the soft cry from the guest suite upstairs where they'd set up two porta-cribs.

"I can come—"

"You stay right here, Raina. This family needs you."

She gave him a grateful smile, just as Dad finished and held up his hands, inviting questions.

For a long moment, there was nothing but silence. Surprised at that, Raina looked around, seeing the emotions etched on every face. Love, pain, fury, disbelief, and the unbridled desire to help.

In the shocked silence, Raina stepped forward.

"I believe she's a scam artist," she said. "I have no doubt she's targeted this family somehow and we need to find out who she is and put a stop to her."

Then the questions started, fired fast and furious. And Raina realized they hadn't been holding back out of shock, but out of respect. They didn't want to bombard their father with an interrogation as they struggled to make sense of something so tender and wrong.

Without any explanation, Raina took over, putting a loving hand on Dad's shoulder while she answered one question after another. Before long, the conversation was mostly between Raina and Adam, who firmly agreed this was the work of a con artist.

And coming from a former FBI agent, his position validated and thrilled Raina.

"But the handwriting matches," Susannah said.

"Forgeries can be stunningly accurate," Adam said. "We have to find out who this woman really is."

"How do we do that?" Madeline asked.

"We ID her. Do you have a picture?" When Raina, Susannah, and Rex all shook their heads, he stood, his law enforcement expertise on full display. "I don't suppose you have fingerprints. That would make this so easy, your head will spin."

"She was at Wingate Properties," Blake said. "Sat in the main office, used the bathroom."

"But it's been cleaned since then," Raina said. "Several times. At Wingate House, Suze?"

Her mother frowned, thinking. "She sat outside the one time she was there and, oh, I threw her coffee cup away!" But they all agreed that was understandable.

"Who else has seen this woman?" Adam asked

"Just us," Susannah said. "Raina, Rex, Blake, and me. But she was following me in town today. When we were talking to you, Isaiah. She was up and down Wingate Way, not trying to hide herself."

"She looked vaguely familiar," Rex said. "But I couldn't place her."

"We need a detailed description," Adam said.

"I can describe her," Susannah said. "She's about five-three, with dark hair, bangs, scrawny, beady-eyed, and has filthy sneakers."

"A woman who looked very much like that came into the bookstore the other day," Grace said, leaning forward. "I noticed her sneakers and the bad hair dye."

"Hair dye says she's trying to cover her real identity," Adam said. "But next time, Grace? Try and surreptitiously get a picture, but more important, get a fingerprint."

"How?" Rose asked.

"You might have to be creative, but all we need is one good print, so have her hold anything. Also, I'll run her name through the FBI database."

"She said she's from Minnesota," Raina said. "Though there's no reason to believe that."

"Do any of these so-called letters have envelopes?" Sadie asked. "With addresses?"

Raina shook her head. "You didn't see any, did you, Blake?"

"Not a one."

"What else can we do to help?" Chloe asked as Chase walked in, holding Lily and walking to the fridge for one of the bottles Raina had placed there when they arrived.

"Think of a way to lure her out," he said, proving he could calm a baby, get a bottle, and still participate in the conversation.

"I can lure her," Raina said. "She's waiting to hear from me, to basically say yes or no. That's the answer. I'll meet up with her, think of a way to delay a decision, and get her fingerprints."

"And we'll all watch for her in our stores," Rose said.

"And pray," Isaiah said, standing up and walking toward Rex.

Raina's father looked at his son-in-law with trepidation in his gaze, and she understood that. The men in this room, with the exception of Rose's husband, Gabe, hadn't known Rex for that long. Surely, they could wonder... even for a second...if there was any credence to what Ivy said Doreen claimed.

"I could use your prayers," Rex said to him.

"I know you're innocent of this, sir," Isaiah said. "And I want to pray for justice right now."

It wasn't something they normally did as a family, at least not outside of church. But these circumstances were well beyond extenuating, and they all felt they could use any help they could get.

With his hand on Rex's shoulder, Isaiah's powerful, deep voice filled the room, quietly asking for divine intervention and help from above. As he did, Chase joined Raina, easing a bottle into Lily's tiny mouth.

Raina looked up at him and held his gaze, silent out of respect for the prayer.

He leaned in and pressed a kiss to her hair and handed her the baby, who'd caught her eye and clearly wanted her mother.

Isaiah finished to a resounding, "Amen!" and they broke into smaller groups to chat about the situation and share thoughts and ideas. As they did, Rex joined Chase and Raina, his expression hard to read.

"You okay, Dad?" she asked.

He gave a whisper of a smile, then looked down at Lily, stroking her tiny chin with his fingers.

"A little overwhelmed," he admitted gruffly.

Raina leaned in and put her head on his shoulder. "You're loved, Daddio."

"I know." He blinked back a tear. "That's why I'm overwhelmed."

She smiled at him, then looked at Chase, who pointed upstairs again. "I hear baby number two."

Without a shred of instruction or encouragement, he walked off.

"Rinse and repeat," she quipped. "He's quite good at it, isn't he?"

Dad smiled in agreement. "He's a keeper. Any news

on the adoption front? They came and interviewed me, you know."

"I'm sure you told them how unfit he is to be a father." She added a playful jab with the elbow holding a bottle.

He laughed. "I wanted to ask you something privately and with all that went on today, I didn't get a chance."

"What's that?"

"The lady. Helen something hyphenated?"

Raina nodded. "I know exactly who you mean. What about her?"

"She asked some weird questions I didn't, well, expect. About the four older girls in this family and Suze." He lifted a brow. "Isn't that strange?"

Raina's eyes widened. "Did you say anything to Suze?"

"I was going to, but then the whole Ivy thing happened. Why?"

She sighed, doubting he could keep a secret from his wife. "Just be sure you and Suze come to the hearing when Chase adopts the babies. That's all I'm going to say. And all *you're* going to say, am I clear?"

"We'll be there." A hint of a smile tugged at his lips as he stroked Lily's head. "Assuming I'm not off defending my ruined reputation."

Chapter Fifteen

Chloe

It was late on a Saturday when Chloe finished baking. She'd spent the day at it, making her banana bread, lemon bars, and cookies. In between, she took care of her boarders and rescues, answered the phone to schedule more, and hummed through the process of running her small animal shelter.

She loved spending time in the sun-filled kitchen, looking out over the kennels and the woods beyond the fence.

With Lady Bug at her feet and Buttercup curled on her bed in the corner keeping watch over her domain, Chloe let the work with her hands and the frequent interruptions distract her from all that was on her mind.

In addition to the latest family crisis, she was in a bit of a personal conundrum of her own. She missed Judah. She ached for him and had to force herself to tamp down her frustration that Travis wasn't feeling the same way.

He was getting there, though. They'd seen Judah, what? Four times now in total, and each visit was lovelier than the last. They'd even applied to have him spend a weekend up here, which required Chloe to have a background check, as well.

They hadn't heard if they'd been approved, but she hoped it happened this week, so they could bring him here next weekend. She already planned how she would give him her room, and sleep in the living room. Long term, she had to live *and* work here, to take care of the animals over night, but it was too small for a family.

It wouldn't be if Travis built the addition off the back they'd talked about.

She let out a groan, just wishing he'd move a little faster on...well, everything. Their life, their future, and, most of all, that child. She couldn't lie—Judah had reached right into Chloe's chest and taken ownership of her heart.

Maybe a bakery's worth of bread and goodies could bring Travis around, she mused as she packed up the treats to take to the fire station.

Judah would love these, too, she decided as she eyed the last golden batch of chocolate chip cookies. On impulse, she took one full container of the cookies and slid them to the side. When she got back, she'd make bags and freeze them for next weekend, in case they got approved to keep Judah overnight. What kid didn't love homemade chocolate chip cookies?

A few minutes later, she packed up the rest of the containers and drove to the station, where Travis was on duty. She knew he'd greet her with his happiest response and gladly accept a gift that would be devoured by the crew before the end of this shift.

But when Travis came out to the front of the station to meet her, she didn't get the smile she expected. In fact, he looked stricken.

"What's wrong?" she asked, lowering her small mountain of Tupperware to the front desk.

"Judah's...been adopted."

She gasped, shocked at how hard the words hit her gut.

"I just heard." He reached for her, pulling her into him for a hug that really didn't require an explanation, clearly shaken by the news.

As was she. He was *adopted*? Gone? He couldn't be theirs?

"Are you upset or...relieved?" she asked, not sure she wanted to hear the answer if it was the latter.

"I'm confused," he admitted. "I thought I'd have a say as his only living relative, but legally, I don't. It's something called an adoption placement, so not final, but still, I'm sad, Chloe. Aren't you?"

Devastated, but telling him that would only etch more misery on his features. "I'm...yeah. Happy for him, but sorry for us. But you weren't ready and—"

"I should have been." He growled the confession, shaking his head. "I didn't know I'd feel this much regret over losing him."

She nodded, not one to say, "I told you so!" even though she wanted to scream the words.

Of *course* they'd feel regret. Judah was *family* and now he...was part of another one and not ever going to spend a weekend with the dogs or eat her chocolate chip cookies. He was part of another family now.

Which was good, but...*oh*. She swallowed a growing lump in her throat.

"Do you know anything about the people who adopted him?" she asked. "Mae said there were two different couples considering him."

"One dropped out and took a baby girl who became available," he said. "They go fast. The babies, I mean." As he said the words, he cringed. "Horrible, isn't it? Like a fire sale on the best kids."

"Judah was the best kid," she said, her voice thick.

"Chloe, I'm sorry."

"You don't have to apologize to me, Travis." She took his hand, digging for kind words and a rationale for why this had happened. "This just wasn't in our hands. And if he—"

The scream of a deafening alarm cut her off.

"Gotta go!" He pivoted and tore through the doors to the station, leaving her dumbfounded and...yes, very, very sad.

She stayed stone still while orders and curt instructions to the team blared through the loudspeakers. She didn't even move while organized chaos erupted in the bays, close enough that she could hear the chief bark out numbers that indicated which gear to pack, followed almost immediately by the roar of the truck engines.

She stared out the window as an ambulance took off, followed by the chief's car, then the ladder truck, all with alarms ripping through the silence of a Saturday night the way this rotten news ripped through her chest.

Judah was adopted!

Finally, she left, too, leaving the containers on the front desk. Someone would find them and get them into the kitchen, but she...

She had to get home and have a good cry.

The tears refused to wait, though, and she was swiping at her cheeks when her phone rang with a call from...Mae Ling?

She was only a little surprised. She and Mae had developed a nice rapport, bonding over Judah. No doubt she wanted to share the joy of his adoption, but Chloe had done a terrible job of hiding how much she wanted Travis to agree to at least foster the little boy, if not adopt him.

"Hey, Mae," she said as she touched the dashboard to answer the phone. "Travis just told me the news."

"Well, he didn't tell you the latest, because I can't reach him," she said.

"Travis? He just went out on a call," Chloe said, tapping the brakes as she neared the turn to her house. "What's the latest?"

"The family backed out on Judah."

"Yes!" She pumped her fist and instantly regretted the reaction, which was heartfelt and impossible to hide, but probably didn't show genuine care for Judah's well-being.

But the woman on the other end of the phone chuckled. "I had a feeling you'd say that."

"No, I want him to be adopted, Mae. I don't want him living in a group home! But...well, you know what I want."

"I do," she said softly. "And you've been approved for a weekend visit."

"That's awesome." She pulled into her driveway and stopped, aware that her heart rate kicked up. "But Travis is—"

"*You* have been approved," she repeated. "You are both certified to have him for a weekend, individually or together."

"Really?" She sat up a little straighter, a smile pulling.

"And, Chloe, I know Travis is on duty this weekend at the fire station, but that little boy is devastated. He was told he was being adopted and they packed him up. Poor Kelly, who just got two more twelve-year-olds, absolutely can't comfort him. Actually, calling you was her idea but it comes with an apology and a box of tissues. You'll need them."

"He's crying that much?"

"He has a bad cold."

Oh, the poor baby. Sick and sad. "I can be there in an hour," she said, squeezing the steering wheel. "If I can bring him here alone. You're sure?"

"Positive. You passed the background check with flying colors."

Well, apparently a runaway bride and a network news failure didn't stop her from qualifying to be a...

Oh, good heavens, she would *love* to be Judah's mom.

"But, Chloe, it's a bad cold. No fever, but you aren't allowed to give him over-the-counter medicine, so—"

"I've got homemade cookies, cute dogs, and a heart full of love," she said, sorry she didn't have more. Like lemonade. Dang. That kid loved his lemonade. "But I'll get that boy healthy before he has to go back. Which is... when?"

"By Sunday night at ten o'clock," she said.

"Perfect. Will you meet me there in about an hour?"

"I most certainly will. Thank you, Chloe."

"No, thank you, Mae. You've made me insanely happy. And I will take such good care of him, you'll see."

"I already know that."

On the way down, she reached Travis, back from putting out a small kitchen fire.

"Well, I have another small fire," she said, and explained the situation, hearing the same relief and joy in his voice as Mae must have heard in Chloe's.

"You're taking him? Tonight? Now?" he asked when she told him she was on the way down to Jax.

"Is that okay?" She held her breath, waiting for his reaction.

"Of course!" he exclaimed, making her wonder why she'd ever worried. "Maybe I can get out of this shift early. Can I just show up in the middle of the night if the captain agrees?"

"I'll be asleep in the living room," she said. "I'm going to let him use my room."

"Aw, babe, I don't know how to thank you for this," he

said, his voice lowering with tenderness. "I'll try to get over there as soon as I can."

"Great. Oh, and Travis? Bring lemonade."

"All I can find," he answered on a laugh.

A COLD? Chloe admittedly didn't know much about colds and kids, but were they always this...*slimy*?

At four-thirty in the morning, she sat at Judah's bedside with an icy washcloth, a tumbler of water, and her arms full of a kid who sneezed and coughed so much, she figured she was officially bathed in germs.

"Oh, baby," she cooed, holding him close while she pressed the cold cloth on his forehead, which was definitely warmer than it should be. "I suppose I could call Rose, but she'd come straight over. If she got sick, it would fly through her whole family. Maybe Tori? Mom? Who knows about sick kids?"

He looked up at her, his eyes foggy, but his gaze... loving.

Her instinct—new and flawed as it may be—was that this cold wasn't serious, just terribly uncomfortable. And messy. He needed love and attention, not another mother in the mix.

On the bed, Lady Bug stayed close, her tail swishing and her gaze locked on this new arrival with that "cause for concern" look in her brown eyes.

"I'm sorry you feel so terrible, Judah."

He nodded, sneezed, and fell against her.

But she wasn't sorry she held him. What would have happened to him tonight? Kelly was torn in ten different directions and couldn't have nursed him through to morning. Not to mention all those kids getting sick! Hopefully, he'd be on the mend tomorrow.

Or, if he spiraled and got worse, she could call Mae and ask if there was anything she could give him or if she could take him to a walk-in clinic.

The answer would probably be no, since these poor babies were just...alone in the world. And she had nothing but love to give. Love and...what else could she offer?

"Oh, Judah," she whispered, sitting up a bit. "Would you like a chocolate chip cookie?"

For the first time, she saw light in those sick-looking eyes. The tiniest glimmer of hope and maybe hunger.

Kelly said he'd had dinner when Chloe picked him up and he hadn't been interested in stopping for food, but his expression looked like he'd been offered the Holy Grail.

"You'd like cookies, wouldn't you?"

He nodded, surprisingly alert for how sick he was, not to mention the hour.

"Come on. Let's get you out of this room and into the kitchen." She grabbed the box of tissues and a fluffy blanket he seemed to like and the two of them—and Lady Bug—padded to the other side of the house.

Buttercup greeted them, rising sleepily, but somehow sensing Judah was not ready to befriend a dog her size.

Judah had been sick enough when she got him here

that she hadn't even taken him in the back to see the kennels. But now, from a seat at the kitchen table, Judah could see the row of dog houses in the soft lights she kept on for her boarders.

"That's where the doggie guests live," she told him as she opened the container of cookies and put two on a paper plate.

He sniffed, still so quiet it broke her heart.

"That's what I do," she said, filling the silence. "I rescue doggies. Sometimes they just stay here, like guests at a hotel, while their owners have to be away. Sometimes people bring doggies that have no home here, and I try to find someone to take them and keep them forever."

"Like me."

She turned at the words, certainly not expecting them, as surprised that he'd spoken as she was that he deeply understood his situation.

"Oh, not...exactly." Except a rescue refuge? It was exactly like a group home and she could see why he'd make the connection.

"Well, all the doggies eventually get homes," she said, bringing the cookies to the table. "And they don't get chocolate chip cookies."

He smiled up at her, true gratitude in his eyes.

"I don't have any lemonade or milk," she said. "But would you like orange juice? It's full of vitamin C, which you obviously need."

He nodded, very carefully picking up a cookie and looking at it for a long time before taking a bite.

"Is it good?"

Another nod, this once slightly more furious and accompanied by another bite.

"That's one thing I can do, bake cookies. Not like, say, my sister's boyfriend, Scout. He owns a whole cookie store, but you want to know the truth?" She found a plastic cup she'd stashed away for when Nikki Lou visited, and poured the OJ. "I'd hold up my chocolate chip cookie to anything he makes. Okay, maybe not the one—"

"More?" he asked, reaching for another cookie, crumbs and a little chocolate on his lips.

"Yes! Do you feel better?"

He shrugged and took the next cookie, trying—and failing—not to shovel it into his little mouth.

"Are you hungry, Judah?"

He nodded and pointed at the cookie container.

"I don't know about three cookies, but..." What did she even have? Spinach salad? Hard-boiled eggs? A chicken breast she could cook? Eww. He was *five*. But Travis said he'd stop and get kid-friendly food after his shift.

"What's your favorite thing to eat?" she asked, hoping for an idea.

"Gwilled cheese."

"Yes!" She popped up, doing a mental inventory of her fridge. Bread, cheese, and butter—check. "And chips!" she announced, remembering an unopened bag in the pantry.

He nodded happily.

"Okay, let's save cookie number three for after

dinner, which we are having twelve hours late, or early, depending on your perspective. Give me ten minutes."

He rested his head on his hand, elbow propped on the table, his face so tender and tired and sick that she nearly cried.

"You look at the dogs and see if any of them come out to go to the bathroom." She buttered bread, turned on the stove, and started peeling deli cheese slices. "That one reddish dog, named Spike, he does that a lot."

"I need my glasses," he whispered.

"Oh! Of course you do."

He slipped out of the chair. "I get them."

She stood for a moment, watching him disappear, with Lady Bug hot on his heels, then she turned to Buttercup, who was back in bed but taking it all in.

"I love him," she admitted. "And nothing's going to change that."

Buttercup responded with a very sleepy sigh and one thump of her tail while Chloe got to work on the grilled cheeses—plural, because he couldn't eat alone.

Judah came back in with his glasses on and Lady Bug in his arms.

"Bug-boo let me pick her up," he said.

"Then Bug-boo loves you," Chloe replied. "She only lets wonderful people hold her, especially at this hour when she gets the crankies."

He giggled at that.

"Have you ever had a middle of the night dinner before?" she asked, flipping the grilled cheese, thrilled with the golden, buttery color gained from the very hot pan. She'd learned that in her short stint as a waitress at the Riverfront Café.

"With Pops." He muttered the word, his face against Lady Bug's head as he pet her.

She slid the sandwiches out and onto plates, cut them, and brought them to the table. "Pops? Your grandfather?"

He nodded, already looking better.

"Why don't you put Bug-boo down, wash your hands, and let's eat."

He followed all the instructions, coming back to the table like an angel. Maybe he was sick or shy or in a strange place, but she couldn't remember a better-behaved child.

She inched the plate closer. "Please. Eat it up."

"Pops says we pray before..."

Goodness, she hadn't thought of that. "Then, by all means, you pray. Will you say one for me, too?"

He pressed his little hands together and put his head down. "Thank you, Jesus, for this food. And for Bug-boo and the nice lady. And Uncah Man."

She practically groaned as her heart swelled with love.

He lifted the sandwich and took a gooey bite, stretching out the cheese with a giggle.

"So tell me about Pops," she said, happy to discuss the man when Travis wasn't here—that topic was off-limits.

"I miss him," he admitted, breaking her heart.

"I bet you do. What did you love most about him?" she asked, plucking at her sandwich.

"Everything," he said through a mouthful of grilled cheese. "He is the best grandpa ever!"

Is. Not *was.* Did he even realize what had happened to his beloved grandpa? She leaned closer and put a hand on his arm.

"You know what, Judah? Pops is in heaven and he's keeping an eye on you. He's going to make sure you get the best family in the whole world."

He didn't answer, his eyes on his plate. "I could..." He hesitated a long time, then finally looked up. "I could live here."

"Oh." The single syllable slipped out, a mix of a whimper and a sigh.

Right at that moment, she never wanted anything more.

"Well, you're here now," she said. "Grilled cheese, chocolate chips, and—"

He let out a wet sneeze and all she could do was laugh and hand him a tissue. And say a little prayer of her own.

Please let Travis see the light...and say yes. Please.

Chapter Sixteen

Sadie

"You don't have to do this, Sadie." Scout reached for her hand to stop her from zipping up the carrier with Wiggles inside.

"But I do," she said. "We've been to see Hank, what? Three times now. Each time you head in determined to take Rhett back—"

"And each time I turn into the world's biggest pushover and let him keep 'Elvis' for a little while longer." Scout dropped onto the couch with a defeated sigh. "It's hard to say no to that sad old man mourning his wife."

She smiled at him. "I love that you can't say no to him, Scout. It's sweet and kind and...nice."

He snorted. "You know what they say about nice guys. Welcome to last place, dude."

"Scout!" She jabbed his arm. "You have a tender heart. So much that..." She zipped the bag closed. "I'm willing to offer my literal firstborn fur child to Old Hank."

He looked up at her with a pained expression. "I just

hate for you to say goodbye to Wiggles. And I hate to let him go. He's such a great cat. We could find another replacement cat."

"It's hard to find orange cats, as we know, and Kitty will be home soon. This is the right answer."

"But you love Wiggles."

"I do, but honestly?" She leaned closer to whisper, "I never really wanted a cat."

He laughed softly. "I know, but he's such a sweet little guy. So affectionate."

"Which is perfect for Hank, who is lonely. I do hope he'll go for the switch."

"Oh, he'll go for it." Scout tapped the carrier. "We like you, buddy, but this will be better."

Sadie let out a sigh, the long day at the chocolate shop leaving her wearier than usual. Maybe it was just this whole stress of the cat. Or the Ivy problem they were facing as a family.

Whatever it was, she was anxious to put this errand to rest...so she could get some.

It didn't take long to get down to the now-familiar complex where Hank lived and Rhett Butler wasn't supposed to live.

When the old man opened the door, he blinked at them in surprise and his whole face fell.

"It's today, isn't it?" he asked sadly. "I think Elvis knows, 'cause he's planted himself under the bed and ain't comin' out for love or money."

As he pushed open the door wider, Scout raised the cat carrier in his right hand. "But we have very good news, Hank. We brought you another cat. Meet Wiggles."

Hank inched back, his scowl deepening the thick creases on his face. "I don't want another cat."

"Oh, you'll want this one," Sadie said brightly. "He's very sweet and—"

"No." He held up both hands. "No, I do not want any other cat in the world. I want the one that's mine, in the back. If I can't have him, then I'm not interested in working to make another one like me. It's taken me darn near a month to get Elvis to come out and see me at night and he still sits on the other side of the sofa and gives me the stink eye."

"But Wiggles won't—"

"I said no!" he growled, cutting Sadie off. "I am not interested in your substitute. There is no substitute for Elvis, and that's that."

She glanced at Scout, who looked like...he was going to cave. Would he? Would he face the wrath of Kitty to avoid breaking this old man's heart? What a predicament for a guy who only wanted to be kind and caring.

But Rhett Butler was Kitty's cat, and she was a few days from coming home. They had to do this, no matter how hard it was.

She put her hand on his shoulder. "I'll go coax Rhett out from under the bed," she said. "Be right back."

He nodded, lifting the carrier in Hank's direction. "Would you like to meet—"

"No, I would not."

Their voices faded as Sadie turned the corner into

Hank's bedroom, lifting a yellow chenille spread that looked like it was as old as the man who slept under it. Peeking into the darkness, she caught the light of Rhett Butler's eyes from the other corner.

"Hey, Rhett. It's time to end your stay at Chez Hank, buddy. Come on." She reached into her pocket to get the little treat she knew would draw him closer and, after a minute, it worked.

She didn't hear any conversation from the living room—probably because Hank was stewing mad and Scout didn't know how to handle that.

Curious, she got ahold of the cat and snuggled him—as much as anyone could snuggle the standoffish animal—and got to her feet.

As she walked down the hall, she heard Scout talking about...the weather. Wasn't he going to even try to pitch Wiggles?

At the end of the hall, she paused, partly because she, too, hated that she'd have to witness Hank saying goodbye, but also because Scout was standing in the doorway holding the cat carrier out of Hank's sight behind the wall.

Did he think Hank would be offended by Wiggles? Or...

Just then, while he was still talking about yesterday's rain, he managed to unzip part of the carrier and open the corner.

Wait. What was he doing?

Sadie held back, watching Scout get the netted

window open enough that Wiggles stuck his little head out, and then Scout moved the bag to tip him out.

"Oh, look who got out," he said, giving Wiggles a nudge toward the living room sofa, following him with Sadie right behind.

Would he bolt, or—

"Oh! My! What the...who is..." Hank stuttered as Wiggles jumped up on the sofa next to him and let out a noisy meow. "Good gracious, you are most definitely not Elvis!"

Sadie bit her lip to keep her reaction in, taking a step closer to Scout.

"Brilliant," she whispered.

"We'll see." He looked down at her with a smile, then fluttered his fingers over Rhett Butler's head. "You certainly wouldn't do that, would you?"

He mewed as if to say, "Not on your life, pal."

Wiggles took a few steps closer, eyeing Hank with interest and another whiny greeting.

"Oh, you're a talker, are you?"

He responded with a long and noisy meow, next to Hank now.

"Excuse me?" Hank had to laugh. "You're a singer. Maybe *you* should be called Elvis."

Sadie and Scout exchanged a hopeful look.

"But there's only one." He gave his little orange head a condescending pat. "And it is not you, my young feline friend."

But Wiggles let out another wail, determined to prove him wrong. And this time, he climbed onto Hank's lap and started making biscuits with his little paws. And Hank, being human and all, had to chuckle.

"You're trying to change my mind, aren't you."

Wiggles mewed and turned his attention to Hank's belly, then his chest, eventually kneading his chest and purring the whole time.

"You know what that means," Scout said, taking a few hopeful steps closer.

"He's hungry and thinks I got milk?" Hank looked up at him. "So he's not the smartest tool in the shed, eh?"

"He's comforting you," he said. "And bonding. And, yeah, a little singing."

Hank took a deep breath, put his hands around Wiggles's torso, and lifted him off, putting him firmly on the sofa with a sigh of rejection.

Sadie bit back a whine of defeat and disappointment nearly as loud as the cat's.

"Now, then, to say goodbye." Hank pushed up with a little effort, then came around the coffee table to Sadie, his gaze on Rhett Butler.

"Wiggles is a good—"

He quieted Sadie with a raised hand. "Let me have my moment, Missy."

She nodded, chastised, when he came closer but made no effort to take the cat from her.

"You know, Elvis," he said, leaning close to the cat's ear. "You liked to sing that only 'fools rush in.' But like the wise men say, I can't help falling in love. I couldn't. And I did. With you, ya little scaredy cat."

"Aww." She made a sad face and looked up at his

watery eyes, pretty sure those were tears and not cataracts. "I'm sorry, Hank. You've given him a great place to stay."

He nodded. "He's not much of a lover, if you get my drift."

She chuckled. "He's definitely more of a loner."

"And that's not what I need," he admitted, reaching out as if he were going to pat Rhett Butler's head. Instead, he touched Sadie's cheek lightly and angled his head toward Scout. "You two remind me of me and Margie. Although she had a sly side, and if we'd been in this predicament, we'd have switched the cats and never told the old guy."

Sadie laughed. "That's what I wanted to do, but Scout said you'd have known."

"Oh, I'd have known." He gave her a yellowed grin. "Just like I know you have a touch of Margie's spunk. And you?" He shifted his gaze to Scout. "You knew what would happen if he got out, didn't you?"

Scout just gave a guilty smile.

"You two belong together," Hank said. "Now, get on your way. I need to spend some time getting to know... What did you say his dumb name was?"

They both gasped softly in surprise.

"Wiggles," Sadie said. "And I can't disagree with that opinion on his name."

"I'll get him a new one." He turned and looked at the new cat, who'd curled right on the most worn section of the sofa, already at home. "Presley. How's that?"

"*Purrr*fect," Scout joked, putting one arm around

Sadie and extending his other for a shake. "And thank you, Hank."

They said goodbye and on the way out, they could hear Hank's wobbly voice singing, *"Wise men say..."*

"You know what I think?" Scout whispered into her ear, tugging her closer as they walked to the car.

"I know what I think. You're a genius. What do you think?"

He smiled. "We should dance to that song at our wedding."

She froze, nearly tripping and dropping the cat she still held. "Our..."

"You heard the man. We belong together like...Hank and Margie."

She looked up at him and felt the words bubbling up, right there, ready to be said.

I love you.

But Rhett Butler squirmed and, once again, the cat killed the moment. Or Sadie's uncertainty did.

WE BELONG TOGETHER.

The echo of Scout's words woke Sadie from a deep, exhausted sleep. She blinked into the darkness of her bedroom, waiting for the impact of her thoughts.

But all she heard was—*wait*. What was that noise? Was that someone downstairs at the door of the chocolate shop? Knocking?

Squinting, she picked up her phone to see it was five-thirty.

Well, yes, she sometimes got up this early if it was a heavy chocolate-making day and she had to restock the displays and boxes, but that didn't give anyone—friend, foe, or family—reason to visit before the sun was up. A vendor? They'd come to the back. A customer? They must *really* want chocolate.

As she set the phone down, a text came in, but there was no vibration or sound, since she had silenced it for the night. The words, however, were loud and clear.

Scout: *Answer your door. Please.*

Oh, no. Did the cat get out again?

Deep inside, she knew this wasn't about Rhett Butler. She *knew*.

Shaking off the remnants of sleep, she tugged at the drawstring on her sleep pants under her T-shirt and slid on a pair of flipflops. All the way down the back stairs, through the kitchen, and out to the front door of Charmed by Chocolate, a bit of déjà vu tapped at her heart.

This is where and how she'd met Martin "Scout" Jacobson, who showed up sweeter than the cookies he made and warmed her with his understated charm and silly expressions.

He took her by surprise, offered unexpected support on her new venture, and nicely smoothed out the rough edges on a heart that Tristan had torn to shreds.

And now...he was here again. Why?

But deep inside, she knew why.

She unlocked the door and opened it slowly, still trying to formulate her answer.

"Shalom," he said.

She wasn't sure she'd heard right, the greeting was so unexpected. Had she ever heard him say that before? It wasn't entirely out of character, since she knew he was proud of his Jewish heritage, and honored his faith, but...

"Shalom?" she volleyed back, a question in her voice.

"Do you know what that means, Sadie?"

No, a lesson in Hebrew before dawn was not on her bingo card this week.

"I think...peace?" she guessed.

"There's so much more to it," he said. "Can you take a walk?"

"Um, yeah, I'm in my pajamas and...don't have a key..."

"You're dressed, and I have a key, remember?"

Of course, they had keys to each other's businesses, and each other's homes. They were much more than friends, close in every way, and...he deserved to know exactly where she stood on love and the future. And that was why he was here, for sure.

"Okay." She closed the door and he locked it for her, taking her hand to walk down a deserted Wingate Way. A few of the businesses had tiny lights on over the windows, and some boats bobbed on the river, their warning lights moving with the current.

Other than that, it was very dark, with the early morning cool that wouldn't be felt once the sun rose. She could smell some tropical flowers in a planter box and a brackish scent wafting from the water, and both those aromas seemed a thousand times sharper than they were during the day. Intense enough to make her stomach grip a little as they walked.

Or maybe that was nerves.

Was Scout ending their relationship? The thought hit her like a two-by-four to the chest.

"This is a surprise," she finally said, but even as the words came out, she realized it wasn't.

They'd parted warmly last night, but something hung in the air between them. Was it...a commitment, or the lack of one? A bout of doubt? Or just the relief of having Rhett Butler home before Kitty was any the wiser.

"I couldn't sleep," he said softly, threading his fingers through hers with a slightly tight grip that always felt like he didn't want to let go of her.

Had any man ever held her hand like that? She'd never noticed. Hand-holding was just...basic. And nice.

However, with Scout, it was so much more. He held her hand with pride and certainty and surprise that she even let him.

"Shalom," he said again as they passed Grace's still-dark bookstore, "is often loosely translated to 'peace.' You're right. But if you dig deeper into the root of the word and the much more subtle meaning, shalom means safety and completeness."

"Which are things that give you peace," she said.

"Exactly. And that, Sadie Wingate, is what I want to offer you." He slowed his step and turned to her, taking her other hand, and looking into her eyes. "Safety and completeness. Shalom."

She looked up at him, mesmerized and terribly confused.

"I had a realization about you and your life last night," he said. "You like things and people and situations that are extraordinary."

"I do?"

"Very much so. Because you, yourself, are extra-ordinary." He said the word as if it was two separate thoughts —*extra* and *ordinary*. "And by that I mean not ordinary at all. I mean above, beyond, and special. And you seek that out in your relationships and jobs and lifestyle and even where and how you live."

She considered that, recognizing enough truth in it that she didn't correct him.

"You call yourself a tumbleweed or a person who won't settle down, but what you are is a person who won't settle for ordinary," he continued. "Your whole life—your career, your years in Europe, even your last relationship—was Sadie seeking *more* than the ordinary."

"Okay. I guess." She'd never really thought of it that way, but it made sense.

"Think about it, Sadie. Tristan was extraordinary—the second son of billionaires with a household name—and even the way you married him by eloping was extraordinary."

"So extraordinary it didn't last ten minutes," she said drolly.

"Yep, and if you think about what I'm going to say, you'll get it."

She frowned at him, searching his face, taking in the soft lines and kind eyes.

"Extraordinary, as attractive as it might be, can be very disingenuous," he said.

"Tristan certainly was," she agreed.

"But ordinary? Now, that is...well, let's be honest. That, my beautiful Sadie, is what I am." He chuckled. "The very definition of ordinary."

"Scout, you aren't—"

He put a finger to her lips. "I'm not ashamed of it. I'm a forty-year-old Jewish accountant-turned-baker who's a little soft in the middle and likes a cliché or two. No private plane, no fancy house, no chiseled jaw, no trips around Europe."

She pressed her hand to her chest, only then realizing she was holding her breath, which must be what was making her dizzy.

"But Sadie, I'm an *ordinary* man who will protect you, adore you, treasure you, and put your needs before mine. I have a steadfast heart and a strong shoulder. Ordinary brings the completeness and safety that is part of a life filled with...*shalom*."

She let out that breath with a whoosh, nearly swaying on the street at his speech.

"I know you call me 'nice,'" he added. "I've heard you refer to me that way a lot."

"Many times," she confessed. "But I never mean it in an unkind way."

"And I don't take it that way," he assured her. "Nice is a key component of the recipe for ordinary. Nice is a level path for walking through life together. Especially when things get rocky or, I don't know, when you're pushing a stroller or losing a parent or trying to navigate the tough stuff. Nice is dependable and solid and lasting and honest."

It was all those things, she agreed. And no one, absolutely no one, was nicer than Scout.

Still studying him, she got another whiff of the salty water, letting out a groan as her unsteady stomach threatened again.

Why? Was she overwhelmed? In love? Or bone-deep terrified? Was it actually making her nauseous to think of spending her life with a man this good?

She swallowed the rising wave and nodded. "I need to...think." What she needed to do was put her head between her legs and *breathe*.

And nothing was more *ordinary* than that.

He nodded. "That's what I want and why I came over now. You don't have to answer me. Just think about it for as long as you like. I'm in no rush and I'm not pressuring you. I just had to be sure you know that I love you. And nothing about that is ordinary."

Still holding her hand, he walked her back to the shop in silence, his plea complete. At her door, he took out his keys and unlocked the shop.

"Will you go back to bed or start making chocolate now?" he asked.

The very idea of pouring nibs into the *melangeur*

nearly turned her stomach. "I don't know," she whispered.

After a moment, he let out a sigh, then leaned in to kiss her cheek. "Shalom, Sadie."

"Shalom," she replied as he took a step back, smiled, and turned to walk down Wingate Way.

She stood with her hand on the doorknob, watching him disappear into the darkness of the north end of the street. She squeezed the metal, her whole body wanting to cry out three simple words that reverberated in her head and heart.

"I love you." She heard them come out of her mouth, the sound reed thin and unstable.

But not as unstable as her stomach.

Somehow, she made it all the way back upstairs to her apartment, where she thoroughly disappointed herself by throwing up.

What was wrong with her that the very thought of loving a man like Scout made her sick to her stomach?

She *did* love him, and somehow, some way, she'd have to show him that or she was going to lose that extra-ordinary man and then she'd have no...*shalom*.

Chapter Seventeen

Raina

No one had seen Ivy Button for well over a week, and she hadn't responded to the texts Raina had sent. She'd used the number that was on Susannah's phone, but it could easily be a disposable phone ringing in a trash can somewhere.

Without her fingerprints or a little more information about her, Adam couldn't do any searches. The name Ivy Button came up with no leads to the woman's identity, and Rose had dug into town archives to discover that Doreen Parrish indeed had a sister who was much older and moved away when their mother died. There was no record of where she'd gone.

Madeline had a friend at the county clerk's office who had done a deeper dive on the notary commissioned on the "contract" that their grandfather had allegedly written, and they absolutely couldn't find that person anywhere in the past fifty years.

Blake had found every record in Wingate Properties related to the ownership of the Inn, but there was nothing that implied it would have changed hands, except for Rex

Wingate officially inheriting it when his parents had both passed away.

Records were in their favor, more or less, but they were all afraid that proving that would encourage Ivy to launch her slander campaign, which was blackmail and illegal, but oh, how everyone wanted to avoid that pain.

Hopes were running thin until Raina got a call late one night from Ivy on an unknown number. She agreed to meet again the next morning.

And from dawn until eleven that day, Raina stewed and stressed.

"We got this," Chase assured her, walking across the kitchen to fold Raina—and the baby she held—in his arms. "You even have the coffee and water set up, I saw."

"Wasn't that smart? I put a coffee carafe and water bottles right in the entry, so I can get something in her hand first thing. Then I'll get her into the living room to touch every surface imaginable. But she won't touch the babies." Raina looked down at Charlie and stroked her sweet face. "I don't want them in the same room as this woman."

"Don't you worry. I'll have them upstairs in the nursery with everything I need."

"With the baby monitor on," she reminded him.

He nodded. "The upstairs unit is set to record, so anything she says, we'll have on tape. I'll be listening, and if you need me, I'll be down in a hurry."

She blew out a breath and walked over to Lily, currently asleep in her bouncy seat in the sunlight, a smile permanently plastered on her happy face.

"They're growing fast," she mused. "Milestone after milestone. Did you see her sit herself up?"

"And this one." He rubbed Charlie's head. "She's practically speaking in sentences."

Raina snorted a laugh at the joke, but Charlie rewarded them with her favorite phrase of, "Ba-ba-ba-baaa!" and a giggle.

"Change that B to D, little one." Chase tapped her chest. "Then you'll be talkin' to your Da-da!"

Raina's shoulders dropped at the thought. "When are we going to hear from Hyphenated Helen? Tim the lawyer said she'd be contacting us any day for the site visit."

"She's started," he assured her. "As you know, she and her assistant have already been to Ocean Song and interviewed half my staff at the hotel, including Jules, who told them I would be the world's greatest dad."

"I hope her interviews are enough to approve our official and surprise adoption as daughters of Suze." She made a face. "I have to admit that side of this process is almost as important to me. For some reason, I want to call Suze 'Mom' now. Isn't that weird? After forty-some years of calling her Suze?"

Smiling, he leaned over and kissed Charlie's head. "Not weird at all. After fifty of being called Chase, all I want to be is Da-da." He rubbed his nose against Charlie's. "With a D, girl."

She blew a bubble and powered out another, "Ba!"

Laughing, Raina turned to check the clock over the

oven. "Eleven-oh-five, Ivy. Where is our little scam artist?"

At that very moment, the front doorbell rang and Raina's eyes flashed.

"As my soon-to-be brother-in-law Isaiah would say," Chase teased, "'Ask and you shall receive.'"

"And as his uber-cautious wife Grace would say, 'Be careful what you wish for.'"

"You'll be fine," he assured her, easing Charlie out of her arms. "And I can carry one baby in one hand and the baby bouncer in the other. Take a video and show *that* to Hyphenated Helen."

The bell rang again.

"All right, all right," Raina muttered, helping Chase with the bouncer seat and watching him head up the stairs.

Giving it a minute to be sure he was set up and listening on the upstairs monitor, she took a deep breath, swiped her damp palms on her jeans, and marched to the door to whip it open and make sure Ivy knew who was in charge. And get a coffee cup in her hand, stat.

"Hello—" She nearly choked on the word as she stared at the woman at the door. It was Hyphenated... "Helen." She croaked the woman's name.

"You remember me," she said, giving a tight smile. "Helen Lensky-Fallon and this is Wendy Holmes, my assistant."

"Wendy."

Her mind went absolutely blank. How was this possible? What was she going to do? She could not let Helen meet Ivy. No, it couldn't happen.

"Oh, I'm so sorry," Raina said, stepping closer and pulling the door behind her, praying Ivy didn't pull up now. "This is not a good time."

"There is no good time," Helen quipped. "In fact, the worse it is, the better for me to see the flaws the soft underbelly of your home, Ms. Wingate. Can I call you Raina?"

She blinked at her. "I'm expecting someone."

"We won't be in your way. Just think of us as disappearing elves in the background, listening and learning. I see your future husband's car—" She gestured to his convertible coupe. "Please tell me he doesn't take the babies in that thing."

"Oh, no. Never. In my sedan, which is so safe. So very safe." She swallowed as a car slowed down at the end of the long driveway, then exhaled when it didn't turn. "But can we reschedule, please? This meeting I have is, um, work. And it's very important."

"I thought you'd stopped working," Helen said, tilting her head with a question in eyes a few shades browner than her auburn hair. "Am I wrong that you are a stay-at-home mother?"

"Not that it matters," the other woman—Wanda? Wilma? Something...Holmes. Like Sherlock. "We approve adoptions for working mothers and fathers all the time. More than SAHMs, I assure you."

Raina winced at the acronym, never a fan. "I simply

have to say no," she finally said. "I have a personal meeting with someone—"

"You just said it was work," Helen volleyed back. "Are you lying, Ms. Wingate?"

She let out a sigh. "It's a little of both, but I can't give you my full attention—"

"I don't want your attention, full or otherwise," she said, flipping her hand in a silent order to be let inside. "I want to speak with Mr. Madison, watch him interact with the babies, tour your house for everything from safety issues to the temperature. The soft underbelly, Ms. Wingate." Another hand flip. "Now or not at all."

Oh, dear. That car was slowing down and pulling in. She'd have to get rid of Ivy if she couldn't get rid of Hyphenated Helen.

On a sigh, she opened the door a little further and let them in.

"Thank you," Helen said, sounding a tad exasperated with the effort. As she stepped inside, she let out a hoot of happiness. "How lovely that you have water and coffee for us. Wendy? Would you like some?"

And both cups were swooped up with the wrong fingers leaving the wrong prints.

"Do you have milk?" Wendy asked. "I can't do heavy cream."

"Yes, I do..." *In my breasts*, she added mentally, glancing as the car rolled in. "But I—"

"If you'd just get that for me, I'd appreciate it," Wendy said with a smile that somehow seemed disingenuous on the forty-something blonde.

"Go ahead." Helen gave her a nudge. "We'll tell your company you'll be right here."

Flattened by this human bulldozer, Raina walked back to the kitchen, grabbed a carton of milk, and paused at the bottom of the stairs, considering a quick run to the top to give Chase a heads-up.

But that would take too long and the one thing Raina didn't want was Ivy and Helen to talk.

She sailed back toward the front door where Ivy and Helen were doing just that.

"Here you go," she called, trying to end the conversation before it started. Ivy did not need any more ammunition and Helen really did not need to know this woman even existed. "And, Ivy, how nice to see you again," Raina added. "Please help yourself to water or coffee while I take these ladies where they need to go."

She fried Helen with a look that said who was boss in this house and ushered the two women down the hall.

"Start upstairs. The nursery is the first door on your left and Chase is there with both babies." She practically pushed them up, then spun around and hurried back to Ivy, who stood in the center of the living room, arms crossed, no cup, glass, or bottle in her hands.

"Please, Ivy. A water or coffee?"

She shook her head, gripping her crossed arms tighter as if...as if she knew Raina wanted her fingerprints. Had she even touched the doorknob, or had Helen let her in?

"I'm done messing around," she spat out. "Give me the keys and the deed now, today, right here, or every person on Amelia Island will know your father took a mentally incapacitated woman by force, made her pregnant, paid her off to go away, and promised her a home, and then refused to deliver."

"Whoa, whoa, whoa. That is not what happened and you know it. He couldn't hurt a fly and their liaison was entirely consensual. She never told him she was pregnant—"

"She told his father," Ivy interjected.

"And he's dead," Raina countered.

"Yes, just like my poor aunt, who didn't have the brainpower to hold off a man determined to have his way with her. Your father ruined her life."

"He did not," she shot back. "He gave her a place to live and work—"

"Out of guilt for what he did to her!" Ivy finished. "And now your whole family is trying to shake me down and get rid of me because you think you're so powerful you own this island. Well, I know the truth about all of you."

"The truth?" Raina scoffed. "About us? That we love each other unconditionally, have given blood, sweat, and tears to our local businesses, and care about everyone we know?"

"That you were married to one man, living with another, and have no idea who the father of your children really is!"

Raina gasped so hard she choked. "Excuse—"

"That one sister is involved with the Cassano mafia gang, another one blackmailed a Belgian billionaire for the money to start her business, and the youngest is such a flake she ran away from the altar in her wedding gown."

Raina's jaw nearly hit the ground. "How do...what have you..."

"People talk, Raina. And they just love to talk about Wingates. Don't get me started on how your twin sister let her son get into an accident when the ink was still drying on his driver's license, and another one hit on your dad's doctor while the old man was dying in the hospital."

Raina just stared at her, waiting for whatever this monster dug up on Grace.

"And the one who owns the bookstore left her baby daughter alone when the place went up in flames."

That. Another lie. Another utter abuse of the facts.

Ivy snorted, probably at the look on Raina's face. "So, believe me when I say they will gobble up this latest dirt about your father, a ra—"

"Stop it!" Raina screamed. "Don't say that word. It isn't true! Not one word of what you said is true."

"Isn't it?"

"Not...not that way. Just get out. Get out of my house. You are not welcome here. You can't do any damage with your lies, so bring 'em on, sweetheart. We will find out who you really are and we will destroy you in the process."

"Oh, sure, just another Wingate casualty." She rolled her eyes and walked toward the entryway, while Raina braced herself for her closing comment.

But she didn't say a word. She merely lifted the

bottom of her sweater, wrapped the material over the doorknob, and let herself out without touching a thing. She turned her face when she walked out, no doubt avoiding being caught on the Ring camera.

Raina stood stone still, fighting the tears that welled up from deep inside.

Only then did she remember the baby monitor had just relayed the entire conversation to Hyphenated Helen and Sherlock Holmes.

For what seemed like an hour but was probably thirty endless seconds, Raina couldn't move. She waited for... something. Chase to come bounding down or Helen to announce the deal was off or one of the babies to wail at the unfairness of life.

But the house was utterly silent, which was weird.

Finally, she walked to the baby monitor—the one they'd so carefully set up to capture every word and broadcast to Chase in the nursery—and touched the switch to turn it off. Too little, too late, she thought as she stuck her nail on the soft button.

She held it down too long, it crackled, and all of a sudden, she heard hushed voices.

Chase...then Helen.

They were still up there? Maybe he'd brilliantly turned off the monitor when he heard Helen coming upstairs. But he didn't know Ivy had arrived. Still, he was smart and resourceful and—

"I know what I heard, Mr. Madison." Helen's disapproval came through loud and clear.

So he was not a miracle worker. They'd heard.

"You heard someone twisting facts, spewing gossip, and outright lying," Chase said.

"Why would that woman say those things about the Wingates?"

Raina turned to hustle upstairs for damage control.

"Let me tell you ladies something about the Wingates." Chase's voice was low and steady, the way it was when he wanted to make his point perfectly clear. Raina froze to listen.

"I don't think you can say much more than what that woman just told us," Helen replied. "I think I've heard enough to—"

"You've heard the vitriol of a greedy con artist who has an agenda and no moral compass."

Helen sniffed, her opinion about who had a broken moral compass pretty clear to Raina even without seeing her face.

"The Wingate family is unlike any I've ever known," Chase said, his voice clear through the small speaker. "And I say that as a man with cousins all over Sicily and two of the finest parents and grandparents that ever lived. I say that as a man who not only knows what makes a good family, but has longed to be a part of one for...well, forever."

Raina dropped on the edge of the sofa, needing to hear this.

"The only reason I met Raina was that she was a

mama bear on a search for a missing cub—who happened to be her nephew, who'd been turned away from his own family because he's gay."

One of the women grunted in sympathy.

"She moved heaven and Earth for that young man, determined for him to know that if he had a drop of Wingate blood in him, he was family. Today, he's helping to run Wingate Properties, mentored by Raina, and loved by all."

"I understand that you—"

"No, no, you don't understand," Chase interjected. "There are seven sisters and they all live within a stone's throw of their parents. They are supportive, they are united, and they love through thick and thin and everything in between."

"But she called Rex a—"

"Rex Wingate is the definition of a kind man, with a heart so big it defies logic. He's fathered seven amazing women, raised four of them alone until he married Susannah, and just celebrated their fortieth anniversary. Men who do what she just said don't fit that mold, Helen."

The other woman was quiet, hopefully shut up by Chase's speech.

"These babies," he continued after a beat, making Raina close her eyes and imagine the scene upstairs, with the twins sleeping, maybe one in his arms. "These two are the luckiest girls in the world. And not because I hope to be the best father imaginable. But because they are Wingates, part of a legacy like I've never seen before. Good women, with open hearts and minds and the willingness to do whatever it takes to help each other."

One of the women sighed, and Raina hoped it was Helen and that it was a sigh of resignation.

"I would bet my life—and in fact, I have, as I will be giving it to Raina soon—that Rex is one hundred percent innocent of these false allegations. And every other incident she mentioned? They happened, not like that, but they did happen. Madeline was 'involved' with the mafia because she put her life on the line to protect this town. Sadie was betrayed by the Belgian billionaire and bounced back with the support of her family. Chloe is a runaway bride because she's too smart to marry the wrong guy and her sisters helped her see that."

"I'm sure there are explanations—"

"There are, Helen. Good explanations. Grace didn't leave Nikki alone in the bookstore—she was with the man who is now her stepfather, and...who did I miss? Oh, Tori. Well, yeah, she did kind of run into Dr. Hottypants while Rex was recovering from his stroke." He chuckled. "That turned out okay, though."

Raina picked up a sofa cushion and smashed her face into it, not sure if they could hear her reaction, which was a squeal of pure love for this man.

"You forgot one allegation," Helen said. "And it has to do with the father of these children, and who Raina lived with while she was pregnant and not yet divorced."

For a long beat, there was just silence, and she squeezed her eyes shut to imagine Chase's handsome face, solid and strong as he considered his response.

"There is no question who is the biological father, who has relinquished his rights. And there is no question who is the emotional father. That would be me. I had the honor of becoming first Raina's tenant—living downstairs in the guest suite when I was in town—and then her friend. The only person who thinks I'm the biological father is in heaven now, and that is my nonna. Raina went against all her instincts and agreed to let my dear grandmother go to the next world happy."

"That was...sweet."

"It was far more than that," he shot back. "It was a selfless act of love, not the first or last that I've seen from Raina. It was also the day I knew I loved her and would wait forever for the honor of marrying her and spending the rest of my life loving, protecting, supporting, and enjoying Raina and these little girls. So, if the rumors say they are mine, then the rumors are right. They will be mine, God willing. And you, Helen. You have to be willing, too, I suppose."

Raina let out a sigh and sat up when, after a moment or two, she heard footsteps coming down the stairs.

Very slowly, she stood, ready to face the music. She came around the corner just as they reached the bottom of the stairs, with Helen in the lead.

"What else can I show you for a tour?" Raina asked.

"I've seen—and heard—enough." She gave a tight smile, handing Raina her coffee cup. "And I have a lot to think about."

Raina stepped back to let her pass, smiling at Wendy as she also handed back her coffee cup.

"I'll walk them to the door," Chase said, giving Raina's cheek a little knuckle-brush as he passed.

She didn't listen to any more of their conversation, but walked up the stairs slowly, turning into the nursery. Both babies were awake, cooing and moving and growing into two more amazing Wingate women.

Except if Chase adopted them and they got married—

"Well, not exactly what we expected, huh?" Chase said with a soft laugh as he came into the room.

"I heard what you said," she whispered, turning to him. "About my family and...well, thank you."

"Meant every word." He stepped closer to her, studying her face.

"You know, I haven't decided about my name. Of course, the girls will be Madison, but..."

"Raina Madison doesn't sound right?" he guessed.

"It's just...a huge change. And, if I'm being honest, I'm worried that it will hurt my dad's feelings. The Wingate name means so much to him."

"We could try again, have a boy and name him Wingate Madison," he said, only half-joking, she could tell.

"I think that ship has sailed," she replied, reaching up to close her hands around his neck and lower him for a kiss. "And your name is beautiful, too. Marrying you is an honor for me, and I'm not sure I want two different last names."

"You know what they say...a rose by any other name."

"That's my sister."

He laughed and she melted into his arms, not caring about names or problems or anything. Right then, she just wanted to hold the most wonderful man in the world and she simply couldn't wait to marry him.

"Tori said you could be Chase Wingate."

He laughed at that, then they kissed while the babies made a few noises, only breaking their contact when Charlie called out, "Da da da!"

And she thought Chase was going to dance with joy.

Chapter Eighteen

Chloe

"Look at McCall strut his stuff." Gabe leaned against the door jamb of the engine bay, arms crossed, a huge grin on his face as he watched Travis walk Judah through the most extensive pumper tour a five-year-old ever got at the Fernandina Beach Fire Department. "You'd think he was Chief instead of just off his probation year."

Chloe laughed and shared a look with Rose, who stood next to her husband, watching Travis and Judah with the same interest and amusement. "I'm so glad I stopped by to see this," she said. "Is Chief Keating around today?"

"Oh, he's here. So's Hutch, who believes it's the Captain's job to personally soak the little guests with a fire hose."

"No!" Chloe said, narrowing her eyes at her brother-in-law. "You will not soak Judah with a fire hose! That's dangerous."

"Don't worry, Mama Bear. It's on the lowest setting. And so's that siren he's about to let Judah turn on."

Chloe turned to the pumper truck, seeing Judah joyfully perched in the driver's seat, his legs swinging with excitement, his eyes wide as he took in the array of dials and gadgets on the massive dashboard.

"Ready?" Travis asked him, leaning in with one hand protectively on the child's back.

"I ready, Uncah Man!" he called out about as loud as any siren.

"You sure?"

"I sure!" His sneakers fluttered wildly.

"Flip that switch. Right there. On three. One...two...three!"

A siren screeched, not much louder than a noisy phone and not nearly enough to even get the attention of any of the firefighters milling about the station on a blessedly slow day.

Travis was off today, but Judah had wanted to see the station so much, they decided to make a trip here.

"You just going to let that slide?" Rose asked, stepping away from Gabe to whisper to Chloe.

"The siren?" she asked with a frown.

"The reference...Mama Bear?"

"Oh, yeah." Chloe gave a laugh. "I didn't even notice."

"Because it's a natural role for you, darling." Rose tenderly slid a lock of Chloe's hair behind her ear, giving her wise big-sister smile. "You three are like a family already."

"Not exactly." Chloe watched Travis hoist Judah out of the seat and let him scamper to the gear wall, holding his hand as he guided him to the hook that said "McCall."

"That's my name!" Judah announced loudly.

"Oh, he can read his name?" Rose asked. "That's awesome for a kid who just turned five."

"He knows every letter, can spell simple words, and can count to fifty." Chloe beamed. "I know I sound like a proud mother, but the credit goes to his late parents, and I suppose Travis's dad, though he'd never say that. I don't think Pops was exactly evil—he taught Judah to say grace."

"Is Travis still struggling with all that?" Rose asked.

"He doesn't seem to be. Judah has become a person to him now, not a symbol of Dale's shortcomings as Travis's father." She smiled as she watched Travis let Judah put on his jacket and stick a whole leg into his boot. "Wait, I have to get a picture of this," she said, reaching into her purse.

But before she found her phone, she sensed Gabe standing a little straighter. Not exactly at attention, but she wasn't surprised to see Chief Keating come into the bay.

"Who do we have here?" the silver-haired boss asked, bending over to look at Judah, swimming in the oversized jacket and boots.

Slipping her phone out, she took a few steps closer, a smile pulling at the adorable sight as she snapped pictures.

"Is this Firefighter McCall Junior?"

Judah looked up, eyes wide, silent.

"This is my nephew, Judah, sir," Travis said, his voice rich with pride. "And I do think he'll make a fine firefighter someday."

"Then he'll need this." He brought a hand out from behind his back, and presented a small plastic firefighter helmet. "Do you want to wear it?"

Judah nodded enthusiastically, grinning while the Chief put the helmet on his curls, carefully placing it over the elastic band that held his glasses in place. Then Judah looked over to Chloe and practically danced on his toes, his joy arcing across the bay.

"Aww." Rose cooed next to her.

"I know, right?" Chloe laughed while she snapped about a hundred shots.

Behind them, Gabe put a hand on Rose's shoulder. "Don't get any ideas just because your twin sister had two babies," he joked to his wife. "Four and done for the D'Angelo family."

She turned and smiled up at him. "No fears, Lieutenant. I'm done. But my baby sister here…"

"It's not up to me," Chloe said. "I'd give up everything for that kid. But Travis…"

"Give him time." Gabe put his other hand on her shoulder. "He's coming around, Chloe. We talk about it every day. He's made major strides and just needs time to process and accept. Not you, obviously. The guy's a goner for you, which I knew he would be when I set you two up."

"Set us up?" Chloe threw him a look. "I ran into him on the street."

"Yeah, but when he came into the station asking everyone about a girl named Chloe, I, uh, might have made sure you were at our house alone the night he needed to pick up some gear."

"It's true," Rose said. "We made the match."

Chloe grinned at both of them. "Well, thank you. You know how I feel about Travis. He's..."

"He's the one," Rose said, dropping her head back to land on Gabe's chest. "Just like my guy, here."

Chloe groaned. "Nobody is as perfect as you two, or your four angelic children."

"Families come in all shapes, sizes, and colors," Gabe said. "And speaking of colors, I'm going to be the one to give that kid the fire station coloring book and crayons or he's going to forget I'm here. And *Uncah Gabe* arranged the tour."

They laughed as he disappeared, while Judah trotted closer with his new red helmet askew on his head.

"We're going to play with the hoses!"

"And he's going to get a little wet," Travis said, right on his heels after he thanked the Chief for his kindness.

"Consider it a bath," Rose said. "I can't tell you how many nights my kids have been here for hose fun and we called them clean."

"I have dry clothes in a bag for him," Chloe said. "Go have fun. Travis, will you take pictures?"

"I'm on hose duty. And we don't need pictures, we'll get them next time we're here."

As they took off for the lawn outside in the back, Rose turned to her.

"Next time? See? I'm optimistic about this, Chloe."

She let out a sigh and admitted the truth. "So am I. In fact, if this kid slips through our fingers, I don't think I could stand it. But it's not up to me, Rosie. Travis has to want it as much as I do."

Rose put a hand on her shoulder and guided her toward another back door that led to a patio and a view of the grassy area. There, they could see Travis gently chasing, teasing, and soaking Judah, and then letting him hold the hose and do the same in return.

Their laughter—one deep and from a masculine chest, one like musical giggles from a wee body—echoed over the space and completely filled Chloe's heart.

"I know what I want," she whispered to her sister. "I just don't know how to convince him to give it to me."

"Don't worry, Chloe. Judah's doing the heavy lifting."

Watching the uncle and nephew laugh with abandon, she had to believe that was true.

Long ago, Chloe realized she hated saying goodbye. But this one? Oh, she despised leaving Judah after a long day of fun.

This evening, they'd delayed the inevitable with a stop at Cracker Barrel, treating Judah to chicken fingers and Travis's legendary "mashed taters."

The meal filled the boy's belly, but not his heart, which looked like it might be aching as Travis took the exit to Mandarin off the Interstate.

Storm clouds with a threat of tears filled his eyes as he recognized it was time to go back to the group home.

Just as she was about to say something cheery and optimistic, Chloe caught sight of the look in Travis's eyes —just as stormy, just as foreboding, same tears on the horizon.

What was stopping him? The next step, according to Mae, was to take over guardianship, then they'd file paperwork that established the blood relation for a "kinship" adoption. All of it would be easy as pie. At least legally it would be.

Emotionally? She couldn't say.

As she'd mentioned to Rose, Travis didn't seem stuck on his issues about his father anymore. Sometime in these weeks—between ice cream cones and dirt-lifting toy trucks, after bath time and over late-night grilled cheese sandwiches, and, of course, today's insanely fun tour of the fire station—Travis stopped mentioning the man who had broken his spirit as a child.

In fact, he more and more frequently referred to "Pops," because they agreed it wasn't fair to just let the man's memory disappear for Judah, who'd now lost a mother, a father, and his beloved grandfather. But there were no more pained expressions on Travis's face, no more anger over his late father's shortcomings, no more resentment toward Judah.

But something still stopped him from going all in.

Travis turned and pulled into the group home, which looked even drearier than the first time they were here.

Now they knew Kelly and Ron, the "home-keepers," as they were called, were lovely but stretched to their limits.

Simple things—a manicured lawn, a neat garage, or a desperately needed fresh coat of paint—were ignored as the middle-aged Christian couple put their hearts and souls into making this temporary stop for so many boys as pleasant and safe as they could.

As far as Chloe was concerned, she had one goal, and that was to stop coming to this place and leaving Judah behind.

Before they were out of the car, the front door opened and they saw Kelly step out, pushing back hair that probably hadn't seen comb or brush in hours. Next to her, and deep in conversation, was the now-familiar face of Mae, who'd become a lifeline for Chloe.

Stopping their discussion, the two women looked at Travis's truck with a mix of expectation and worry in their expressions...and Chloe's heart sank.

He'd been placed for adoption. It was bound to happen again, and soon.

She shook it off and turned a happy smile to the only person who mattered in the mix—the sweet angel whose glasses were crooked as he stared down at the red plastic helmet on his lap.

"There's Miss Kelly," Chloe said with a high-pitched voice of excitement. "You can tell her all about how you sat in a fire engine today, Judah!"

He gave a half-smile, which she interpreted as, "If Miss Kelly has time."

"Oh, buddy," Travis said on a heavy sigh as he pulled into the driveway. "Guess it's time to say so long."

Judah's lower lip quivered and protruded, instantly making Chloe reach into the back seat to his booster chair. "But we'll see you again soon. I promise! On Travis's next day off from being a fireman!"

The lip just came out a little more.

Oh, yeah. The goodbyes were getting hard for everyone.

He looked down and gripped the helmet, then reached for the coloring book with a netted bag of crayons that "Uncah Gabe" had given him. As his fingers rubbed the gold firefighter seal on the cover, he shuddered, fighting tears.

Oh, good gracious, this was no way for a child to live!

"I'll get your stuff, buddy," Travis said, already out of his seatbelt and pushing open his door.

Chloe climbed out of the passenger side and waved to Mae and Kelly. Immediately, Mae beckoned her closer. While Travis got Judah, Chloe walked over, noticing that neither one of them looked happy and with each step, her heart dropped, expecting the worst.

"Wait until you hear about the day he had," Chloe said first, hoping to delay the bad news. "The personal one-on-one fire station tour—"

"He's going to be leaving here," Mae said quickly and softly.

She knew it. On a sigh, she nodded. "He was placed for adoption."

"Actually, no, not yet," Mae replied.

"Oh, really?" And back her heart went chugging up the Judah rollercoaster. "But...where..."

Kelly's shoulders slumped. "I'm sorry, Chloe. We'd love to keep him but Ron and I have got to thin down the population at this home," she said, glancing at Mae to give the impression they'd just been talking about this. "My husband and I love helping the 'in-betweeners' as we call them—the kids who are on the cusp of a new life but fresh out of their old one. It's a challenge, but it's a blessing, too, as I'm sure you understand."

Chloe nodded, but she didn't understand a thing. What did they mean he was leaving?

"Judah is the last boy I want to let go," she continued. "He's a good, good child. But we've got three teenagers at the moment and desperately need the space."

"There's another home that can take Judah," Mae said.

"Oh, okay." Did they hear the total relief in Chloe's voice? There was still a chance for them. If only Travis...

She glanced over her shoulder to see what was taking him so long and caught sight of Travis crouched down, his hands on Judah's shoulders, clearly calming the little boy down. Time was all they needed—she was certain of that.

"Then we can see him at the new home," she said.

Mae and Kelly shared a look that spoke volumes, but nothing Chloe could decipher.

"We can't?" she asked.

"It's not in Jacksonville," Mae said. "But it will be in Florida, of course."

Which was a massive state. "Where?"

"Near Fort Myers Beach and it's so pretty—"

"The west coast? And that far south?" Southwest Florida was a good six-hour drive from Amelia Island. They'd never see Judah! "When is he going?"

Mae made an apologetic face. "I'll be driving him down in a couple of days."

A couple of *days*?

"But it's a good home," Kelly said, reaching out her arm because Chloe was probably doing a terrible job of hiding her feelings. "I know the people and they're terrific. Plus, I promise you he'll be adopted in no time. The babies and toddlers go first, but Judah is special."

Chloe swallowed against a growing lump in her throat. "I know. He is. He's..."

"Hey, Judah!" Kelly interrupted her by bending over and smiling at the little guy who shuffled over to them. "Is that a fireman's hat you're wearing? You look like you could climb a ladder and put out the blazes!"

He offered a half-hearted smile, then took off the hat and turned to Travis, arms up. "Ride, Uncah Man?"

"Aw, bud, we can't do a piggyback now. You'll get all sweaty and you had a hose bath! Wait until you tell everyone about that." He held out the small bag that contained Judah's change of clothes to Kelly. "Probably not officially clean, but..."

"Clean enough for a woman with seven kids in one bathroom," she said, taking the bag. "Did you get dinner, Judah?"

"Oh, he visited his first Cracker Barrel," Travis

announced proudly. "Chicken fingers until he bawked!" He imitated the bawking chicken, complete with flapping wings, but the stunt didn't get the cascade of giggles it had while they'd been in the restaurant off the highway.

"Come on, now, Judah," Kelly said, reaching for his hand. "I bet Mr. Ronald would like to hear about your trip to the fire station. We have a lot to do to get the house ready for lights out, so say goodbye to your friends."

Friends? Was that what they were to him? The thought sucker-punched Chloe.

Judah hung his head from one side to the other. "Bye," he whispered.

Travis put out both hands for a double high-five, their standard way of saying hello and goodbye, but Chloe had to reach down and squeeze his little body with love. She added a kiss on his cheek, which was probably against some dumb foster kid rule, but she didn't know when she'd see him again.

And he didn't even know he was leaving, which would destroy him.

Still holding him, she looked up at Mae, who gave an infinitesimal shake of her head, which Chloe interpreted as an instruction not to say anything just yet. She'd let Kelly break the news, and wipe the ensuing tears.

"Bye," Judah repeated, patting her back like he was the one giving comfort.

She straightened slowly and backed away with another wave, watching Kelly take him inside.

They stood with Mae, and Chloe waited for her to

tell Travis the news but she just took a deep, slow inhale, silent.

"He's being moved to another home in Fort Myers," Chloe finally said softly. "Sometime this week."

Travis's jaw loosened as he blinked and processed that.

"So, we may not see him for a while," she added. "Or you, Mae. Thank you for all you've done for us and for Judah."

The woman nodded, clearly emotional. "Judah loves you two. You'd make great—"

Travis held his hand up to stop her. "Wait. Wait. *What*? He's moving?"

"This house is jammed and Kelly is ready to break, so we've done some shuffling and we're moving him," Mae said. "There's nothing we can do unless he gets an adoption placement or a foster family opens up."

For a long moment, Travis just stared at her, his face growing pale and the small vein in his neck throbbing.

"We need to go," he said gruffly, reaching for Chloe. "Right now."

A little stunned by that, she leaned in and gave Mae a quick hug. "We'll be in touch," Chloe promised, and let Travis hustle her back to the truck.

She climbed in the passenger side, waiting as he settled behind the wheel, staring ahead, his Adam's apple rising and falling like he was fighting the same sob threatening to come out of her.

"One caveat," he said.

She shook her head. "Excuse me?"

"I have one simple requirement before we go in there and declare that kid is ours. Foster, adoption, forever, whatever. One condition."

And it didn't matter a lick what it was. "Yes," she rasped, her eyes stinging with hope and the sense that they were truly turning a corner.

He turned to her. "I haven't told you what it is."

"I don't care, Travis. I don't care if I have to fly to the moon and bring back a rock. I don't care if I have to run through Times Square naked. I don't care if we have to move, change, empty our bank accounts, or stand on our heads. I don't care! I love that child and I want to—"

"Marry me."

She gasped.

"We can't raise him separately. We have to be his parents, a unit, a family. I won't let history repeat itself with single parents and...instability. I want to be the father to Judah that mine wasn't to me and there is no way in heaven or hell I can do that without you, so we have to get...Chloe?" He lifted his hand, swiping a tear she didn't know had fallen.

"You heard me," she said in a hushed whisper. "Yes."

His face lit up as he threw his arms around her and pulled her closer and both of them let go of the tears they'd been holding in since...well, since the moment they met the boy who would become their son.

Chapter Nineteen

Susannah

We have news.

Susannah stared at Madeline's text for the longest time, a little unwilling to let a lovely Friday afternoon on the deck be ruined by...whatever Adam and his team of FBI friends had learned about Ivy Button.

Raina's doorbell camera had given them a blurry image, but Adam seemed certain it was enough to begin the process of learning more about their nemesis. It had taken some time, but he had said a few days ago they were making progress and he'd be getting a report before the end of the week.

That must be the news. But was it good? Wouldn't Madeline have said so?

Susannah turned as she heard Rex's footsteps behind her as he walked through the French doors to join her in their favorite sitting area, ready to watch evening fall over the coastline of Amelia Island.

"Okay, this is not Tori-level charcuterie, but—"

"You made a board?"

"I sliced cheese, found crackers, opened olives, and

finished that hummus in the fridge—the one without peppers, I promise. Oh, I threw on some grapes for decoration and you can call it what you want. Charcuterie sounds a little upscale for this mess." He set the tray on the coffee table, careful not to tip two champagne flutes or the large bottle of Pellegrino that would be used to fill them. "I call it a celebration of life."

"It's perfect, Rex, but 'celebration of life' sounds like a funeral."

"Which..." He bent over and kissed her on the top of her head. "It most certainly is not, and I have every scan, probe, test result, and medical opinion to prove it." He straightened and grinned toward the ocean, his shoulders seeming broader this afternoon.

She suspected that was because they'd met with his cardiology and neurology teams today and was given a perfect bill of health.

Except for a little heartburn, which he could manage by skipping certain foods, like peppers and alcohol, which they agreed was a small sacrifice for a long life ahead.

Rex was happy with the news, but repeatedly said he wasn't surprised. Susannah, on the other hand, cried for joy in the car all the way home.

"I really had no idea how worried I was," she admitted, smiling up at him. "But not anymore."

"No worries for Wingates," he said with true Rex confidence. "And now I can take that Ivy Button creature to the mat and fight her all the way to the Supreme Court if I have to."

If they did that, Susannah knew it would be ugly. Maybe Rex could handle it physically. But emotionally? She wasn't sure.

"That may happen sooner than you think," she said, holding up her phone as he sat next to her.

"She called you?"

"No, but Madeline and Adam said they have news."

"What kind of news?"

"I don't know. There's no adjective like...good, happy, life-changing, or wretched. Just news."

"When do we find out what it is?" Rex twisted the sparkling water open and poured it with the same flourish he'd use if it were Moët. "Get them over here. I can add to my board if they're hungry."

She let out a sigh and wrinkled her nose. "Is it wrong that I don't want to think about that nastiness on the horizon and just gaze happily at this one?" She gestured toward the blue-on-blue slice of sea and sky in front of them. "You are completely healthy and I want to bask in that for today."

"I'd be healthier if I heard good news," Rex said, picking up a champagne flute and offering the bubbly water to her for a toast. "To the future," Rex said, dinging their crystals. "May it be filled with love, laughter, daughters, sons-in-law, and so many grandchildren, we lose count of them all."

She just smiled, but the tears stung again.

"More waterworks?" he joked.

"I just love you and want to protect you, Rex. It's what I've always wanted." She sipped when he did, setting down the glass and leaning back to watch the waves crash on the sand.

"What you've protected," Rex said after he took a drink, "is the Wingate family name."

She threw him a look, not sure what he meant.

"Obviously, you've been the best imaginable mother," he continued. "But you've cared so deeply about the family name all these years. From the day I told you I was Rex Wingate—"

"After you walked out on your check at the Riverfront Café without telling me you *owned* the place," she reminded him with a laugh. "I had to march after you to get my seven dollars and forty-two cents."

"But I slipped you a five-dollar tip."

"That's what your grandson Zach would call a flex."

He chuckled. "I remember turning around when I heard this high-pitched squawk of, 'Hey, Mister! Hey! You didn't pay your bill!'"

"How was I supposed to know you were a Wingate? I'd only been on Amelia Island about a week or two, dead broke after running away from Georgia, and so happy to have been hired at the waterfront diner. I couldn't lose that job because I let some hotshot guy in a suit flirt with me."

"How could I not?" Rex countered. "You were so perky and cute and had that fresh-out-of-Savannah Southern accent."

"But you could have paid or at least told me you had the same name as the street."

"I did!" His dark eyes danced with mirth at the

memory they never tired of sharing. He pointed upwards to an imaginary street sign, exactly as he'd done that day when she'd demanded to know just who the heck he thought he was. "And that changed—"

"Everything," she said on a sigh. "And not because I was impressed by your money or businesses."

"I know." He reached for her hand. "From Day One, you had a bone-deep respect for my family's reputation. You honored the name far more than some people who were born with it."

She closed her eyes, remembering how she'd felt when she learned the heritage and history of the Wingates.

"I came from nothing, Rex," she said, even though this wasn't news to him. "And I felt shame for my family. My father was a drunk who never contributed a thing to his community and I always longed for the self-respect that I imagined came with having a solid name and family."

"I knew that." He squeezed her hand. "I sensed that from the moment I met you. And I was terrified to ask you on a date because I had so much baggage."

"Four daughters." She smiled. "Hardly baggage. Four amazing, beautiful, spectacular daughters who..." She made a face. "I never adopted."

"Excuse me?" he scoffed.

"You know I never did the paperwork. Sadie came along, then Grace, and Chloe. We were too busy and—"

"Does it matter now?" Rex asked with that pragmatic look he gave when she got just a tad too emotional.

"I guess not, but..." She sighed. "It's a small regret in a life with very few of them. I wouldn't hate it if the four older girls called me Mom."

"Just ask them to."

"Well, it's a little late after forty years."

"Why didn't you ask them to when they were little?"

"Oh, I don't know. Out of respect for Charlotte, I suppose. But maybe it was deeper than that." She thought about it, then nodded as the thoughts formed.

"I wasn't sure I could be a mother," she admitted on a whisper. "My own disappeared when I was a child and I had no role model other than TV moms or women I observed doing the job. I wasn't sure I could earn the title, and 'Suze' rolled off their lips."

He studied her for a long time, his gaze full of affection. "Didn't hurt your relationship with them. You couldn't be closer to those four daughters, or the three you gave birth to."

"No, I couldn't." She glanced at the phone lighting up on the table. "Oh, it's Madeline. Hang on."

She tapped the screen and put it on speaker. "Hey, there—"

"Can we come over?" Madeline asked without preamble. "We want to tell you what Adam found out."

"Is it good or bad news?" Susannah asked, holding Rex's gaze.

"Just...news."

Oh, that did not sound good.

"Come over now," Rex said, leaning closer to the phone. "We're on the deck."

"Good. We're in the driveway. Be right up."

They didn't say anything, but looked at each other with that insanely deep connection that started under that street sign more than forty years ago, and showed no signs of ending.

"Whatever it is," Rex said softly, "we'll handle it together."

"You bet we will," she agreed, standing when she saw Adam and Madeline walking up the side steps, hand in hand.

"Hey, Suze." Madeline reached for her and gave a warm hug, and Susannah fleetingly wondered how it would feel if she'd said, "Hey, Mom," instead.

Different? Better? She'd never know. Plus, there were far more important things to discuss.

They gathered around the coffee table and charcuterie, but no one seemed interested in chatting or enjoying appetizers. Adam's expression was too serious.

"Doreen Parrish does have a sister," he started after a beat. "Her name is Felicity Button and she does live in a very expensive private assisted-living facility in Minneapolis."

Susannah felt her heart drop. "So, that much of Ivy's story is true. I wonder why Doreen never mentioned a sister. She never even took a vacation or time off to visit family."

"We may never know," he said. "Felicity has dementia and has been going downhill rapidly this past year. The sisters were raised in Yulee."

Rex nodded. "I recall that Doreen was from the mainland."

"No father that anyone knows of, but their mother died when they were young. Doreen came here, got a job at the inn, and Felicity followed a guy she was dating up to Minneapolis. Not sure if that's the same person she married, but she does have one daughter."

"Ivy?" Susannah asked.

"Her legal married name is Olivia Button Beattie, but..." He swallowed. "Ivy is her nickname."

Susannah dropped back with a grunt. "So her story holds up."

"It gets worse," Madeline said softly, sharing a look with her husband.

How could it, Susannah wondered. But she just squeezed the armrests of her chair and waited for whatever bomb they'd drop.

"I spoke with a nurse at the assisted-living facility," Adam said. "She confirmed that Ivy is a frequent visitor, that she has dark hair and is petite, and that for years, Felicity received letters from her sister in Florida. They stopped about a year ago."

Rex closed his eyes. "Then they're real letters," he said.

"We simply have to prove they're full of lies," Susannah countered. "Because you didn't assault that woman and I don't know why she would say you did."

"A million reasons," Rex murmured. "She wasn't that bright and maybe it seemed harmless to her to make up a story like the romance novels she read. Maybe she was jealous of anyone who came near me—including both my wives. You were her boss at Wingate House, Suze, and constantly had run-ins because no housekeeper in the county wanted to work for her."

Susannah groaned and put her head in her hands.

"Don't give up yet," Madeline said.

"*I'm* not giving up," Rex insisted. "Whatever she wrote was a lie and we have to prove that. I just don't know how you interrogate a dead woman."

"We do," Adam said with the confidence of a former FBI agent. "We'll comb the letters for inconsistencies, and I've called in a favor with a special agent in St. Paul, who agreed to snoop around Ivy's life, home, family, whatever he can find. I have her phone number and current address. If she's been caught in lies before, we'll find out."

"But when?" Madeline asked, voicing what they were all thinking. "By the time we've cleared Dad's name, real damage could have been done."

"Rex Wingate's name stands on its own," Susannah declared, taking his hand. "And regardless of what it puts us through, we will make sure this lie doesn't stick."

Rex pressed her knuckles to his cheek. "Thank you, Suze. There's no one else I'd rather have by my side in battle. And that, my dear wife, has been true since that fateful and wonderful day we met."

She didn't want this fight, but now that she had it? She'd win it. For Rex. For her family. For the Wingate name.

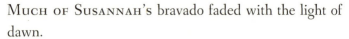

Much of Susannah's bravado faded with the light of dawn.

After a long and mostly sleepless night, she was back on her beachfront deck, watching her husband dive into the Atlantic Ocean, as he did every morning. At this time of year, the water wasn't freezing, only a bit chilly at sunrise, but he still loved his "cold plunge therapy."

In fact, he'd told his medical team yesterday that he credited the morning routine with his clean bill of health. They'd humored him with smiles and nods, but Rex believed in his morning dips that left him shivering on the sand.

Susannah didn't feel the same about a morning swim, but she had taken to standing here at the deck railing almost every morning. She could breathe in the salt-infused air and keep an eye on the man she loved as he walked down to the sea and stepped into the waves.

This morning—especially after the medical meeting—she wasn't watching for him to clutch his chest or falter on the sand. She wanted to see if his shoulders were still square with steadfast resolve or if he hung his head in dread of the war they had to fight with some stranger who...just appeared.

Why hadn't this Olivia "Ivy" Button Beattie looked up her Aunt Doreen sooner? What kind of relationship did Doreen and Felicity really have? Why wait a year to press for the transfer of the deed? Why steal a house or wear filthy sneakers when your mother could afford a private assisted-living facility?

She hated the circular thoughts and unanswered questions that had haunted her all night. She'd rather watch Rex. She'd rather let the rising sun warm her face. She'd rather do anything—

"You're here every day, aren't you?"

Susannah gasped and whipped around to see the familiar and unwelcome face of Ivy Button coming up the side stairs to the deck.

"What are you doing here?" she asked on a shocked breath.

"You're *never* not with him," Ivy said. "Trust me, I keep an eye on your comings and goings, Suze, and this is the one sliver of time I can get you without Rex."

Her heart slammed against her ribs as she backed against the railing.

"Why don't you want to talk to Rex?" Susannah asked. "Are you scared of him?"

"Of Sexy Rexy? That's what my aunt said everyone called him."

Did they? She'd never heard the expression and he said it was a handle hung on him by fraternity brothers in college. Doreen could have known that, though. He was in college when...when this all happened.

"What do you want from me?" Susannah asked, forcing strength into a voice that felt like it could easily waver.

Ivy notched a thin brown upwards. "To avoid the

trouble of what you know I can do to this family," she said. "Put my name on the deed and let's call this thing."

The deed that Raina had located and was on Susannah's desk.

Yes, it would be easy, but what kind of "warrior" would it make her to give up so easily?

"Over my dead body," Susannah ground out.

Ivy's eyes flickered just enough to make Susannah's blood run cold.

"I had a feeling you'd be difficult," the other woman said on a sigh, taking a split-second look at the water, but Susannah didn't take her eyes off Ivy.

Was she scared of Rex? She didn't want to face him. Why not? Had they met before? Did she know him from work or life or was she just intimidated because he was so much more formidable than Susannah?

Ivy crossed her arms and cocked her head. "Then why don't we make a deal, Suze?"

Susannah drew back, not expecting that.

"Raina offered money," Ivy said. "I think that would be easier for you."

Really. Well, now she was truly getting into blackmail territory.

"You guys are loaded." Ivy flipped a hand at the expansive beach house. "Let's come up with a number. Say three hundred thousand? Four? I can be reasonable."

Reasonable? She was out of her ever-loving mind. Disgust rolled through Susannah as a powerful realization hit. Ivy wanted to negotiate? Why? To pay for the assisted-living facility?

It didn't matter. Right now, Susannah had the upper hand. She just needed to figure out how to use it.

"So, can I take your silence as a yes, Suze?"

"No."

"Then let me up the ante." She took a few steps closer. "Because I've been having conversations with a nice lady named Helen from a law firm that handles adoptions and such."

Her heart slid around in her chest as she waited for the rest.

"And it occurred to me that if I showed up at the hearing scheduled for...Monday, is it?"

Raina and Chase's adoption was on the books for Monday morning at the courthouse. They'd already planned to attend as a family to celebrate Chase becoming Charlie and Lily's father.

"Well, I could cause some trouble, don't you think?" Ivy asked. "The judge will offer up time for open commentary and ask if there's anyone who has objections. I know this is true, because my friend Helen told me."

Susannah just stared at her, her pulse pounding so hard she could barely hear what the woman was saying.

"Unless we work out...an arrangement."

"A three- or four-hundred-thousand-dollar arrangement," Susannah said under her breath, suddenly wondering if they could get that much money if they cashed out some investments.

Because now it wasn't about Rex's reputation, but Raina's babies and their father!

They stared at each other for a few heartbeats, then Ivy stole another glance at the water, almost, but not completely, hiding her reaction. Suze turned, too, just in time to see Rex step out of the frothy waves and reach for the neatly folded towel he'd left next to his sandals.

"Think about it, Suze. Fast. Clock's ticking." She turned and started to walk away, while Susannah clung to the railing.

They could get that kind of money and this nightmare could be over. All she had to do was say yes, because if she ruined Chase's adoption...

"Ivy," she called, but there wasn't enough force in her voice and the woman kept walking. "Olivia!" she shouted.

Nothing made a person hesitate like the use of their full given name.

But not Ivy. She didn't even react. She just disappeared to the bottom of the steps and around the house.

Susannah sucked in a soft breath, a sudden realization hitting her. Ivy didn't know her name. That changed everything.

Now she knew exactly what to do with that upper hand...and pray it hit the target that was just revealed to her.

Chapter Twenty

Sadie

Was it the new cocoa nibs? The latest batch of lavender? Or just that last rush of tourists that put Sadie over the edge?

Whatever was eating away at her, she just wanted to curl up in a ball, drink green tea, and sleep. Or cry. Or relax. Or...something.

And since when did she like green tea? Since never, but she kept thinking about it lately.

On a heavy sigh, she held up her hands to the empty kitchen and mentally called it a day at just after six. After all, it was Saturday and she had a night crew to run the store for the tourists who brought the shops of downtown Fernandina Beach to life when the sun set.

But all Sadie wanted to do was sleep, which wasn't easy when the apartment upstairs faced that lively town. She'd go to Scout's for sure, where it was quiet and secluded and they could cuddle up and watch a movie and talk. And *sleep*.

He'd left a while ago to pick up Kitty and Val from the airport, still debating if he should be completely honest with the adventures of Rhett Butler. If Sadie were a betting woman, she'd put her life savings on the fact that he would—Scout didn't have a disingenuous bone in his body.

Just as she was taking off her apron, the shop door dinged with a new arrival, making her look up and smile at the sight of her baby sister looking...anxious or excited. Something had lit a fire in Chloe Wingate's sky blue eyes.

Regardless of her current state of exhaustion, Sadie flipped her apron on the counter and hustled out to the front, waving to her sister as she came around the display counter.

"Chloe, are you—"

"Getting married!" she announced, loud enough to get a few smiles from the three customers in line.

"What?" Sadie flattened her hands on her chest as if the news nearly pushed her right back through the kitchen door. "That's fantastic!"

"But that's just half of it. We're officially filing the paperwork to become Judah's legal guardians on Monday!"

Sadie bit back a totally unprofessional squeal and danced a little, getting even more amused looks from her customers and cashier.

"Come here, come here!" She grabbed Chloe's hand and pulled her through the swinging door back to the kitchen for privacy and a big, fat hug.

"Congrats!" she exclaimed, throwing her arms around Chloe so they could squeeze and sway and squish each other with joy. "Chloe Wingate, you're getting married!"

When they finally separated, both of them had tears in their eyes.

"You're happy for me?" Chloe asked.

"What? Of course!" Sadie squeezed her again. "You won the lottery, Chloe! Great guy, adorable boy, and you have...the thing."

Chloe laughed. "We sure do have the thing."

They hugged again, ending on a sisterly sigh.

"Am I the first to know?" Sadie asked, suddenly realizing that there hadn't been any buzz on the 7 *Sis* group chat.

"You are."

"Why? Are you asking me to be maid of honor? 'Cause I'm pretty sure we have an unwritten Wingate rule that it's six sisters or nothing. But please, Chloe! Not in Pepto Bismol pink again!"

Chloe giggled at the memory. "That was my last fiancé. This one wants it way low-key and fast. No, I just wanted to tell you first because we need a witness for the guardianship, which is step one of an official adoption. Someone who'll vouch for us, and sign an affidavit stating we will be loving and responsible parents."

"And you will! I'd love to have that role, Chloe. It's *almost* like being maid of honor. When are you telling everyone?"

"Actually, we want to wait until the paperwork's filed and all the T's are crossed and I's are dotted. With Raina and Chase doing the baby thing and the whole Ivy situation, we thought we should wait to announce. But I had to tell you."

"Oh, my goodness, Chloe, I'm so happy." Sadie sighed, beaming at her baby sister.

"You're sure?" Chloe pressed.

"Yes! Why would you even ask that?"

Taking Sadie's hand, Chloe pulled her closer. "You've seemed off these past few weeks and I didn't want to throw you, since I know you've been trying to figure things out with Scout."

"That's sweet and considerate and I expect nothing less from you, but..." She thought about it, nodding. "You know, I think the whole Rhett Butler ordeal got to me. A lot of stress and, yeah, Scout..."

"What about him?"

"He's kind of...serious."

"And you're not?" Chloe asked.

"It's weird, because normally, I would be. His declaration of love was just swoony, if I must say so."

"And the problem is..."

"Everything is swoony," she said on a laugh. "I just feel so lightheaded all the time, like my feet aren't touching the ground and I kind of feel nauseous and all I want to do is close my eyes and lay down. But when I do, I feel dizzy. And I can't eat, but I really want to."

Chloe was staring at her, a mix of amusement and maybe a little shock in her eyes.

"Is that...the thing?" Sadie asked.

"If the thing is a *baby*, then maybe, yeah."

"A..." Sadie threw her arms up with a noisy gasp. "A... did you say...Chloe, *am I pregnant?*"

Chloe laughed. "I think you're the only person who can answer that, Sadie. I mean, unless you're sick."

"Only when I pass the nib grinder. The smell of chocolate makes me..." She tapped her belly with horror and disbelief. "I thought maybe I just had too much of it."

"I think it's Scout you've had too much of," she cracked.

"Stop! This is serious! How can I have a baby?"

"I'm guessing the usual way," Chloe quipped. "But then, who am I to talk? I'm having a five-year-old."

The nausea rolled again, but this time...it kind of made sense.

"Do you have a test?" Chloe asked.

"A test? No. I...I..." She shook her head. "It's been a while since I've had a period," she admitted. "A long while. Like...I can't remember when I had one."

Chloe looked astonished. "You don't track them? There are apps for that, you know."

"I haven't...well, Scout and I just...it would be so soon, Chloe. Only a month or so. Is that possible?"

"Did you not pay attention when our mother taught us the facts of life? Of course it's possible! Especially for you, Miss Spontaneous. You spontaneously conceived."

It was Sadie's turn to give a look. "Not *exactly*."

Chloe laughed and added a hug. "It's fine. It happens."

And it just might have happened to Sadie.

She backed away from the hug, suddenly burning with the need to know. "Where can I get a test?"

"Walgreens or CVS, I guess. Want me to drive you? 'Cause, honey, you're in no condition to go yourself." Chloe stood and put her arms around Sadie, giving her a squeeze. "And what if you are? What are you going to do?"

She blinked, nowhere near close to considering the ramifications of...*a baby.*

"I guess...I don't know. Drive me. Take me. I need to think."

They hopped in Sadie's car in the back lot, but she let Chloe drive. She tried to have a conversation—ask about the unorthodox engagement, get more details on Judah—but she couldn't do small-talk.

Not when something this big was on the horizon.

Of course it was possible! Unlikely, shocking, but it was certainly possible.

"Anyway, to answer a question you asked a lifetime ago," Chloe said as they pulled into the pharmacy parking lot, "our wedding will be small and simple. I don't want to do the whole St. Peter's thing again. I'm still scarred from my last walk down the aisle, U-turn and all. I should be the one terrified of getting married, not you."

"I'm not terrified," Sadie said quickly.

"Aren't you?" Chloe challenged. "I mean, Scout is, well, he's the second-greatest unmarried guy on Amelia Island, if you ask me. He's good as gold, caring, funny, talented, and looks at you like he's never seen a more beautiful woman in his life and—"

"He's ordinary," Sadie whispered.

Chloe choked. "Sadie, you think that's a bad thing?"

"I don't. It's the greatest thing. It's the perfect thing. It's the real thing, and it's what every woman wants, needs, and deserves," Sadie whispered the last word. "Except...do I?"

Chloe turned off the ignition and whipped to face her. "Are you asking if you deserve love, Sadie Wingate? Because I will lecture you so hard, you *will* throw up in this car."

"Don't suggest things you aren't willing to clean up."

"I'm dead serious. You are so deserving of love. Why would you even question that?"

"I don't know," she said, feeling deeply honest as she said the words. "But Tristan really, really messed me up. I know it looked like I just recovered in a flash, opened the chocolate shop, and started falling for Scout. But I loved Tristan—or the idea of him. And his family made it their life's mission to drive home how unworthy I was of his love."

Chloe winced. "I hate those billionaires."

"And then I land Martin Jacobson! Literally the nicest guy in the universe."

"Martin?" She lifted a brow, but slipped into a smile. "Girl, you cannot give Tristan the power to hold you back. You made a mistake. And I say that as a bona fide runaway bride. We make mistakes, but they can't haunt us forever."

"At least you backed out at the last minute. I signed paperwork and clung to hope and gave him my secret ingredient. And he still allowed his family to erase our marriage from the face of the earth."

"Forgive yourself, Sadie." Chloe reached over the console and took her hand. "You will heal from that. And I can't think of a better way than as a wife and mother."

Sadie put her hand up to her mouth, realizing just then how much she wanted...this. Scout. A baby. Stability. A beautiful, safe, perfectly *ordinary* life.

Biting back tears, she nodded. "I'm going to take the test at Scout's, with him. I want to be with him when I find out."

"Good call," Chloe said, reaching for her seatbelt. "Come on. Let's get a few, just in case one's wrong."

Sadie let out a little squeal of joy when she saw Scout's car parked in his driveway. He was back from the airport, and it was time—time to tell him those three words she'd been holding back for no reason she could truly understand.

And they weren't "I am pregnant."

She could say those later, but first, she wanted to take that man's hands, look him in the eye, and tell him what she'd known for weeks...but apparently pregnancy hormones had pickled her brain.

I love you, Scout Jacobson!

Holding the CVS bag in one hand and her purse in the other, she darted out of the car and practically danced to his front door, twisting the knob with a smile from ear to ear.

And that smile disappeared in an instant.

"Hello...Kitty." She stared at the woman visible on the couch from the front door, petting Rhett Butler.

"Oh, hello, Sadie."

Disappointment thudded down to her feet. "Welcome back," Sadie added, so she didn't sound as sad as she felt. "Where's Scout?"

"He drove Val over to Raina's house but I couldn't wait for one more moment to see my little baby, Rhett, so he dropped me off here for a reunion. And we're enjoying our time together!" She lifted the cat by the belly so his front and back legs hung limply and he let out a yowl of unhappiness. "Yes, I know you missed me!"

"He sure did."

Kitty lowered the cat and gave a disapproving look over her glasses. "Don't lie to me, Sadie. Scout told me everything."

"Of course he did." And that, she decided in her heart, was why she loved him. That and so many other reasons. "What did he tell you?" she asked, letting herself all the way in as she casually stuffed the CVS bag carrying three pregnancy tests into her purse.

"*Everything*," she repeated with slow emphasis. "From beginning to end. Including the part about you wanting to fool me with another orange cat."

Whoa, he *had* told her everything.

"I wasn't serious," she said. "And Rhett's little adventure wasn't a bad thing, you know."

"Oh, I know. Nothing bad about my little darling running off into the night—"

"It was daytime."

"—only to be kidnapped by a stranger."

"The neighbor's really nice cleaning lady, who had no idea Rhett was staying here."

"Then he was hidden in the bowels of south Amelia Island with a recluse who could have been a mass murderer for all I know."

Sadie snorted, so not wanting to deal with this right now. "Hank wouldn't hurt a fly and he renamed your baby Elvis, but only temporarily."

"Still." She stuck her face in Rhett's and shook her head but, of course, her hair-sprayed helmet didn't move. "It was *vewwwy twaumatic!*"

Sadie rolled her eyes at the baby talk.

"It was a demonstration," she said to Kitty, who gave her a sharp, questioning look. "A demonstration that Scout would have moved heaven and Earth for that cat. He was destroyed at the idea of hurting you, or Rhett. He lost sleep, didn't eat, missed hours of work, and shed real tears of worry. Nothing mattered to him but finding Rhett Butler."

Kitty stared at her, then stood up very slowly, cuddling a cat who clearly did not want to be nestled to her bosom. "He said the same thing about you."

"He did? Well, I was worried about him, so..."

A smile tugged. "Gayla would approve."

"Scout's mother?" she asked, remembering the late baker's name, though they'd never met.

"She was my best friend," Kitty said. "I mean, until Val came along. I have such a fondness for women with whip-sharp tongues and a sarcastic sense of humor."

Sadie smiled at the dead-on description of Raina's former mother-in-law and the new insight into the woman who'd raised Scout.

"Funny women are fun," she agreed.

"But it wasn't that. Gayla had a huge heart. Huge. Like her son."

Both of them sat down again and Sadie resigned herself to the conversation, trying to forget about the pregnancy test—tests—burning a hole in her bag.

"He does have a good heart," Sadie agreed. "And it was on full display with Rhett Butler."

"It's on full display with you," the other woman said softly.

Sadie smiled at that, not sure how to respond.

"It was Gayla's deepest wish, you know. All she wanted was for Scout to find someone who could truly love him. I mean, let's be real, he's not a hunk and a half."

Sadie sat up a little. "He's very cute!"

"Yes, if you like that...what do the kids call it? A Dad bod? And he's forty and kind of nerdy and drives—I don't even know what that little thing is."

"A Toyota."

"Right. And look at Raina, engaged to Chase Madison, who is handsome and drives a Mercedes."

"Who cares what he drives? Does that matter?" Sadie fired back at her. "I'm not comparing my boyfriend to any of the men in my family. If I'm comparing him to anyone, it's the last guy I thought I loved—rich, handsome, and... and...extraordinary."

Kitty shrugged. "Oh, the Belgian chocolate guy. Yes. Now he sounds like the kind of guy a Wingate woman would love."

"Then you don't know us at all," Sadie replied. "The men we love are good-hearted, steady, kind, patient, and wonderful. Just like our father. And Scout is all those things and I love him with every fiber of my being. I'd be insane not to! Men like Scout come along once in a lifetime, and I intend to keep him for mine. I love everything about him...so...so..."

A throat cleared noisily. "One more time for the guy at the door who didn't get to record that."

She turned to see Scout standing at the open door, with no idea how long he'd been listening. But it didn't matter. She meant every word.

He stepped inside, his eyes glistening with unshed tears. Of course they were, because his ordinary heart was not only good, it was soft.

"I better be going," Kitty said, putting Rhett in the carrier. "Scout, can you drive me?"

He flipped her the keys without taking his eyes off Sadie, a move that was pretty darn cool for a guy with a Dad bod.

"Take yourself, Kitty. Sadie and I will be over later to get my car." He took a few steps closer, his arms out, his gaze locked. "We have some things to talk about."

Kitty couldn't fight a smile as she looked from one to the other, then zipped the carrier closed.

"We can tell when we're not wanted, right, Mr. Butler? Thank you for trying to babysit him and not replacing him with an imposter and...and..." She smiled wider. "And good luck, you two. You deserve each other and I say that in the kindest way I know. Good people belong together. Bye!"

She stepped out with the carrier, and closed the door. Not one second too soon, either.

Scout pulled Sadie closer and kissed her on the mouth, hugging her like she might slip away and he had no intention of letting that happen.

"Say everything again," he murmured against her lips. "Really slowly and with all the pretty words."

She laughed at his sweet desperation. "I will, many times." Putting her palm on his cheek, she looked into his eyes and finally said the words she so deeply meant. "I love you, Martin Jacobson."

He let out a noisy sigh. "Aw, Sadie. I love you, too."

"And..." She reached down to her purse, open on the sofa, and pulled out the CVS bag. "There's something in here that might interest you."

"Really? You got me a present?" He looked down at the bag.

"Maybe. I'll have to take the test."

He looked up, shock in his eyes, then opened the bag to see what was inside.

"Oh. Oh! *Oh!*"

"Yeah, I bought three in case we don't believe the first two."

He tossed the bag on the sofa, reaching for her. "I don't care."

"You don't...*care?* That I might be pregnant?"

"I don't care what that test says. Positive, negative, maybe. Because no matter what it says, Sadie Wingate, you are going to marry me and have the most ordinary and happy life a woman has ever had."

She slid into his embrace, laying a head on his soft shoulder.

"Yeah," she whispered. "I am."

"Now, take the test." He kissed her forehead. "Because nothing about our baby is going to be *ordinary*."

Chapter Twenty-one

Raina

Where was Susannah?

How could she not be here yet?

Since the judge hadn't yet left his chambers, Raina looked around the small courtroom from her vantage point at the front table between their attorney, Tim Sherwood, and Chase.

"I have to find out where my mother is," she leaned over to whisper to Chase. "She can't miss the second half of this hearing."

"She'll be here," he assured her. "What could be more important?"

"Nothing, but remember, she doesn't know the surprise I'm cooking up at the end." Standing, Raina quickly scanned the familiar faces scattered through a few rows of mahogany seating, sun-washed by the large windows along the second floor of the Old Nassau County Courthouse.

From two rows behind Raina, Rose gave a hopeful, excited wave. She tenderly lifted baby Lily, who was doing her best to get the pink ribbon off her head.

"You got this, Raindrop!" Rose stage-whispered while her daughters, Alyson and Avery, giggled over Lily and the hair bow. Next to them, Gabe and the boys sat solemnly in their Sunday best in the same row.

With two fingers to her lips, Raina blew the crew a kiss, then mouthed, "Where's Suze?"

From behind Rose, flanked by her fiancé and her two teens, Tori leaned forward, concern in her eyes, Charlie in her arms.

"I haven't heard a word!" she whispered.

Chloe and Sadie weren't here yet, either, but they'd both texted the 7 *Sis* group chat to say that they had a quick errand and promised to be there as soon as they could.

Once again, Raina had to wonder what could be more important than six adoptions.

They knew that Raina had planned the big surprise for Susannah, so maybe they were getting flowers? Balloons? Something?

Just then, Dad and Madeline walked in, deep in conversation—but without Susannah! Unable to stop herself, Raina pushed her chair back and darted down the aisle to talk to them.

"Good luck, Raina," Grace called as she passed, looking up from the book she was flipping through with Nikki Lou on her lap.

Raina smiled and gave her sister a thumbs-up and the same to Blake and Dani, sitting further down with smiles of love and support.

Behind Grace, Valerie Wallace, looking fresh from her weeks abroad, reached out a hand.

As much as Raina wanted to get to Dad, she had to stop and acknowledge how incredibly sweet it was of her former mother-in-law to be here.

"Thank you, Val," she said, leaning over to give her a kiss. "You're an angel for this."

Yes, the babies were Val's grandchildren—but their biological father was her son. And for her to stand with Raina and support another man adopting them showed just how much Val's formerly crusty heart had softened.

"But where is their other grandmother?" Val asked.

"I'm trying to figure that out," she replied, just as Dad barked something to Madeline, his face flushed. "'Scuze me."

She rushed to Madeline and Dad. "You still don't know where she is?" Raina asked.

"He's called her ten times and so have I," Madeline said. "She left at seven while Dad was in the shower and didn't say where she was going. How weird is that?"

"It's got to do with that Ivy woman," Dad grumbled. "I just know she's trying to put an end to this, even though I'm willing to go to court to fight her."

"She'd do that *now*?" Raina asked, having a hard time believing her mother would put that situation above this moment, even if she had no idea that Raina was planning a surprise. "Plus, she told me she was resolute that she was fighting that woman through legal measures."

"I don't know," Dad said, shaking his head with palpable frustration. "She left a note that said she'd meet me here. I just wish she'd answer my texts. The only thing that would keep her from answering is if she's driving. But where would she go?"

"Where's Adam?" Raina asked Madeline.

"He had to take a call, which he said was an emergency, and he took off to handle it. He did tell me that Susannah had asked for the phone number and address the FBI found for Ivy Button in Minnesota, but she didn't drive there, for heaven's sake."

Raina sighed, not liking the way this was going at all.

"You'd better get seated," she told Dad and Madeline, ushering them to the row in front of Grace and Isaiah. "She has to show up soon."

"From your lips to God's ears," her father said.

"Then I hope He's listening," she replied softly.

Isaiah leaned forward and gave his typical huge smile. "Oh, He's listening, Raina. And He's got this. Probably in a way you've never imagined, but that's how our Lord works."

"Thanks, brother." She put a hand on his sturdy shoulder, so grateful to have this man of faith in their family. "I want you to be right."

Next to him, Grace chuckled. "Trust me—and God. He's right."

Clinging to their confidence, Raina hustled to the front table but she'd barely hit the chair when the back door slammed open with force, making every head in the place swivel, except Raina's. She just closed her eyes and said a silent prayer, grateful Isaiah had been right.

But when she turned to give her mother a "where have you been" scowl, her gasp was the loudest of all.

Ivy Button stood in the back of the room, her beady gaze straight ahead.

That was awful enough, but what really made Raina sick was the fact that Hyphenated Helen, who held her fate in her hands, was right next to her. And behind them, two writers for the local newspaper that Raina knew personally.

A breath whooshed out of Raina's mouth. This just got...*ugly*.

"All rise for the Honorable Francis John Strayton."

Raina was so frozen in shock that Chase had to take her by the arm and ease her up when the judge walked in.

A gray-haired man well past sixty and a local well-known to this group, Judge Strayton gave a warm smile as he took the bench. He wore a dark suit and tie, with no robes or overt formality, as if to remind them that this was a happy occasion—no crimes, no sentencing, no victims. They were here for adoptions.

She *hoped*.

She squeezed Chase's hand. "Do you see—"

"Yeah. But first things first, Raina." His dark eyes shuttered as he swallowed. "I want my girls. I want my daughters."

The words touched her, along with his calm but determined demeanor, and that excellent advice. She couldn't do anything about Ivy or Helen or her missing mother and two sisters.

What mattered was this man who loved her—and her

babies—so much that he wanted to take the wholehearted responsibility of being their father on his broad shoulders.

The "four sisters" adoption was icing on the cake, but this was the real reason they were in the room.

The judge flipped open a file. "The matter before this court is the formal adoption of minors Lillian Susannah and Charlotte Rose Wingate by Charles James Madison, who has petitioned for legal fatherhood."

Just hearing that gave Raina a thrill, and she and Chase tightened the grip on their still-connected hands. When the judge invited the attorney to speak, Tim rose and cleared his throat to begin a short speech about the appropriate paperwork, the forms that had been signed, the interviews that had been conducted, the background checks that were now complete.

Judge Strayton looked bored, so much so that he held up his hand to politely cut off the speech, his attention shifting to Chase.

"Mr. Madison, could you approach the bench?"

"Of course, Your Honor." Chase stood and the judge pointed to him, and then behind him.

"With your soon-to-be daughters, please. Assuming you can hold both at once."

"Oh, I can." Chase gave a quick smile and turned to the rows behind them, taking Lily from Rose and meeting Tori in the aisle to take Charlie.

No surprise to anyone but maybe the judge, Chase was an expert at perching those two, one in each arm, carrying them like princesses on display for their adoring subjects.

As always, his face lit up as he looked from one to the other. Lily smiled at Chase like he hung the moon. Charlie pulled his earlobe and made a raspberry.

Chuckling, he took a few steps closer, standing to the side so Raina could see and hear the judge, whose eyes danced with amusement at the sight.

"Do you have a favorite?" the judge asked, making Chase's eyes widen.

"No, sir. I love them both equally. Lily's a great sleeper, and I can already tell she's going to be the peacemaker in the family. And Charlie? Well, I think she'll be unstoppable." He grew serious. "But I'll stop her from anything not...right, sir."

The judge gave a quick laugh. "You'll try, but as the father of three girls, I can tell you, it ain't easy." He looked at the group, his gaze resting on Rex. "Ced Bet your future father-in-law could back me up."

Again, everyone laughed, the whole vibe shifting to relaxed and happy.

"So, Mr. Madison," he continued. "You're not a young man. You'll be nearly seventy when they graduate from high school, correct?"

Chase lifted a shoulder. "But I'll be there, for that day and every one before. Including their dates. You don't think they'll mind if I chaperone?"

That made the judge laugh. "Brace yourself for dating. You'll hate every guy until...you don't."

Chase smiled and nodded, waiting for the next question in the unorthodox interview.

Quiet for a beat, the judge looked at him, then the

babies, then back to Chase. "If you had to give your daughters a piece of advice on their wedding day, right now, in advance, what would it be?"

He thought about that for a moment, then rested his head on top of Lily's when she nestled closer.

"I'd tell them that whenever they need to make a decision in life, they should ask themselves: what would their mother do," he finally said. "Raina is the wisest, strongest, best person I've ever known, and if they grow up to be exactly like her, they will help make the world a better place."

"Oh." Raina pressed her fingers to her lips to hold back the tears that were threatening.

"And," he continued, "I'd tell them both that their last name might be Madison, but they are Wingate women. That carries weight and responsibility, and tremendous blessings. That means they are ladies who love first, forgive fast, laugh constantly, and stick together through thick and thin."

For a second, there was silence, then a chorus of, "Aww!" and, "Yes!" and a noisy sniff from Rex.

Just as Raina dabbed under her eye and turned to look at Tori, the back door opened and Susannah walked in.

Hallelujah!

But right behind her was another woman, a complete stranger with stylish dark hair swooping around an attractive face. She was dressed in navy Chanel from head to toe, and, like Susannah, wore a stoic, unreadable expression.

With the riveting exchange happening in the front of the courtroom, no one else noticed the new arrivals, and Raina quickly turned back to hear what the judge said next.

"Good answer for this crowd, Mr. Madison," he joked. "I predict a happy life for you, and am confident you'll be a terrific father." He picked up his gavel. "I hereby decree you are the legal father of Lillian and Charlotte, with the full burden of responsibility as their parent to protect, guide, educate, feed, clothe, and inspire. Best of luck to you, Dad. Remember all this when they're sixteen and want to drive your car."

He slammed the gavel down to a noisy cheer from the rest of the room.

Raina rose to round the table and take Charlie, giving Chase a celebratory kiss on the lips. All around them, the family clapped and called their congrats—until the gavel came down again, hard.

"We are not done here," the judge announced noisily, bringing instant quiet to the room.

With a quick intake of breath, Raina glanced around, noticing Susannah and the other woman had stayed standing in the back. She tried to get her mother's attention to beckon her closer for this part.

But Susannah had her gaze locked on the back of Ivy Button's head, so fierce it was a miracle the woman's hair didn't ignite.

"The next matter before the court is the formal adoption of Madeline Anne Logan, Victoria Lucille Wingate, Rose Lydia D'Angelo, and Raina Deborah Wingate by

Susannah Jean Wingate, to be named their legal mother..."

With each word the judge spoke, Raina—and her sisters—took in the expression on Susannah's face.

Confusion made her frown. Her mouth opened to a round O of shock. She shook her head, searched the room, and let her gaze stop on Raina, then the judge. Even from across the courtroom, Raina could see her struggle to get her next breath, pressing her hands to her breastbone as she let out a soft mew of delight and disbelief.

In that split second, Ivy was forgotten. The only thing that mattered was the love between this mother and her daughters and the joy of seeing someone receive the perfect gift.

"Mrs. Wingate, can you come forward?" the judge asked.

"Of course!" she exclaimed, throwing a quick glance at the stranger with her, then gliding up the aisle with her usual grace and poise.

Madeline rose to get next to her, beaming through a teary smile. Tori and Rose slid out to the center aisle to join them and as they came to the front, Raina reached her hand to Susannah.

"Surprise," she whispered.

"Oh...oh..." She blinked back tears. "I don't know what to say."

"Well, I do." Ivy Button shot into the middle of the aisle, her gaze piercing, stunning them all. "And I say, not so fast, Your Honor. I think there are a few things you need to know about this family."

As shock reverberated through the room, the little brunette barreled closer.

"Let's start with the fact that their father is a rapist, the mother is an extortionist, and every one of these seven sisters is guilty of cruel and unusual punishment inflicted on a family employee."

Instantly, everyone in the room tried to talk over everyone else, only silenced when that gavel hit three times.

"Everyone sit down. Order. And you, ma'am. Who are you and what are you trying to claim?"

"I understand I get to say my piece before this sham of an adoption goes through," Ivy said.

The judge just stared at her and dipped his head in concession. "Fine. Name and purpose, please."

"My name is Ivy Button, my purpose is—"

"Oh, no, it's not!" The woman in Chanel marched forward. "She is *not* Ivy Button. I am. *My* name is Ivy Button and this woman is an imposter and a con artist."

The judge quieted the next noisy response again with a furious gavel. "Everyone sit down! Everyone except... these two women."

The family slid into seats obediently, but Raina was certain no one could actually breathe as the scene unfolded. Every single person in the courtroom looked dumbfounded and riveted...except Susannah, she suddenly noticed.

She was the only person, along with the new Ivy

Button, who didn't look confused. In fact, she smiled like the cat who ate the canary.

And Raina had a feeling Ivy Button—or whatever she called herself—was the canary about to be devoured.

For once, Raina hadn't done the fixing. But then, she'd probably learned all her problem-solving techniques from Susannah Wingate, the woman she couldn't wait to call Mom.

So she sat back, let out a breath, and trusted whoever was in charge, because, this time, it wasn't Raina.

Chapter Twenty-two

Susannah

Susannah stood stone still, except, yeah. This was even better than she'd hoped. Everything had fallen into place, starting with one phone call to the number Adam had given her. Yes, it belonged to Olivia "Ivy" Button—the real one.

Susannah had suspected Ivy was an imposter when she didn't answer to her full name, which told her she didn't even know it. That meant Susannah had to find out who did, so she called the woman named Olivia Button Beattie—known to friends and family as Ivy— who was married and living in Minnesota. She confirmed that her ill and elderly mother, Felicity Parrish Button, was a resident of a private assisted-living facility called Sunrise Vista Home.

After one long conversation that offered more answers than questions, Olivia instantly arranged for a flight, arriving this morning. With her, she brought...

Well, the court was about to find out what she'd brought.

As everyone took a seat, her gaze stayed on Olivia

Beattie, who, she'd learned in the car this morning on the ride back from the airport, utterly despised the sharp-tongued volunteer—who she knew as Alice—who was always up in her mother's business.

Olivia wasn't at all surprised that Alice was a scammer who stole her name for nefarious purposes. When she'd found out, she'd been willing to do anything to help the family—including fly right into Jacksonville and do whatever necessary to send this con artist to jail.

Until that happened, Susannah couldn't actually wallow in the utter delight that her daughters had arranged the adoption she'd long ago let go. But if the imposter won? Then it would cast a pall over everything.

Olivia joined her and gave a soft smile as they took the last few steps to stand in front of the judge next to Fake Ivy.

Susannah slipped into the row next to Rex, whose expression was a mix of baffled and relieved. Before they could talk, the gavel hit again.

"What is going on?" Judge Strayton asked without preamble. "Which one of you is Ivy Button? Is that a real name?"

"I am," Olivia said. "My name is Olivia Button Beattie and I'm frequently called Ivy. This woman is impersonating me. I know her as Alice Quimble, a volunteer at the assisted-living home where my mother, Felicity Button, is currently living."

"Is Alice Quimble your real name?" the judge asked.

"It'll do," Ivy—Alice—fired back.

All of Judge Strayton's homespun benevolence evaporated as he scowled at her. "May I remind you that you are in a court of law, and I have full authority to fine you for contempt if you don't show the proper respect I demand in this room."

Alice took a step backwards, her dirty sneakers squeaking on the linoleum. "I can, uh, just..." She thumbed over her shoulder. "Leave now."

"Not on your life," the judge said. "You made some extremely serious allegations, and I want details."

Susannah didn't want details, but she bit her lip, hoping the judge would give Olivia a chance to speak first.

"I, um..." Alice shuffled again. "I might have... misspoke."

The judge's furry brows lifted. "Misspoke? You accused a pillar of our local community of a despicable crime, made a similar allegation of a woman who is clearly adored by everyone who knows her, and dragged the entire family—and the local media—to your circus. So now, Ms. Alice Quimble, you will speak."

She took a slow and shuddering breath, and shot a look at Olivia. "You want to go first?"

"Ms. Quimble," the judge boomed. "Speak or pay a fine that you won't like."

"I, um, read some letters that were sent to a woman I was helping at an assisted-living facility," she said, her words halting and so soft, Susannah had to lean closer to hear her. "And I thought it seemed like she'd been... mistreated. Yeah, like she'd worked for this family forever and this guy"— she pointed to Rex—"took advantage of her, and she never really got compensated. So I sort of used this woman's name to gain access and...and..."

"And blackmail them for that compensation?" the judge guessed, intelligent enough to put two and two together and come up with the con.

She looked down at the ground.

"Do you have those letters?" he asked.

"I have them," Olivia said, sliding a file folder from her bag, the contents of which she'd read to Susannah on the way up I-95 from the airport. "The letters I have—which are originals, I might add—don't say anything about an assault or being mistreated." She put the folder on his desk. "They were sent by Doreen Parrish, my aunt, to my mother over a period of about thirty years. You'll see they are mostly the ramblings of a woman who suffered from a mild disability and read a lot of love stories. She readily admits that as a teenager, she had a crush on Mr. Wingate, and threw herself at a man she heard a college friend refer to as Sexy Rexy."

The judge slid a look at Rex, who he'd known for years, but neither reacted.

"My mother left this area long ago," Olivia explained. "She married, and married well, I will say. She became active in her community and lived a full life, but now she's suffering from dementia. She had a distant relationship with her sister. Despite many offers by my mother to move Doreen to Minnesota and support her, her sister insisted she wanted to stay at Wingate House. Change terrified her and she felt comfortable with the family, although she admitted to being awkward around Rex for having pressured him when they were young."

As she spoke, the judge sifted through the contents of the folder.

"As you can tell from what she writes," Olivia continued, "she was treated fairly, well-compensated, but could have a caustic tone. She once heard one of the girls, who was ten at the time, call her Dor-mean. I think it was Victoria."

The judge looked out into the group and Tori let out a little grunt when she raised her hand like a shy schoolgirl. "I'm probably guilty of that."

"She also said the little girl apologized," Olivia added.

Judge Strayton nodded, his body language saying he'd heard enough, then he looked at Alice. "And you have letters that say something different?"

"Not on me—"

"I have them right here."

Every head turned to the back of the room as Adam's voice boomed over the heads of the others. He strode into the room, a phone in one hand, the familiar manila envelope in the other. He moved with the confidence that bespoke his years as an FBI agent, and a man certain he was about to close a case.

"And I have proof that they were all forgeries, handwritten by this woman"—he pointed to Alice—"who has made quite a criminal career out of conning vulnerable and wealthy residents of nursing homes. That was exactly what she did when she read those letters and rewrote them in a way that she could use against the

Wingate family. Then she dyed her hair and showed up here as Ivy Button, demanding a house she knew she'd never get, and would eventually push for a financial settlement to make her go away."

"She already has," Susannah said as a soft gasp and rumble rolled through the courtroom.

"She uses multiple aliases," Adam continued, "and is wanted in the state of Minnesota for..." He glanced at his phone. "Intent to defraud, falsifying documents, altering a prescription, signature forgery, financial exploitation of seniors for personal gain...it goes on. Do you need specifics, Your Honor, or can I just turn her over to the federal agents waiting downstairs?"

"You may take her and add perjury to her list." He looked at Olivia. "Will you go with them and supply a statement? I have very important adoptions to take care of."

She smiled at him and nodded, pausing at the row where Susannah was perched next to Rex. Ever the gentleman, he stood and took the hands she held out to him.

"Mrs. Beattie, I'm sorry for any inconvenience—"

"No inconvenience at all," she said quickly. "When Susannah called me and told me what was happening, I couldn't get on a plane fast enough. Mr. Wingate, I want you to know that my aunt was not unhappy with her life at Wingate House. Doreen was born with a disability due to, they thought at the time, a lack of oxygen during birth. But if you read those letters, and I hope you do, you'll see that she always appreciated your whole family. She acknowledged her very aggressive behavior toward you, too. She never mentioned having a baby, or I assure you, my mother would have stepped in to raise it."

"Thank you," Rex said simply. "I appreciate you telling me that."

"You're quite welcome and I thank you for giving her a purpose for so many years." She smiled and glanced around. "But I believe I have a long-lost cousin named Blake whom I've never met. Is he here?"

"I'm right here!" Blake popped up and they met in the aisle, sliding arms around each other as they followed Adam out.

For a moment, Rex stood frozen, watching them. Then suddenly, he exhaled on a whoosh and threw his arms around Susannah. "Thank you, darling. Thank you."

"It's over, Rex." She leaned back and smiled at him. "It's all over."

"Not quite," the judge interjected. "Mrs. Wingate, can you approach the bench? I'd like to close one more matter during this most eventful day."

Madeline, Tori, Raina, and Rose practically sprinted to the front, group-hugging, high-fiving, and doing a terrible job of being very somber.

Susannah couldn't blame them. She was three seconds—and four daughters—away from doing a jig on the judge's bench herself.

"Adult adoptions are usually done for specific legal reasons," Judge Strayton said when they settled down. "To establish inheritance rights, to formalize a stepparent relationship, or to ensure legal access in a crisis or hospitalization."

They all just looked at him, finally silent and serious.

"My guess is that this one is for sentimental reasons."

Susannah stepped forward, her arms around as many of her daughters as she could hold.

"Yes, sir. You are correct. But I also want the world to know that these four women are...mine." She gave a laugh that caught in her throat. "They always have been. Ever since Raina and Rose were toddlers, Tori was a little girl, and Madeline just wanted to be my helper, I have loved them, cared for them, and actually learned from them every single day."

She took a slow breath, looking from one to the other, swamped with gratitude.

"And if I might say a word, Your Honor?"

He nodded, giving her a chance to find composure and say what was on her heart.

"There is one woman who isn't here today but should be recognized, and that is their biological mother, Charlotte. At the time of her death, this small family was rocked, and Rex was...lost." She glanced at him, not surprised to see the tears pouring. "But from that deep sadness and grief, this family emerged. I'm so grateful and humbled and hope I've...I've honored her by being their stepmother."

For a long moment, the room stayed silent while Susannah caught her breath to finish.

"But if you can help us make it official in the eyes of the law and God, then I will sleep better knowing I've been blessed with seven of the most amazing daughters a mother could have."

He nodded slowly, his intentional gaze moving over all of them with warmth and approval. "It is done. You are now their mother."

The sound of his ubiquitous gavel was drowned out by the loudest squeal of happy Wingates that Susannah had ever heard. She was smashed in their arms, kissed by their lips, and thrilled when one after another called her Mom.

On a cloud of love and laughter, they all floated together, picking up sisters and husbands and babies on the way, happy to see that Chloe and Sadie had joined and witnessed the adoption, with Scout standing just a few feet away.

They spilled into the hall and everyone talked at once, with opinions and jokes and replays ricocheting through the small hallway. There, Chloe turned and looked around.

"Travis!" she called. "Come and join us."

He walked toward the group, with little Judah on his hip, the child looking overwhelmed by the mass of noisy people, but quite comfortable on his uncle's shoulder. "We stayed outside but it sounds like everything went well in there," he said.

"You have no idea," Susannah said breathlessly,

sliding her arm around Rex as he stayed right beside her. "This family is..." She shook her head, not even trying to fight the tears.

"I don't know how to thank you all for everything," Rex said. "I've spent fifty years being proud of my daughters, and that last hour was the highlight of all those years."

As they cooed and hugged, Susannah held up her hand.

"Well, I know how to thank you," she said. "We can start with a party this coming weekend—the best double-ring ceremony you can imagine."

"Um, Mom. About that." Chloe came closer, one hand on Travis's shoulder. "You should know why we were late and not there for the first part of the hearing."

The chatter died down as Chloe moved into the center of the whole group, tugging Travis's arm so that he and Judah joined her.

"Where were you?" Raina asked. "I couldn't believe you and Sadie didn't make it."

"We had something very important to do, and Sadie was a witness," Chloe said.

"To what?" Rex asked, looking from one to the other.

Travis slid into a grin and put his free arm around Chloe, the three of them a picture of...a family!

"You're keeping him!" Susannah exclaimed.

Travis hugged them both. "We sure are."

Chloe practically danced with excitement, reaching for Judah's hand. "Travis McCall and I just became the legal guardians and future parents of Judah McCall, so please welcome him to the family."

Raina whooped the loudest. "We did it!" she exclaimed. "Seven adoptions in one family in one day! It's gotta be an Amelia Island record!"

They joined her in the celebration, with Chloe beaming in a way Susannah had never seen before. She'd never had that expression on her face when she looked at Hunter Landry, that was for sure. This was...this was... Oh, goodness.

She knew what Chloe was going to say next.

"Is there any chance we could make that a triple-ring ceremony?" she asked.

Travis tugged her closer. "We'd like this unit to be legal and official as soon as possible."

One more time, the Wingate family cheered, hugged, and hooted so loud that two babies cried and Judah put his hands over his ears.

"I'd say the answer is yes," Susannah assured Chloe as she hugged them both and gave a kiss to Judah.

They started to walk toward the stairs in a pack, pairing up, laughing, talking, reliving the emotionally-charged morning.

All but Sadie, who took Susannah's arm and eased her back before they got to the top of the stairs, with Scout doing the same to Rex.

"Could we talk for a second?" Sadie asked, as all the others disappeared around the landing, laughter and talking floating up through the open stairs.

"Of course," Rex said, slowing his step as they stood and formed a small circle of four. "Is everything okay?"

Scout and Sadie shared a secret, warm look that... that...

"Another one?" Rex asked on a laugh, echoing exactly what Susannah was thinking.

The couple slid their arms around each other, unified and clearly very much in love.

"This day could only be better, sir," Scout said, "if you give me your blessing to marry Sadie. I love her with all my heart and I will make her very happy."

Rex drew back, his jaw loose. "Well, at least you asked," he said on a chuckle. "That last one just told me."

"I'm asking with humility and high hopes," Scout said. "And I realize we're a different faith, but—"

Rex held up his hand. "You're of one mind," he said. "I've noticed that from the beginning. Yes, you most certainly have my blessing."

"Thank you, Dad!" Sadie reached up and hugged him, then turned to Susannah. "And a question for you, Mom."

"You could ask me anything today, Sadie," Susannah replied. "I'm pretty sure the answer will be yes."

"Wait until you hear it."

Susannah lifted both brows. "Okay."

Sadie glanced in the general direction of the noise still coming from the group that had made it down to the lobby but couldn't be quieted.

"We'd like to get married quickly and, as a matter of fact, after Chloe and Travis finished the guardianship,

Scout and I slipped down to the marriage license office. Do you think we could make it...a four-ring ceremony?"

Susannah's laugh morphed into a gasp, then nearly a sob of joy. "Of course!"

"What's the hurry?" Rex asked.

Sadie bit her lip and put her hand on her stomach. "Well, we...we just want...no fuss and—"

"Sadie's having a baby," Scout said, his whole face lit with pride. "But even if she weren't, I cannot wait to marry this woman."

Rex and Susannah exchanged a quick look, then folded the other two in their arms, no more words needed to show their love and approval of this decision. After more hugs and kisses and congrats, Susannah let out a sigh of ecstasy.

"Join the others," she said, gesturing for Scout and Sadie to go downstairs. "Dad and I need a moment."

"Of course." Sadie kissed them both and walked out arm in arm with one of the nicest men Susannah had ever met.

"Well." Susannah sighed, almost dizzy from the day. "You wanted more grandchildren."

Rex just smiled at her, his eyes misty from all the tears. "You did this, Susannah Wingate. I just worked and doled out advice, but you made these beautiful women who love the same way they breathe—without thinking. Thank you for giving me this life. Thank you."

She slid into his arms just as the door they were next to popped open. Judge Strayton stepped out, then stopped and did a double-take when he saw them.

"Don't move, you two," he said.

He pivoted and went right back inside, leaving them perplexed.

"I hope he doesn't change his mind," Susannah said, only half joking.

"Maybe you were supposed to sign something."

The door opened again, and the judge held out his gavel to Rex. "It occurred to me you'd like to keep this."

"A wonderful memento of a spectacular day," Rex said, taking it. "Thank you."

"And..." The judge's wry smile grew. "You might need it with that crew."

They heard him chuckling as he walked down the hall.

Chapter Twenty-three

Raina

Looking out over the grounds of Wingate House from the third-floor balcony, Raina let the warm breeze from the Amelia River flutter her just-styled hair. From this vantage point, she had a perfect view of the ceremony setup—a large semicircle of about fifty chairs, with one aisle that would accommodate four brides in four back-to-back ceremonies.

Massive sprays of flowers in four distinct shades of pink, from deep magenta to a sweet blush, flanked the aisle and spilled over an archway where Isaiah stood preparing to perform four weddings.

She caught sight of Grace walking toward him, already dressed in a flowered maxi. What was Grace doing down there? Raina turned, frowning into the apartment behind her just as Tori and Rose walked out to the balcony to join her.

"I'm done with hair and makeup and they're starting on Sadie and Chloe," Tori said.

"Want a mimosa?" Rose asked. "With no champagne for the breast-feeder among us?"

Raina laughed and reached for them, pulling her sisters closer. "I don't need anything but you two."

She circled her arms around them and turned so they could see over the grounds all the way to the blue waters of the river, which would be gold at sunset when four Wingate women took their respective walks down the aisle.

After a minute of admiring the view and each other, Raina asked, "Why did Grace leave?"

"She wants to practice the scripture readings one more time," Tori said.

"And be close to Isaiah," Rose added on a sigh. "I think she's pregnant."

"What?" Raina and Tori both asked the question in perfect unison.

"Just a guess," Rose told them. "She skipped champagne, barely touched a drop of food, and could not stop talking to Sadie about baby names. Now, maybe that's me being my super optimistic self but—"

"Nope. She's pregnant," Tori said.

"And she doesn't want to steal any attention from our wedding day by announcing her news," Raina added. "God love that girl."

"He certainly does," Rose said on a sigh. "In fact, I'd say He loves us all."

"These are good days," Raina agreed. "Everyone is happy and healthy, married and pregnant—"

"Not necessarily in that order," Tori cracked. "Sadie always has to break the rules, huh?"

"And Dad is strong," Raina added, shaking her head.

"What was it? A year and a half ago, not even, when I got the call that he'd had a stroke."

"Kenzie and I were at Logan so fast getting on the first plane from Boston," Tori recalled. "I remember you two were at the beach house at midnight when we got in." She leaned into Raina. "You were worried about your marriage."

Raina gave a dry laugh. "And here I am, doing it again with a different man."

"A better man," Rose said.

"The best man," Raina whispered, then held up two hands at their expressions. "The best man for me. Angel Gabriel for you," she said to Rose. "And Dr. Hottypants for you." She smiled at Tori.

"It's been an unbelievable year and a half," Tori mused, taking a sip of her mimosa. "So much change."

"And yet so much has stayed the same," Rose said. "Relationships change, babies are born, we even have a new legal mother. But through it all..."

"We stay together," Raina said.

"What are you three talking about out there?" Chloe called from the makeup chair. "I have FOMO."

"Once the baby, always the baby," Tori joked, guiding them back into the spacious living room that had been transformed into the perfect bridal party dressing room. "No fear of missing out, Chloe. We're just talking about what an incredible year and a half we've been through."

"Oh, really?" Sadie looked over from the hair chair, where the stylist was attempting to tame her curls. "I thought you were talking about Grace being pregnant."

"What?" Madeline shrieked from the bedroom where she was steaming out four very different wedding dresses.

Still holding the steamer, she marched in. "Did I hear you say—"

"Exactly," Rose insisted. "*Hearsay*. We shouldn't start rumors, no matter how much we want them to be true."

"And we do," Sadie said. "I'd love a pregnancy pal. Although she didn't look green around the gills like I always do."

"That's 'cause you're having a girl," Rose announced. "There's no nausea with boys."

At least three of them choked in disbelief.

"And that's what they call an old wives' tale," Tori quipped.

"Well, then, I'm an old wife," Rose said. "Because that folklore held true for me and I've had four kids."

"I'm here!" Susannah called from out in the hall.

Raina rushed to open the door, anxious to see how the deep pink silk gown Madeline had made looked on her.

"The mother of the brides is here!" Susannah announced with her arms held out to all of them. "How do I look?"

"Gorgeous!" they exclaimed.

And she did. Despite all she'd been through—perhaps because of it—their mother looked vibrant, fresh, joyous, and ready to send four daughters into the arms of loving men.

After a group hug, Susannah looked around as if she were mentally counting heads. "Where's Grace? I just left Kenzie in the nursery with all the kids and Nikki is in wonderful spirits."

"Grace didn't go to check on Nikki," Raina said. "She went down to the ceremony setting to practice reading her scriptures."

"And be with Isaiah," Rose added.

"Because she's...*ahem*, not nauseous," Tori said under her breath.

"Wait. What? Is she sick?" Susannah asked.

None of them said a word, but the silence and a few raised brows spoke for them.

"No!" Susannah gasped, dropping onto the sofa. "Why wouldn't she tell us?"

Raina sat next to her. "Maybe it's too soon or maybe she doesn't want to step on our wedding days. Weddings day? What's the right way to say that?"

Suze—Mom, now, if she could ever get used to that—slid her arm behind Raina. "Perfect day, is what I call it. The weather cooperated, the inn looks spectacular, and all my daughters are full of love and joy. How could it get any better?"

Just then, the door opened and Grace stepped in and they went completely silent. She froze, looked from one to the other, a look of amusement on her features.

"You know that feeling when you walk into a room and you know everyone was talking about you?" She put her hands on her hips. "Well..."

The sisters all stayed quiet, but one of the stylists gave it away with a not very well hidden snicker.

"You *were* talking about me!" Grace said, taking a

few more steps and zeroing in on Rose. "You can't tell a lie, Rosie. You're not capable of it. Were you?"

"None of us can tell a lie," Tori countered, pretending to be miffed.

But Rose didn't say a word.

"What were you talking about?" Grace insisted.

From her makeup chair, while blush was brushed on her beautiful cheekbones, Chloe beckoned Grace closer. And closer. Until she could whisper in Grace's ear, which she did while everyone watched, listened, and waited.

After a second, Grace stepped back, her color deepening to one of the many shades of pink they'd picked for their group wedding.

"Grace?" Susannah's voice rose with the need to know.

"Mom," she countered in the same tone.

"What aren't you telling us?" Tori pressed.

Grace gave a soft laugh. "I guess there is no such thing as a secret in this family. Of *course* you know."

No one needed any more than that before the uproarious response.

"It's early days," she finally said. "I think..." She looked at Sadie. "I think we have almost the same due date."

"Yes!" Sadie jumped up from the hair chair and threw her arms around her sister, dancing like a loon.

Watching the two sisters, not two years apart in age, hugging and celebrating, Susannah took Raina's hand and squeezed it.

"I know," Raina said, already wiping the recently applied mascara from under her eyes. "It's perfect. Everything is perfect for your girls...Mom."

Her mother just dropped her head back and smiled.

THEY HELD the ceremonies in order of age. After Tori and Justin's laughter-filled vows and a happy dance back down the aisle side by side with their attendants, Kenzie and Finn, the sound system played soft music while the sisters regrouped for the second wedding.

For her ceremony, Raina had Rose and Madeline as her attendants, but instead of flowers, they carried babies. Lily and Charlie were in cheery moods, too, cooing as they were carried down the aisle in their fluffy pink dresses with bows on their heads. Charlie's rested on her soft tufts of hair, and Lily's wrapped around her dear bald head.

The beautiful angels elicited cheers and applause from everyone but their father, who stood next to Isaiah with a look of wonder and awe, a tear meandering down his cheek as he absorbed the moment.

When the song changed to the processional and everyone stood, Raina slipped her arm into her father's and looked up at him.

It was time. He had to know one last thing.

"Um, Dad," she whispered. "I made kind of a big decision."

He gave her that sly Rex smile. "I know. I'm taking you to him right now."

She laughed. "I mean, about that...I'm going to..." She sucked in a deep breath just as he was about to take a step. "I'm changing my name to Madison."

The words tumbled out really fast, and she clung tighter, hoping Dad didn't tumble with them.

But he didn't move, staying still at the beginning of the stone path that led to a wedding pergola that framed the setting sun.

"I expected you to."

"You did?"

"He's the man in your life, Rain. You're sharing a home, a life, children, finances, faith, hopes, dreams, and your heart. Of course you should share a name."

"But...there just aren't going to be any more Wingate women after today. Well, Suze, but we're all married and I know you don't want the name to end."

He looked into her eyes, happy tears in his. "It's not a name, Raina. It's a spirit. It's in our DNA and we will continue to carry on that spirit for generations. Lily and Charlie will do their bit. You watch."

He was so right. So very, very right.

"Now," he whispered. "Can I give you away to the only man I've ever met who is deserving of a prize as great as you?'"

She laughed softly. "Yes, please."

They started down the stone path slowly, her gaze locked on Chase standing under the flower-laden trellis.

His tall, strong silhouette stood out from the sunset on the water, beckoning her closer with every step.

In the golden glow, she could see every angle and shadow of his expression. The light in his eyes, the upward curl of his lips, the teeth as he grinned with joy at the sight of her.

Two more steps and her father brought her to a gentle stop, turning to her.

"I love you, Regina Wingate," he whispered as he hugged her. And into her ear, he added, "Now go be Raina Madison and carry on the spirit."

"I love you, Daddio." She gave his cheek a light kiss, then inched back when he turned to hug Chase.

She gave her bouquet to her mother with another hug and kiss, then stepped up to the platform to stand in front of Chase, with Isaiah in the middle, holding the Wingate family Bible.

Both of them were trembling when they took each other's hands.

"Hey," Chase whispered. "You're the most beautiful woman I've ever seen."

She let a shiver roll over her. "Back at you, Charles."

They shared another nervous laugh, and then settled into the short ceremony that Raina and Chase, like the other three couples today, had written themselves.

Isaiah welcomed the guests to wedding number two for the day, earning laughs, and then asking them to bow their heads in prayer.

Raina wasn't much of a pray-er. She liked to take matters into her own hands, as God and anyone who knew her would attest. But right then, she wanted to pray. If there was a divine power that could bless this union, protect them and guide them, then Raina wanted to lift those words and get that blessing.

As Isaiah began the prayer, she looked down at their joined hands, then slowly lifted her gaze to meet Chase's. There was no smile, no glimmer, no humor right then.

They stared into each other's eyes and connected. Just like that. They were one.

"...Your Word proclaims that what God joined, no man can tear asunder." Isaiah's baritone boomed over the crowd, barely needing a microphone. "And to that end, we ask Your blessing on this couple as they begin a life together, as parents and husband and wife. Let their family grow and honor You with every decision. Father, bless this marriage from today into eternity..."

When they finally broke eye contact and the prayer ended, Isaiah invited them to exchange rings while he took them through the traditional wedding vows.

Raina's hands trembled again as they slipped on rings, repeating words, making the promises to love, honor, and cherish until death parted them.

With every word, all she could think was how this man had come into her broken life and healed her heart. He'd shown her love with patience and friendship, taught her how to laugh again with teasing and a deep understanding of what made her tick, and nurtured her with attention and care and a whole lot of homemade pasta.

And the next thing she knew, Isaiah pronounced

them husband and wife and Chase swept her off her feet with a soul-melting kiss.

As the applause died down, they took a step down, just below where Isaiah stood.

"Ladies and gentlemen," the big man exclaimed, then he waited a beat and leaned in right between them to whisper, "Raina?"

She slid him a look and whispered, "Madison."

"Allow me to present Mr. and Mrs. Madison!"

She managed one quick look at her very happy husband, then clung to his arm as they floated back down the stone path to start their life as husband, wife, and parents.

At the end, he wrapped his arms around her and spun her in a full circle that kept her feet off the ground.

In fact, she floated through two more beautiful weddings—Scout and Sadie broke a glass and everyone said, "Mazel tov!" After much applause, music, and chatter, the youngest Wingate started her trip on Rex's arm.

Ring bearer Judah preceded Chloe down the aisle with Lady Bug, the flower girl, on a leash next to him. The sweet little boy carried the rings with great style and grace, and stood next to Travis while the couple exchanged vows and were pronounced "husband, wife, and future son."

And while that meant that not one of the seven sisters remained a Wingate any longer, Raina knew the spirit would carry on for many generations to come.

What a gift to be part of that legacy. What a blessing, indeed.

Love Hope Holloway's books? If you haven't read her first two series, you're in for a treat! Chock full of family feels and beachy Florida settings, these sagas are for lovers of riveting and inspirational sagas about sisters, secrets, romance, mothers, and daughters…and the moments that make life worth living.

These series are complete, and available in e-book (also in Kindle Unlimited), paperback, and audio.

The Coconut Key Series

Set in the heart of the Florida Keys, these seven delightful novels will make you laugh out loud, wipe a happy tear, and believe in all the hope and happiness of a second chance at life.

A Secret in the Keys – Book 1
A Reunion in the Keys – Book 2
A Season in the Keys – Book 3
A Haven in the Keys – Book 4
A Return to the Keys – Book 5
A Wedding in the Keys – Book 6
A Promise in the Keys – Book 7

The Shellseeker Beach Series

Come to Shellseeker Beach and fall in love with a "found family" of unforgettable characters who face life's challenges with humor, heart, and hope.

Sanibel Dreams - Book 1
Sanibel Treasures - Book 2
Sanibel Mornings – Book 3
Sanibel Sisters – Book 4
Sanibel Tides – Book 5
Sanibel Sunsets – Book 6
Sanibel Moonlight – Book 7

The Carolina Christmas Series

If you need a little family Christmas, later-in-life romance, and sweet holiday feels, come to the Blue Ridge Mountains for a Carolina Christmas, co-authored by Hope Holloway and Cecelia Scott.

The Asheville Christmas Cabin – Book 1
The Asheville Christmas Gift – Book 2
The Asheville Christmas Wedding – Book 3
The Asheville Christmas Tradition – Book 4

About the Author

Hope Holloway is the author of charming, heartwarming women's fiction featuring unforgettable families and friends, and the emotional challenges they conquer. After more than twenty years in marketing, she launched a new career as an author of beach reads and feel-good fiction. A mother of two adult children, Hope and her husband of thirty years live in Florida. When not writing, she can be found walking the beach with her two rescue dogs, who beg her to include animals in every book. Visit her site at www.hopeholloway.com.

Made in the USA
Columbia, SC
01 June 2025